third time Lucky

THE BENNETT'S BASTARDS SERIES

JENNIE KEW

THIRD TIME LUCKY

Copyright © 2018 by Jennie Kew
Published by Wooden Key Press
Edited by Hot Tree Editing
Cover design by Mayhem Cover Creations

ISBN: 9780648209416

www.jenniekew.com

For Katie, love always.

This Time Around – Koru Award of Excellence 2020
Short Romance – 2nd Place

This Time Around – Stiletto Award 2020
Mid-length Romance – Finalist

Third Time Lucky – Passionate Plume Award 2019
BDSM Romance – Finalist

Third Time Lucky – Stiletto Award 2019
Erotic/BDSM Romance – Finalist

Revenge and Redemption – Sexy Scribbles Award 2018
Contemporary Romance – Finalist

"Be prepared to be taken along on a
wonderful, sexy, heartwarming, sometimes
tear inducing, slightly kinky joy ride!"
Review for *Third Time Lucky*

"The story is heartwarming and empowering.
The plot is gripping and keeps you turning
pages. Definitely one click worthy."
Review for *Third Time Lucky*

"This novel was so romantic! I'm in love, love, love with
Rafe! I will read this book again it was so good!"
Review for *This Time Around*

"Couldn't put it down! Great characters with funny/quirky personalities...some steamy scenes full of emotion."
Review for *This Time Around*

"This sexy story is not for the weak of heart but those that enjoy a story with heart and grit and passion."
Review for *His Own Heaven*

"...there is a doozy of insecurity, emotional growth, vulnerability, trust, strength, and many more emotions swirling underneath, ready to suck you in."
Review for *His Own Heaven*

"The characters will pull on your heart strings and leave you breathless."
Review for *Revenge and Redemption*

"The chemistry between the hero and heroine is incredible."
Review for *Sacrifice and Seduction*

"...enough steam to have you needing a cold shower..."
Review for *Dirty*

"...fun, unique, and just the right side of twisted."
Review for *Grind*

Prologue

Crooking her finger at handsome strangers was not something Abigail Bennett did on a regular basis. Or ever, really. Skinny-dipping in the creek that cut through her father's property, on the other hand, was a semi-regular activity, so it was only a matter of time before someone caught her in the act.

She'd considered sinking under the water and waiting until the motorcycle had ridden past, then she figured the chances of anyone seeing her with their helmet on were pretty slim and thought, *bugger it.*

The bike rider only made it two metres past the clearing before slowly rolling backwards and kicking the stand into place, cutting the engine and removing his helmet.

Abby's first thought upon seeing the man underneath was a stream of unintelligible noise akin to that of a drooling dog chewing on a bone.

A big, sexy, leather-clad bone.

Was this guy for real? Had her prayers been answered?

I mean, talk about great timing.

Before she knew what she was doing, she was crooking her finger at him in wanton invitation.

An invitation he eagerly accepted, the impropriety of skinny-dipping within full view of a dusty country road apparently as meaningless to him as it was to her.

With a devilish grin, he stripped out of his clothes, discarded his heavy leather jacket on the grass by his feet and yanked his T-shirt over his head, revealing a muscled slab of tattooed perfection.

And then he unzipped his pants.

Abby bit her lip and whimpered as he peeled back the leather and tugged down his briefs to reveal his hardening cock.

Handsome held her gaze as he toed off his boots and stripped off his pants. Well, he tried to, but Abby's gaze was constantly drawn down his body to the impressive cock standing proud between his thighs. The one he'd wrapped his fist around as he walked to the edge of the creek and stared down at her.

The man was quintessentially male.

He looked to be a good half foot taller than her—and she stood at six feet tall. Maybe a few years older too, his short mop of brown hair peppered with the beginnings of grey. His stubbled face was punctuated by intelligent hazel eyes and his big, broad body was chiselled to athletic precision, his strength undeniable.

His collection of intricate tattoos wrapped around his thick biceps, stretched across the solid expanse of his chest, and trailed down one tightly muscled thigh, displaying a variety of scenes and creatures such as dragons and wolves and vine covered castles.

He was gorgeous.

"What's your name," he asked. Dark and smooth like

velvet, his voice slipped over her sex-starved body, making her shiver with awareness.

When she answered, she barely recognised the sultry timbre that had taken over her voice. "Let's not ruin this with names, okay, Handsome?"

His grin broadened. "Whatever you want, little nymph." And then he lowered himself into the water. "Fuck that's cold!"

Abby laughed and swiped her hand through the water, splashing his chest and face. He dove for her, caught her and they both fell under the surface. Both came up laughing. But their laughter quickly died, and the frigid temperature of the water was forgotten as Handsome slid his hands around her waist and bent his head towards her.

Stopping short of kissing her, he held his mouth above hers, his fresh breath brushing over her lips. "I want you, but... I don't have any protection."

Abby smoothed a droplet of water off his cheek and forced a smile. "I have birth control."

Handsome licked his lips, concern warring with lust in his heated gaze. "Are you sure?" His deep voice sent another shiver of awareness through her sadly neglected nether region.

And her answer was a no-brainer. "Yes."

As soon as she said the word, Handsome's mouth was on hers, hot, soft and fierce. And as they explored each other's bodies, tasted and tested and pushed and pulled, as they licked and fucked and cried out in pleasure, Abby forgot that her world was cold and lonely.

Because for a few blissful moments, her world ceased to exist.

Chapter One

As her body jolted from sleep, it took Abby a moment to remember where she was—the creek. And another moment to remember why she was still there—sex.

Mind-blowing sex.

But why the hell had she let herself fall asleep?

Slowly lifting her head from the pillow of an outstretched arm—*his* outstretched arm—she froze when his bicep twitched. He made a snuffly sound like a contented dog—a really big contented dog—and a lazy smile split her face. He should be content after what they'd done.

She was.

Even so, she repressed the urge to snuggle back into the warmth of his embrace. The last thing she needed was for Sleeping Handsome to wake up and foil her escape. Scratch that, the last thing she needed was for him to take her again. Because *take her* was exactly what he'd done.

Handsome's brand of sex was addictive. Powerful. Vital. Yet at the same time he was almost tender, his touch

4

reverent and gentle, igniting in her a passion she'd thought long since dead.

It had been exactly what she'd needed, and until today she hadn't realised just how much she'd missed it.

Human contact.

Male human contact.

Skin-on-skin contact.

And the way Handsome had handled her, as though her size meant nothing, as though her body was his to do with as he pleased, and what he'd pleased was to make her mindless with pleasure. She could see herself craving more from this guy—*eagerly*. Handsome had reawakened her submissive side, and that was not good.

She'd already learned the hard way: good sex didn't equal good man.

Lifting her head a little higher, she peered over her shoulder. She couldn't see his face, buried in her hair as it was, but she could feel his breath brush over her neck and shoulders like a gentle caress. The scents of leather and sandalwood radiated off his warm skin to envelop her senses, sending shivers of arousal straight to her core.

She closed her eyes and swallowed a moan. It took all her will not to squirm and wiggle her arse against his cock.

One large, hot hand rested possessively on her side, his strong fingers curled around her fleshy hip, and one long leg sat heavily atop hers, pinning them under his weight, but she didn't feel caged. No, he held her against him in all the right places, and if anything she felt protected, as though his embrace would keep her safe from the world.

It was an odd sensation for someone who'd come to rely on no one but herself.

Abby looked towards her feet, her mouth twisting with a wry grimace. Her belly and breasts sagged towards the ground, completely at the mercy of gravity. She wondered if Handsome would have been so eager to take her had he seen her like this to begin with. Probably not. Not that it mattered. She wouldn't be seeing him again anyway. He'd wake up and be glad she'd done a runner because it would mean no awkward silences as he tried to find just the right words to say, "Thanks for the fuck but I really must be going", and be on his merry way.

She stifled a laugh. The gorgeous wall of muscle behind her had taken what she'd freely offered and probably thought he was doing her a favour to boot. He didn't need to know he'd been used.

Now if only she could get out of here before he woke up.

Gingerly, Abby pried each of his long, lean fingers from her hip, slipped her legs out from under his, and slowly rolled forwards out of his grasp. With a stealth that belied her size, she got to her feet... and then like an idiot she stopped to stare at him and drank in his rough masculine beauty, sighing with both longing and awe.

Until her attention snagged on one distinguishing feature.

Even as it slumbered against his thigh, his cock was a magnificent sight to behold, long and thick and dangerous to her capacity for rational thought. Erect and proud, it had been a thing of beauty, its proportions the stuff of myth and legend, and as she stared at it now, she muffled an amused snort behind her hand.

How the hell does he walk straight with that thing between his legs?

Sudden heat blossomed low in her belly and her skin prickled with a rush of lust, her mind suddenly filled with an erotic montage of everything he'd done to her with that *thing*. Not only could the man walk straight, but he had a pretty damn good idea what to do with it while standing up, lying down, and kneeling, in water and on land.

Handsome was a big man, and she'd not had sex in a very long time. He'd stretched her wide and filled her completely, and her body had melted with the sensation of total abandon. The way he'd touched her had made her forget herself, forget everything until nothing existed on her horizon but him.

Sex hadn't just been good with this guy, it had been breathtaking.

Just then Handsome shifted and snuffled again. He reached for her. The gesture made her heart flutter.

She frowned. *Stupid heart.*

But it also reminded her that it was time to leave, to return to reality. Stubbornly ignoring her body's cry of protest, and leaving Handsome to come to his own conclusions when he found her gone, she quietly turned away and headed home.

Keeping his eyes closed against the dappled autumn sunlight, Wolf breathed deep and sucked in the clean country air. The scents of fresh water, green grass, and hot-blooded woman clung to his nostrils and made him smile. Yawning loudly, he stretched the sleep from his body, his riding leathers creaking under his naked weight. The makeshift bed felt warm against his skin compared with the coolness of the lush grass around him. He barked a laugh as he remembered sharing that warmth with the mischievous beauty he'd found skinny-dipping in the creek, all glistening wet curves and long black hair, crooking her finger at him in silent invitation like some mythical water nymph.

He grinned as his cock stiffened in anticipation of having that soft, feminine body under him again, of hearing her moan as he teased her to the peak of arousal, then whimper with frustration when he stopped. His grin softened to a satisfied smile as he thought of her eyes, deep brown like melted chocolate and glazed with passion as he'd rolled her nipples between his fingers, increasing the pressure until she'd gasped, until her back had arched and her eyes had rolled back, and she'd gifted him with a husky groan of pleasure.

It'd been a long time since he'd enjoyed a woman so much.

The Dominant in him eager to push her limits further, he reached for the warm little bundle he'd fallen asleep with. Maybe he'd bite her some more—she'd responded very nicely to that—or a sound spanking perhaps? Her responsiveness to the few exploratory slaps he'd placed along her thighs and bottom had been encouraging, had indicated she'd be open to something more intense.

His hand alighting on an empty space, Wolf opened his eyes—and his gut fell to his feet.

Where is she?

He bolted upright, narrowed his eyes and scanned the clearing but found no sign of her. Nothing. He sprang to his feet and looked back up the gently sloping bank to the road beyond. His motorcycle was still there. He snatched his backpack off the ground and tore it open. His keys, wallet and—most importantly—his laptop were still inside. She hadn't robbed him. That was something, he supposed. But she'd stung his pride, and *that* he did not appreciate.

Wolf planted his hands on his hips, his brow pulled

together in a deep frown as he scoured the clearing and again found no sign she'd ever been there.

Was it possible he'd only dreamt her?

He looked down. The fading bite marks on his lower abdomen were evidence enough of her presence. His lips turned up at the corners. His little nymph liked to bite almost as much as he did. So no, while the fifteen-hour journey north from Sydney to Melville's Cross had certainly made Wolf tired, he wasn't delusional. He hadn't imagined the mischievous beauty.

She was real. Whoever she was.

And now she was really gone.

"Damn it!"

Wolf dragged a hand down his face and huffed out a sigh. He should have demanded her name instead of indulging her little game of anonymity. After months of nothing but sycophantic subs tripping all over him, he'd been thirsty for a real challenge, and lo and behold if he didn't actually find one in the middle of bloody nowhere and at the most inconvenient time of his life.

He felt like roaring at the sky.

Why here? Why now?

He knew it was time to move on, time to put the past behind him once and for all and get on with his life. Hell, that was one of the reasons he'd agreed to this retreat bull-shit. But why couldn't he have found his little nymph *after* he'd appeased the gods of publishing and finished the manuscript he'd been procrastinating over for months?

The one he had simply lost the will to write.

The one he had a month to finish or forfeit his substantial advance cheque.

Wolf closed his eyes and rubbed away the tension gathering at his temples. His mysterious little nymph was a distraction he could ill afford, but one that was now burned on his brain, a searing reminder of what could have been had their timing been better.

A mixture of disappointment and betrayal churned in his gut as he swiped his clothes from the ground. "Fuck."

A short time later, after one wrong turn, a subsequent backtrack and a lot of swearing, Wolf stopped his motorcycle in front of the only house he'd found along the dirt trail from hell and wiped away the film of dust that blanketed his visor. He pulled a scrap of paper from his pocket and checked it against the faded signage that sat propped against the low stone wall bordering the property.

The Forge
4 Bennett's Road
Melville's Cross

This was the place, all right. The Bennett family home and current residence of his agent's spinster aunt. The house he'd be holed up in for the next four weeks of his miserable life.

Wolf growled, his frustration palpable. He didn't need a babysitter. He didn't need someone watching over his shoulder, making sure he put words on the page. He knew he had a deadline, knew he'd made commitments, and knew he was failing to uphold them. He didn't need a walking, talking reminder of that fact.

Talk about pouring salt on a wound.

The whole situation was ludicrous. It wasn't as if he was suffering from writer's block or anything as asinine as that. The entire book was mapped out inside his brain and scribbled down on notes. And he would've gotten around to it. Eventually. Once he'd straightened out his life.

And his head.

Unfortunately, his agent, Sally "my bite is worse than my bark" Bennett, didn't agree with his current timetable of "you'll get it when you get it", which was why she'd arranged this little sojourn into the wilds of South East Queensland.

To force the city boy out of his comfort zone.

To force him to finish the book.

Cutting the engine, he dismounted the bike, gritting his teeth as he caught sight of a large stone chip in the finish of the fuel tank.

Wolf was beginning to think God hated him. Or maybe the atheists were right and He simply didn't exist.

That would certainly explain the last twelve months.

As he approached the house, he removed his helmet and absorbed his surroundings, his sharp eyes roving over the building sprawled before him and the overgrown cottage-style garden that enveloped it. On any other day, he would have considered the house quite charming. Its heritage design and vine-covered walls were an artist's dream, the stuff postcards were made of.

Today, however, the house was anything but a dream. Today it was more like a nightmare, looming before him like a mausoleum just waiting for him to crawl inside and rot.

With a resigned sigh, he knocked on the door and waited.

As the door swung open, Wolf lifted his head, his gaze colliding with the most beautiful pair of chocolate-brown eyes he'd ever seen, eyes that were wide with surprise, and for a moment he didn't dare breathe nor move for fear she would vanish again. But then those eyes narrowed and darkened with anger, and the door began to swing shut.

Fuck that!

She wasn't getting away twice.

Adrenaline shot through his limbs and he released the breath he'd been holding. His arm shot out, shoving the door open, breaching the barrier between them. She stepped back as he stepped inside, and she gasped as he slid his hand around her nape, squeezing with just enough force to prevent her retreat.

Wolf grinned as he stared down at her, watching the tip of her pretty pink tongue flick nervously over her full upper lip.

"There is a God."

Chapter Two

Abby struggled against Handsome's hold on her and glared up at him.

"What the hell are you doing here? Go away!"

She barely registered him kicking the front door shut before his mouth came crashing down, his lips hot and soft, moving over hers with such passionate ferocity that her anger melted into a gooey puddle at her feet.

She didn't—*couldn't*—resist when his tongue slid along the seam of her lips, pressing for entry. Opening up, she let him inside, let him ravish her senses and steal her sanity, proving the latter by wrapping her arms around his neck as he wrapped her legs around his hips and pushed her against the wall.

She yelped as he squeezed her arse in his big hands, causing just enough pain to shutter her eyelids with pleasure. He rocked his hips into her, his toughened leather pants doing little to buffer the feel of his erection as it pushed between her thighs. Their eyes locked and Abby shivered, drowning in the ferocity of the lust reflected in Handsome's predatory gaze.

"Still want me to go away?" he asked, his grin cocky, his voice a dark rumble in his chest.

"Shut up," she said, and surrendered herself to the moment. Tunnelling her fingers through his hair, she brought her mouth to his, moaned as she teased his lips apart with a flick of her tongue. She tasted him, tested him, until his jaw clenched, his eyes narrowed, and he pushed himself forwards and took her mouth without further ado, crushing her lips under his.

But the more he sought to control her, the more her brain fought to shut him out, to remind her of where she was, of who *he* was. He was a stranger, and it didn't matter how devastatingly erotic his kisses were.

This isn't right.

This was her home, her sanctuary. What right did this man have to barge in here and throw her world off-kilter? It seemed as if leaving him alone, naked and in the middle of nowhere was too subtle a gesture for this guy.

How the hell did he find her? And what was it going to take to make him put her down and go away?

Handsome chose that exact moment to spank her, his big hand delivering a sharp sting to her fleshy rump. Delicious sensation danced across her arse, and her fresh resolve to be rid of the man was crushed under the weight of her arousal surging to the fore.

What could it hurt to indulge in a little more fun before returning to the real world?

Abby considered the words as they whispered through her head. She was a woman after all, allowed to change her mind. And she wasn't a nun. She had no need to endure a celibate life. Abby had needs—and wants. And what she wanted right then was this big man touching her. *Every-*

where. What she needed was his powerful body pressed against her, overpowering her, dominating her.

Making her feel things she hadn't felt in years.

Soft, feminine, helpless....

Warning bells sounded in her head. There was something seriously wrong with her if these were the tracks her train of thought was headed down.

She was an independent woman.

A freethinking, strong-willed, independent woman.

Sure, she was into kink in the bedroom, not that she'd had much of that lately—okay, not just lately—but that this... *caveman* could waltz in there, treat her like his personal plaything *and* make her crave more was proof positive that Handsome was a dangerous man.

Abby needed her independence. She'd fought long and hard to regain her identity, and she wasn't giving it up again. She needed to resist him. And with a much-anticipated houseguest due to arrive within the hour, she needed Handsome long gone.

If only she could muster the willpower to push him away.

He nipped the soft flesh beneath her earlobe, the small sting shooting bolts of sensation along every taut nerve in her body and straight to her core. She tried to resist him, she truly did, but the way he held her, so familiar, so intimate, her body shivered with anticipation and she found herself wishing she could burrow under his skin, melt into his muscles and bond with his bones—anything to keep him close, to prolong the pleasure.

Tilting her head back, she allowed his lips to graze a trail down her throat, sucking in her breath as he retraced the path with the tip of his tongue. He nipped at her chin and toyed with her lips, teasing her with feather-light kisses only to pull away, making her chase him, crazy with wanting.

His breath whispered over her lips. "Is anyone else here?"

A strangled noise escaped her throat, her brain rejoining the party. She was supposed to be getting rid of this guy, not indulging her baser desires.

She had to put a stop to this.

"No," she said. "But I'm expecting someone soon," she hastened to add, hoping the threat of discovery would deter him from anything further.

Slowly lifting his head, Handsome's eyes narrowed, piercing her with their intensity. "Another lover?"

Abby swallowed hard, the seductive rumble of his deep voice making her heart race and her pussy throb.

Oh God.

Lie, lie, lie.

"No."

Damn it!

Handsome studied her for a moment before a satisfied smile stretched across his face. "Good, then they won't mind waiting," he said. Reaching between them, he yanked her skirt out of his way and slid his hand inside her panties. Gently, he pushed two callused fingers inside her wet and willing flesh, sliding them in and out in slow, measured thrusts. Thumb circling her clit, he spread her moisture around and around but never quite touched the aching nub, never satisfied her growing need, just teased her, made her squirm.

This is bad. So very, very bad.

So why does it feel so good?

Putting her hands on his shoulders, she half-heartedly tried to push him away, the toughened red and black leather of his motorcycle jacket cold and creaking beneath her hands. She may as well have been pushing on a mountain for all the good it did her. The man didn't move; he just grinned at her, a devilish grin that promised all sorts of wicked delights. The same grin he'd used on her earlier when she'd thrown caution to the wind, taken advantage of his timely arrival and crooked her finger at him in blatant invitation.

He slid his fingers out of her body, and her pussy clenched around the emptiness he left behind. Abby quivered expectantly as he shifted against her, keeping her pinned against the wall with his body, with his eyes, as he unzipped his pants.

Oh crap!

He was going to take her again. And there was nothing she could do to stop him.

Scratch that, there was plenty she could do to stop him.

I just don't want to.

"I enjoy watching your face, pretty nymph," Handsome said. "All those thoughts shooting back and forth. Yes, I am going to fuck you again, but this time it will be purely for *my* pleasure."

Before Abby could offer any sort of protest, Handsome wrapped his fist around her panties, pulled them to the side and impaled her on his thick cock, forcing a cry from her lips that heralded her unconditional surrender. A cry that dulled to a lustful groan as he bit her neck and marked her flesh.

Handsome fucked her with deep, purposeful thrusts while his hot tongue laved the ache his teeth had left in their wake. Abby moaned deep in her throat as her hands scrunched the hard leather that covered his chest, her fingers digging in and holding on as he rode her with ever-increasing force. He caught her mouth in a brutal kiss, punishing her with lips and teeth and tongue until she was positively sobbing, begging for sexual release.

Wait. Begging?

No way would she beg.

Never again.

But how was she supposed to stop herself from drifting away to the place she'd been before, where there'd been nothing but him and her and the pain and the pleasure?

So much pleasure.

Handsome had her wrapped around his little finger, his every touch, every thrust, every kiss perfectly timed to keep her teetering on the edge of the abyss. An abyss she would happily plunge into head first—if it weren't for the fact that he wasn't supposed to be there.

She had to keep her wits about her this time, couldn't let him take over again. Maybe, if she thought about what he was doing to her, actually analysed his actions, turning them into something cold and clinical instead of hot... and sensual... then maybe....

Handsome nibbled the shell of her ear.

Abby bit her lip, stifled a whimper.

Oh God....

No. She could do this. She could pull herself back from the brink of total abandon and salvage control over the situation. Yes, of course she could. All she had to do was think about his hips—his thrusting, rhythmic, powerful hips.

And concentrate on the way he held her, the way his fingers dug into her fleshy thighs, the arrogance of his stance as he pulled her into him, his hard body holding her immobile, captive....

But then her gaze collided with those stern hazel eyes and she was ensnared, trapped. Bound to him.

How was she supposed to concentrate when she was being watched by such an unrelenting gaze, determined to unravel her mind just as his measured thrusts were unravelling the final remnants of her control?

Wolf slammed inside her one more time, then stopped.

He knew she was close, had felt her pussy clenching around him, had seen her pupils dilate and the telltale flush begin to rise up her neck, but this was supposed to be a punishment.

So he stopped.

The way her face changed from blissful to irate delighted him. His little nymph had spunk. Punishing her was fun. Not that he'd let her know that, so he schooled his features accordingly.

"Why did you stop?" she demanded, her brow pulling tighter together.

Loosening his grip on her thighs, Wolf gently stroked her soft skin, savouring her warmth and the way she filled his hands to overflowing. There was just so much of her. He could spend a lifetime worshipping her body.

But now wasn't the time. "You want me to keep going?" he said, his mouth a firm line, one brow raised.

"Yes!"

Wolf smirked at the hint of desperation in her sultry voice. "Beg me."

Panic lighted her eyes. "What?"

"Beg me, little nymph. Beg me to fuck you."

Her panic receded as her eyes narrowed and she struggled against him. "Fuck you!"

Wolf tightened his grip and she squealed her outrage. A

surge of pleasure washed through him at the sight of her face contorting with that magical combination of malice and arousal. His groin tightened beyond the point of discomfort, and it was a test of his self-control to keep his voice even. "Beg me to let you come."

She shook her head, lips set in a tight line. Stubborn little nymph. He moved a hand to her breast and gently squeezed. "I know you're close. I know if I pinch you like this," he said as he found her nipple and twisted just hard enough to make her gasp, "the pain heightens your pleasure. But the pleasure creates a new pain, doesn't it? The pain of an orgasm that just." *Pinch.* "Won't." *Twist.* "Come." *Pull.*

Chest heaving with every draw of her breath, she sank her teeth into her bottom lip, tried to contain her whimpering, failed. Her body shivered against him, shook with need, and he kept his voice low and gentle as he continued tormenting her. Releasing her breast, Wolf reached between them and slowly stroked the pad of his thumb around her hard little nub.

"The unrelenting throb of a clit that just needs a few more seconds of touch. How can you stand it?" he whispered by her ear. "I know what you want. I can give you what you need. Beg me, *liebchen*. Beg me to let you come and I will give you an orgasm so intense I will ruin you for other men."

He knew it was a ridiculous boast, but the way she looked at him when he said it was breathtaking. All anger, all panic was replaced with something new. He saw determination and willingness. He saw pain, raw and unrelenting. He saw resolve and it touched his heart. But he couldn't soften now, not when he was so close to getting what he wanted from her, what he *needed*.

Her throat bobbed as she swallowed. "Please, let me come," she said through tight lips, eyes lowered.

"Again."

She wriggled against him, and the agony of holding still and denying them their pleasure was incalculable. He slapped her thigh hard, forcing them both to concentrate. Her look was one of frustrated irritation, and he was certain his face looked much the same.

"Please," she ground out between gritted teeth. "Please, let me come."

"Again," Wolf barked, her obstinate pride testing his patience. Silent tears slid down her cheeks. *Shit.* "Again," he said more gently.

Her mouth clamped shut and a little crinkle appeared between her eyebrows, her gaze darting back and forth. She was warring with herself as much as she was with him. As the seconds stretched between them, he considered pulling out, of leaving her in a state of wanting, but then she sagged against him in defeat, a look of utter capitulation washing over her. She met his gaze and whispered, "Please, please won't you let me come? Please. Make me forget other men."

Her plea didn't just tug at Wolf's vitals, it ripped them clean out.

Moving in her again, thrusting slowly at first, he circled her clit with his thumb and suckled her neck with an open-mouthed kiss. Her breathing hitched, her shallow gasps the sound of a woman near completion.

"Please," she whispered again, and he was undone.

Wolf took her.

Keeping her poised on the brink of ecstasy, he rode her hard, teased her, fucked her, until his own body demanded satisfaction, until he could hold back no longer.

"Scream for me, *liebchen*. When I let you come, you will

scream for me." Her eyes were glazed with unrepentant submission, and his chest tightened with a long-forgotten emotion, the thrill of it driving him to thrust harder, faster until her pussy clenched around him. He squeezed her thigh and she bit her lip. "Come. Now." He pinched her clit and she came with such an almighty scream that he followed immediately with his own roar of fulfilment.

Her pussy continued to clench around his cock even as it softened and he slid from her body. Her cry of protest turned to great sobs of anguish as her legs crumpled beneath her. Wolf lifted her easily and cradled her against his chest, absorbing her distress and her tears.

"Hush now, little nymph," he cooed as he gently rocked her in his arms. She burrowed her head into the crook of his neck and he chuckled as he held her trembling body tighter, marvelling at the trust that emanated from her, revelling in it.

It has been too long since I felt this good.

He smiled, content with the woman in his arms, just as he had been at the creek, and chuckled again as her sobbing eased to little more than a laboured breath. "Oh, you came hard, didn't you? But you're safe now. Punishment is over. I've got you, *liebchen*. You're safe."

Slowly lifting her head from Handsome's shoulder, Abby's pleasure-soaked brain finally sobered enough for his words to fully register.

Did he just say *punishment?*

Punishment for what?

And what right did he have to punish her for anything,

anyway? Suddenly the warmth of his embrace felt like the fires of Hell, a Hell she had no intention of revisiting.

Needing to get away from him, she shoved on his chest and struck at his face, but Handsome was quick for a man of his size. He dropped her body, caught her wrists and had her pinned against that damned wall again faster than she could blink.

Lips peeling back from her teeth, she yelled at him. "Let me go!"

"Hmm... no, I don't think so." His response nonchalant at best, he reminded Abby of someone trying to decide what colour they should paint the wall, not someone forcibly invading her personal space.

"Get out of my house!"

Handsome raised an eyebrow and smirked—*infuriating man*—but made no move to leave. "Don't you think it's about time you told me your name?"

She gritted her teeth. "Fuck you! That's my name!"

Handsome's mouth thinned and his eyes narrowed dangerously, the hazel darkening, reflecting his mood. "Now, now, *liebchen*," he snarled as he tightened his grip on her wrists. "There's no need to be rude."

Abby knew the tactic well and winced, pain shooting through her wrists, but she refused to be intimidated. "I don't know what you think is going on, mate, but it's time for you to go now."

He stared her down. "Tell me your name."

She stared right back. "I don't have to tell you anything."

"You do if you want your hands back," Handsome said, a sudden grin splitting his face.

Abby growled in frustration. The man was impossible. Maybe she hadn't been blunt enough. "Look, you arrogant jerk, I had an itch. You helped me scratch it. End of story. Thank you very much. Goodbye!"

His grin broadened.

He found her amusing, huh?

Let's see how amusing he finds my knee in his sack.

She lifted her leg with malicious intent, but he anticipated the move and pressed his full body weight against her, trapping her legs by spreading them wide. His cock, already hard again, pushed against her lower belly.

"Your name, little nymph. I won't let you go until I have it."

Abby glared up at him as she silently debated her options, then gave up, rolled her eyes and groaned loudly, exasperated. "It's Abby, all right? My name is Abby. Now. Leave."

Handsome let go of her wrists but didn't step away. Instead he slid his warm, callused hands down her arms and around her back, pulling her into his embrace.

His disconcertingly gentle embrace.

He brushed his lips against her ear and whispered, "Abby. Oh, *liebchen*, I'm not going anywhere. Not for a month at least."

Abby froze and squeezed her eyes shut as realisation dawned. "Oh no. No, no, no. Please tell me you're not him," she said as she opened her eyes and looked up at his grinning face, so very close to her own and oh so very kissable. "You can't be him. Sally said he was old, and you're not old so you can't be him. Oh, please tell me you're not him."

"I'm him."

"Oh no," she groaned again, making Handsome—correction, making Wolf Adams, aka Adam Wolfe, international bestselling fantasy fiction writer, her niece's top client, her *much anticipated houseguest* laugh out loud.

His laugh quickly simmered to a lazy smile as he gently stroked her cheek with one hand while he slid the other down her back, cupped her bottom and pulled her hard against his leather-clad body, his thigh slipping between her own and rubbing against her still-sensitive core.

Abby's knees almost buckled, the overwhelming sensation of prolonged pleasure keeping her moving against him. She slid her hands over his chest and knitted her fingers behind his neck, snuggling closer to the man she now knew was far more dangerous than just some crazed stalker intent on fucking her to death, and finding she couldn't bring herself to care.

Her body hadn't been this sated in years.

"Did Sally really say I was old?" Wolf said, frowning as he scratched his grizzled chin.

Abby snorted. "I was told to expect, and I quote, 'a cantankerous old fart with half-moon spectacles and a penchant for missing his deadlines'."

Wolf harrumphed. "I do not wear half-moon spectacles. They're bifocals, far more manly. And you're not exactly what I was expecting either, you know?"

"Really?" she said. "I can't wait to hear this."

"Freakishly tall bohemian fringe-dweller with a great rack. I wasn't really sure what to expect, but I certainly wasn't expecting you."

She raised one brow. "Sally said I have a great rack?"

He traced his roughened fingertips along the neckline of her dress, over the swell of her ample breasts. "I might be paraphrasing." His gaze flicked back to hers. "Why does Sally call you Aunty Abby?"

"Because I'm her father's sister," Abby said, refraining from adding the obvious "duh". Her breathy voice sounded foreign to her ears.

Brows pulling together, he continued, "But you look barely a day older than her. To be honest, when you answered the door I thought maybe you were Abby's daughter, not Abby herself."

Abby stiffened as Wolf's spell over her was broken, her arousal doused by a cold wave of reality that left her feeling lost and wary.

What the hell am I doing?

She jerked away from him and smoothed her dress down, then looked up at Wolf's warm hazel eyes, eyes that were narrowed in curiosity, and just a little hurt.

Shit.

Jaw tightening against the guilt, she straightened her back and stood her ground. "Suffice it to say we have an unusual family. Now move."

He raised his brow, his face stern again. "I beg your pardon?"

Abby chose to ignore him, her need to get away from him far outweighing her will to ask his forgiveness for being so rude. And really, what was he going to do, *punish* her again?

Death by orgasm?

"I said move. I have scones in the oven."

Wolf's eyelids fluttered and he moaned with pleasure as he bit into the oven-fresh, butter-drenched scone in his hand. He hadn't realised how hungry he was until he saw Abby pull the baking tray from the oven and smelled warm pastry mingling with the scents of jam and cream and freshly brewed tea. But he must have moaned louder than he thought, because she stopped what she was doing and stared at him, confusion writ across her brow.

"One of the upsides to having a German mum," he explained between mouthfuls. "An ingrained appreciation for all things cake."

Curiosity replaced her confusion. "And what are the downsides to having a German mum?"

He patted his waistline. "An ingrained appreciation for all things cake."

Her mouth twitched, but just when he thought she was about to smile, she shook her head as if shaking herself out of a trance and returned her attention to the task of spooning whipped cream on top of her scone.

Abby.

Whipped cream....

Wolf's brain went to its happy place.

He bit the inside of his cheek to stem the tide of wicked thoughts flooding his imagination, especially now she locked so prim and proper, sitting across the table from him, pouring tea and offering him food. She seemed very uncomfortable for a woman who less than ten minutes before had been rubbing herself against him, tiny moans of pleasure floating from within her like little clouds of happiness.

She'd practically purred.

He watched as she squeezed lemon juice into her tea and wondered what he'd done to bring about this change in mood, or if she was always like this—scorching hot one moment and stone cold the next?

Wolf didn't like secrets, so whatever she was hiding wouldn't stay hidden for long. He was here for an entire month, and he intended to put that time to good use.

Starting now.

Waiting until she was sipping her tea, he said, "Tell me, did you enjoy being fucked against a wall?"

Her little splutter was highly enjoyable, as was watching her prim façade slip away as she hurriedly swiped at the droplets of tea that clung to her lips with the back of her hand in a very unladylike fashion.

She frowned as she set down the fine china, staring at it intently as she traced her fingertip around the rim of the cup. "If I'd known who you were, I would never have—"

"Offered yourself up for my use? Submitted to my will? Come over and over again, screaming like a banshee?"

When she raised her eyes, they shot daggers at him. "I'm so glad I amuse you."

Ignoring her damning expression and derisive tone, he continued, "Why did you offer yourself? If you don't mind me asking."

"I told you why. I had an itch."

"Ah, yes. The infamous itch." Guessing there was more to it than that, he cocked one brow. "And?"

She squirmed in her seat and her eyes darted away from his. "And... I didn't think I'd ever see you again."

Something tightened in Wolf's gut, the knowledge that she'd used him for her own means more irritating than it should have been. He clenched his jaw as his thoughts darkened. Was she a nymph or a siren? At least she had the good grace to be embarrassed by her behaviour. Unlike someone else he knew.

"And do you get these *itches* often?"

Her eyes snapped back to his, her ire firmly in place once more. "No. I don't. So don't expect what happened today to happen again."

His fear assuaged by her affronted tone, Wolf leaned back in the kitchen chair and stretched his long legs under the table, purposefully brushing them against Abby's bare ones. His lips turned up at the corners, a feeling of satisfaction replacing his annoyance when he saw her eyes soften and her cheeks heat at his touch, small gesture that it was.

"That's a shame. I quite enjoyed myself. Well, except for waking up alone. Although I have to admit, you took your punishment well, and I enjoyed that, too."

She frowned. "Are you saying you punished me because I left you alone by the creek?"

"You promised you'd stay in my arms," he admonished as he reached for another scone.

"Not all day. And as punishments go, having an orgasm was hardly an ordeal."

Wolf's smile broadened. "An orgasm you were made to beg for. Tell me, Abby, did you enjoy begging?" Her lips pursed and her eyes narrowed. "I'll take that as a no. Now, why don't you tell me why such an obviously submissive woman fights so hard against her submissive nature?"

Instead of answering his question, Abby rose to her feet and pushed in her chair, her face blank and her eyes hard. "If you're done eating, I'll show you to your room."

Wolf sighed quietly and rose also. "You can't avoid the question forever, *liebchen*."

She threw him a look that said, "Watch me".

Poor little nymph.

She had no idea who she was up against.

Chapter Three

Wolf Adams was a colossal pain in the arse.

He thought he was so superior with his big words and his designer horn-rimmed glasses and his smug face with that sinful smile that tempted her to misbehave *every single time* she walked past him—but he was nothing more than an arrogant know-it-all.

The man had only been in her house for half a day and he was already driving her mad.

After they'd eaten, Abby had shown him where he could sleep and work and then left him to his own devices, which apparently involved staring out the window while drumming his long, lean fingers on the desk.

Fingers that had done things to her.

Wicked things.

Wonderful things.

But he hadn't typed a single word.

And when he wasn't staring out the window and tapping his fingers on the desk, he was watching her. Do. Everything. It was unsettling to say the least, which was probably why he was doing it.

Annoying man.

His penetrating hazel stare scrutinised her every move as though she were his opponent in some damned chess game, that detestable grin playing around the corners of his sensuous mouth, taunting her with decadent memories of what those lips had done to her, how they'd teased her, tasted her, made her erupt in wild abandon.

Finally, she decided to leave the house. It was cowardly, she knew, but the alternative was unthinkable. To give in to her urges, to submit to him, to strip naked before him, kneel at his feet with her head hung low and beg him to use her as he wished would be to admit defeat.

To admit her weakness.

And anyway, after the cold shoulder she'd given him earlier, she wasn't sure submitting to him again was such a good idea. Goodness only knew how he'd punish her for her insolence this time, but she doubted it would be as pleasurable as his last reprimand. Wolf didn't strike her as the lenient sort.

And doesn't that thought just make your body tingle with excitement?

No. She needed to resist him. She needed to stay in control and ignore her baser impulses.

No matter how tempting they were.

Abby wasn't in the habit of repeating her mistakes—

Her chest tightened against the thought that what she'd enjoyed with Wolf had been a mistake. How could she possibly think what they'd shared was wrong? It had been erotic, sensual, beautiful....

Dangerous.

And it couldn't happen again.

Standing by the back door, she stomped her feet into her work boots, her lips pressed together in a thin line of irritation, Wolf's infuriatingly charming chuckle and her own determination propelling her through the doorway into the garden beyond.

Smug bastard.

Her reprieve was short lived. No sooner had she opened the forge doors than she heard her best friend's Jeep rattle to a halt on the road out front. With a heavy sigh she forced herself to go back to the house.

Once inside, Abby leaned against the doorframe and watched the spectacle unfolding before her. "This should be interesting," she muttered to herself.

Wolf Adams, respected wordsmith, going head-to-head with her best friend, Jane Melville, a woman renowned throughout these parts to be missing the filter between her brain and her mouth.

What she had not expected was to find her friend flirting with Wolf, or anticipated the visceral jealousy twisting her gut as her friend's fingers walked up his chest and tangled in the neckline of his T-shirt. The twisting eased a little when Wolf wrapped his large hand around Jane's smaller one and removed it from his clothing.

Stepping forwards, Abby revealed her presence, folding her arms over her chest.

Wolf saw her first, one corner of his mouth edging up in that wicked grin of his. "Speak of the devil. Why don't you ask her yourself?"

"Ask me what?" she said.

Jane spun to face her, her cheeks slightly flushed, though from embarrassment or arousal it was difficult to tell.

She recovered quickly. "How the sex was with Mr Tall, Dark, and Fuckable here," Jane said, thumbing over her shoulder at Wolf.

Abby raised a brow. "And you're basing that assumption on...?"

"Well, that is what he's here for, isn't it?"

"Is it?" Wolf stared over the top of Jane's head, those deep hazel eyes sparkling with amusement.

She answered through gritted teeth. "No, it isn't."

Jane's eyes widened hopefully. "Really? In that case, can I have him?"

"No."

Jane pouted. "Why not?"

"Yeah. Why not?" Wolf said, obviously enjoying the attention.

Abby suppressed a growl of irritation, then focused on her pain-in-the-arse friend. "One, you're engaged to be married," she said, feeling a modicum of smugness when Wolf's grin disappeared and his eyes narrowed on the back of Jane's head. "And two, he's not who you think he is."

"I'm not?" Wolf said, shifting his piercing gaze back to her.

"No, you're not." She sighed heavily. "Why didn't you tell her who you are? Or was one anonymous encounter not enough for you today?"

Wolf's grin returned. "It was more than once, *liebchen*. And I thought anonymity was the name of the game around these parts."

Jane looked from Abby to Wolf, her brow scrunched in a deep frown. "I'm confused."

Abby sighed again. "Jane, meet Adam Wolfe. Adam, Jane Melville."

"Adam Wolfe?" said Jane, eyeing him dubiously.

"Yes."

"The author?"

"Yes."

"So... you're *not* an escort, then?"

Unbiddable heat flooded Abby's body, flushing her cheeks, yet she felt chilled to the bone. She shivered and her eyelids fluttered closed as she sucked in a steadying breath. To say Jane's blunt, albeit not unexpected question left her mortified was an understatement, and if ever she'd wished to be invisible, it was right then. She could only imagine what Wolf was thinking as his eyebrows arched into his hairline.

"Escort?" he said, his grin broadening with every second that ticked by. "No, *definitely* not an escort."

"But you did have sex with her, didn't you?" Jane persisted. "Please tell me you had sex with her, because if anyone needs to get laid, it's Abby."

"Jane!"

Jane shrugged. "What? It's true. And—oh!" she gasped, her eyes wide. "This is perfect. Him not being an escort is perfect. That means he's staying. That means he can be your date," she said as she grabbed Abby's hands and jumped up and down like an overexcited toddler.

"No, he can't." Abby shot a pleading glance at Wolf, silently begging him to help her put an end to Jane's idiotic plans, but all he did was fold his strong arms over his expansive chest and continue grinning.

"Of course I can," he said with a shrug. "Your date to what?"

Jane practically squealed as she spun around to stare up at him. "Only the two biggest social events of the year!"

"They're not *that* big a deal," Abby grumbled, her jaw tight.

"Not a big deal?" Jane shot her a hurt look as she choked out the words. "I'm going to pretend you didn't say that. The town's one hundredth anniversary and, more importantly, *my* engagement party *are* a big deal."

"Can we discuss this later, please?"

"No, we'll discuss it now," Jane insisted. "Or are you still pissy because I'm making you wear a dress?"

"I'd like to see you wear a dress," Wolf chimed in, his dark gaze sliding over her in a way that made her body flush with a different kind of heat. Her nipples pebbled under her T-shirt and she knew *exactly* why he wanted her to wear a dress. She folded her arms across her chest.

Not. Happening.

Abby rubbed at her temples and scowled at them both. It was bad enough she and Jane were arguing this topic for the umpteenth time, but to do so in front of Wolf was bloody embarrassing, and the fact that Jane had somehow garnered his support against her was utterly infuriating. Not only was this man never having sex with her again, at this rate he'd be lucky not to have his laptop smashed over his disgustingly handsome head.

"I'm not wearing a dress because I'm not going, and if I'm not going I certainly won't need a date."

"You *are* going, you *will* wear a dress, and that's final. Besides," Jane added, her eyes narrowing, "if you don't show up, he'll gloat, and you know how much I hate it when he gloats."

"When who gloats?"

Wolf winced at the force behind his words. Was that jealousy darkening his voice? He clenched his jaw and scrubbed a hand down his face to hide his indiscretion, but when he glanced back at Abby, she was staring at him, her scowl softened to a slight frown, her eyes questioning.

"My brother," Jane said, her elven-like features twisting with disgust. "Abby's husband."

Wolf's hands tightened into fists. Yep, jealousy. And something darker. "Husband?"

"*Ex*-husband," Abby corrected.

Wolf popped his jaw and stifled a snort. His intense reaction was illogical at best, but it forced him to acknowledge, if only to himself, he'd known Abigail Bennett for half a day and she already had him tied up in knots.

He allowed himself to study her, half-listening as her friend prattled on and on in her unveiled attempts to bully her into doing what she wanted. Abby's body was stiff as she shifted her weight from one foot to the other, the movement less mesmerising than it was defensive. Fists clenched by her side, her pretty face flickered between hurt and rage, and her eyes shimmered with unshed tears.

It was obvious—to him, at least—she did not want to see her ex, apparently even if it meant missing her best friend's engagement party.

Why?

And what the hell was all that talk about an escort?

This odd little place was becoming more and more interesting as the day wore on. And his desire for answers to his mounting pile of questions was multiplying exponentially.

"... and what about—"

"Jane, I'm sorry," Wolf interrupted, his need to protect Abby overriding his curiosity, "but it's been a *really* long day for me and I'm very tired. Is it possible for you to finish this discussion another day?" Jane stopped in her tracks and gaped at him, as though being interrupted had never happened to her before. Gently taking her arm, he guided her towards the front door. "I'm sure you understand," he said, his voice deepening with authority.

"Well, uh... yes. Of course. But listen, Abby, this discussion is far from over," she had to call over her shoulder as he led her away. "I'm still taking you shopping on Friday. For a dress." Then to Wolf she said, "I really thought you'd be older."

Wolf harrumphed and shut the door in her face, then returned to the living room. He caught a glimpse of Abby through the window, stalking off towards the same building as before, her long legs eating the distance quickly, but instead of leaving her alone to stew in her emotions, he followed her.

As he neared the sandstone building, one of the large wooden doors flew open, almost knocking him on his arse. Grabbing the door to steady himself, he stumbled again as Abby walked smack into his chest.

"Whoa! Are you all right?" he said, locking his hands around her arms and keeping them both upright.

She ducked her head, but not before he saw she'd been crying. "I'm fine."

"No, you're not."

Sniffing loudly, she raised her head, confirming his suspicion. Her eyes were rimmed with red. "What do you want?" she said, then pursed her lips and lifted her chin as though readying herself for the next fight.

Stubborn little nymph.

He wanted to lift his hand and wipe away the errant tears drying on her cheek, but her stiff posture and narrowed eyes made him try a different approach. He arched a brow. "So, Jane seems like a handful. Is she always like that?"

Her lips twitched with the beginnings of a smile, then flattened. "Pretty much."

Stroking his thumbs against the soft flesh of her upper arms, he said, "Do you want to talk about what happened in there?"

She looked away again. "Not really."

Wolf relaxed his grip and took a step back, giving her the space her short answers and stilted body language told him she needed. "You mean not with me." Head snapping forwards again, Abby opened her mouth to respond, but Wolf threw up his hands in surrender and cut her off. "It's okay. You don't have to tell me if you don't want to. I was just thinking that if you wanted to talk, sometimes it's easier to talk to a stranger." Abby shot him a quizzical look but said nothing. He took the hint. "You know where to find me when you're ready," he said, then turned back to the house.

He only took two steps before she spoke up.

"Wolf?"

"Hmm?"

"What if... I want *more* than talking?"

Wolf's pulse hitched up a notch—or ten—at the very thought of Abby wanting *more* from him, and he had to bite back a smile before turning to face her. "You're not in the right frame of mind for more right now."

"I know, but... what if I was?"

Wolf took a deep breath and let it out slowly, calming his urge to toss this woman over his shoulder caveman-style and have his wicked way with her. No way was it going to be that easy. Not again. Not after her declaration at lunch.

"What are you suggesting, Abby?"

"I don't really know," she said with a slight frown before hurrying on, "But I do know that Jane is my best friend, and I know her brother is an arsehole, and I know having sex with you gave me the confidence boost I needed to face him again. You know, before I found out who you really are and my clever plan was shot to hell."

"Okay."

Wolf felt like he'd stepped out of reality for a moment. He was sure Abby thought she was making perfect sense, but he had no idea what the hell she was talking about. Except for the feeling of pride that was currently swelling his chest.

And possibly his head.

Just a bit.

Sex with me gave her confidence.

Tamping down his ego, he put his focus back on Abby who was staring up at him, those lovely dark eyes wide with expectation. But what *exactly* was she expecting?

"I think you and I need to have that talk now." And he knew just what he wanted to talk about. "Tell me about the escort."

Chapter Four

Of course he'd want to talk about *that* first.

Damn Jane and her big mouth.

But if Abby wanted Wolf to help her regain her confidence—*again*—and put her ex-husband back in his box where he belonged, she first had to gain his trust, and that meant telling him about the escort. And everything else he wanted to know.

Well, maybe not *everything*.

He didn't need to know every nitty-gritty detail about her life. The short version would do fine.

Before she sat down, she offered him a drink—a stalling tactic as she tried to figure out what to say—but he just pointed at the old daybed that sat on the back veranda. A silent command to sit.

Feeling like a child about to be scolded, she took a seat and rested her hands in her lap.

Wolf stood with his arms folded across his chest and stared at her, his face set, expressionless, as he waited for her answer. How the hell was she supposed to explain this?

She took a deep breath. "Okay. The escort. Well, he was

supposed to do what you did," she said before looking away and rushing to add, "only I chickened out and cancelled the service two days ago."

"Why?"

"Because it felt... wrong." And because she'd had serious doubts that Jane's insane plan to pay a guy for sex and a spanking would have produced the desired effect anyway. It was too impersonal. Too cold. Not like sex with Wolf. There'd been nothing cold about him.

"No, I mean why did you want an escort in the first place?"

"Like I said, to do what you did. To have sex with me, to feed my ego and boost my confidence."

Wolf raised a brow. "You don't strike me as a woman lacking in confidence, Abby."

She mimicked his expression but kept her tone dry. "Is that so?"

"It takes confidence to swim naked anywhere, let alone in a creek within full view of a country road. Your confidence is what made me stop my bike. Your confidence is what made me get off that bike when you crooked your finger at me. So the question becomes what makes such a confident woman doubt herself?"

That was the real question, wasn't it?

The blood drained from her face at the prospect of answering, of sharing her greatest torment. Her chest tightened, her emotions crushing it, and she struggled to draw breath. Scrunching her toes in her boots, she forced herself to focus.

She loathed that question.

But she loathed the answer more. Because it still hurt. No matter how much time passed, it still hurt. Richard had broken her in a way that Kurt with his kinky toys and cold heart had never been able to duplicate.

Tears fought their way to the surface, but Abby refused to let them out. She clenched her jaw and raised her chin, but when Wolf crouched in front of her and gently rested his big warm hands on her knees, those sneaky tears escaped and tracked silently down her cheeks.

"What happened to you, Abby?"

She sucked in a shuddering breath. "He left me for another woman," she said quietly, twisting her fingers in her lap. "Richard. My ex-husband. He left me for a woman who —" Sighing heavily, she locked her gaze to his, ready to read his reaction. "For a woman who can have children."

Wolf's face displayed none of the emotions Abby had come to associate with people when speaking about her *defect*. She saw no pity, no disappointment, no revulsion, as though being unable to bear fruit from her loins made her less of a woman. But when his hands tightened over her knees, his fingers biting into her flesh, making her cry out in pain, her heart sank nonetheless.

Wolf wanted to punch something... or *someone*.

This beautiful woman had been robbed of one of life's greatest joys and then made to suffer humiliation at her husband's—*ex*-husband's—hands because of it.

He could have kicked himself.

No wonder she'd become so frigid towards him when he'd thought she was Abby's *daughter*. It also explained why she wasn't concerned about his lack of protection when they'd made love.

Snapping out of his momentary rage, he refocussed his

attention on Abby. She was scowling at him again. Why was she scowling at him again? Then he realised his hands were locked, his fingers aching from the strain of gripping Abby's knees. He relaxed his hold and her expression changed to one of relief, and his to one of remorse.

"Did I hurt you?"

"A little bit, yeah."

Wolf swore softly. The last thing he'd wanted to do was hurt her. "I'm sorry."

Abby rubbed her knees and sighed, her warm breath brushing his face. "No, I'm sorry. This was a bad idea. I shouldn't be dumping my problems on you like this. You have enough to do while you're here. You don't need the distraction."

He brushed his thumb across her cheek and smoothed away a stray tear. "No, I don't."

"That settles it, then. I'm not going. If I don't go, I don't have to see him, and if I don't see him, he can't—"

Wolf frowned at Abby's abrupt ending. "Can't what?"

She dropped her gaze. "Nothing. It doesn't matter."

"Can't what, Abby?" he asked again, hooking a knuckle under her jaw and lifting her face to his.

"It doesn't matter," she said again, a hard edge creeping into her voice. "Really."

Wolf shook his head. "You've just told me it doesn't matter twice in ten seconds, so obviously it matters." Abby's eyes narrowed, her mouth flattened. Clearly there was more to this story, and her obstinacy on the matter was beginning to annoy him. "Abby, what aren't you telling me?" She raised a brow, tried to stare him down. *Silly nymph.* "We can do this the easy way or the hard way," he said. "The easy way, you tell me what I want to know. The hard way, I spank you until you tell me what I want to know. The choice is yours."

Her eyes softened and her lips parted, like a lover waiting to be kissed. She leaned towards him just ever so slightly before pulling back and looking away across the garden.

Wolf bit back a grin as he realised her dilemma. Tilting his head, he said, "Abby, do you *want* me to spank you?"

"No," she said, a little too quickly.

"I was a high-school teacher for more than a decade, *liebchen*. I know bullshit when I hear it. Now I'll ask you again, and you will answer me truthfully. Do you want me to spank you?"

The pursed lips were back, as was her scowl. She really was adorable, but why did she fight so hard to deny what she was, what she wanted?

What was she so afraid of?

Abby was a submissive woman. She knew it. He knew it. Even so, he almost fell on his arse in surprise when she answered his question.

"Yes," she grumbled.

Wolf raised a brow. "Yes, what?"

Her lips softened and her eyes darkened. Her breathing grew shallow and she shifted in her seat, pressing her thighs together before answering him. He'd bet a thousand dollars she was wet. "Yes, Sir. I want you to spank me."

"Good girl," he said, smiling as he stroked her cheek. He was gifted with a tentative smile in return, one that dropped as quickly as it had appeared when he added, "Now, tell me what I want to know or I *won't* spank you. What can't your ex-husband do if you don't see him?"

Abby's lips pulled back from her teeth and she hissed out a breath before growling her answer. "Kiss me. He can't kiss me."

Wolf jerked to his feet as another wave of jealousy

steamrolled over him and his urge to punch someone returned with a vengeance. First this guy abandoned his wife for someone else, and now he was trying to seduce her?

No wonder Abby doubted herself.

And if this wanker was the cause of her distress, then Wolf wanted to help. It was the least he could do for the woman who had opened her home to him in his time of need.

The fact he had more selfish motives was purely coincidental.

"That settles it," he said. "You *are* going, you *will* wear a dress and I *will* be your date."

Abby gaped at him like he'd gone mad. "What? No."

"You said you wanted more than talking," he reminded her.

"Yes. I want more sex."

Wolf's groin tightened as his earlier hopes were confirmed, but he held his desire in check. "You need more than just sex, Abby."

"I don't want more than just sex," she protested, jumping to her feet, ready to defend her position. Ready to fight him.

"What you want and what you need are not necessarily the same things."

Abby planted her hands on her hips and glared at him. "And who the hell are you to tell me what I want or need? You only met me today. You know nothing about me."

Wolf straightened to his full height and folded his arms over his chest, but Abby refused to back down. His cock hardened at the challenge. "Oh, I could tell you a few things about yourself, Miss Bennett," he said, crowding her against the wall and caging her between his arms.

She lifted her chin. "Like what?"

"You're stubborn, passionate and submissive to the core,

and you're behaving like an insecure little girl, too scared to take responsibility for your true feelings. You doubt yourself when you have no reason to."

"I have every reason to."

"Why?"

"Because I kissed him back!"

Abby's head throbbed in the ensuing silence, and her chest heaved with a need to scream. Anger coursed through her veins like a lava flow, blistering her from the inside out. Anger at Richard for kissing her, anger at herself for letting it happen, and anger at Wolf for making her relive her shame.

Before she could embarrass herself further, she ducked under his outstretched arm and stormed off into the house, the screen door slamming behind her. The chill in the air and a quick glance at the clock told her it was time to get a fire lit and dinner started, so she squared her shoulders and steadfastly ignored the massive presence of the man who had followed her inside.

She'd have known Wolf was standing behind her even if she hadn't heard him quietly close the door. She could feel his eyes on her, could smell the cloying scent of sex that had clung to him since lunch. The creak of the floorboards as he shifted his weight propelled her into action, away from him and his judgements.

"You should shower," she said over her shoulder, crouching to light the fire.

Abby didn't want to look at Wolf. She didn't want to see the displeasure written across his handsome face, the same displeasure that had narrowed his eyes and twisted his perfect masculine lips when she'd revealed Jane's duplicitous flirting. With that one look, he'd made it perfectly clear how he felt about infidelity.

She listened for retreating footsteps but heard nothing, and a quick glance over her shoulder revealed he hadn't moved. Filling the doorway with his broad body, he silently watched her, his stare potent, unnerving.

"I wasn't kidding about the shower," she said, striking a match and setting it to the kindling. "You smell."

"Do you still love him?"

Wolf's quiet question startled her. Frowning, she shook her head. "No," she said, standing up and turning to face him. "I stopped loving Richard a long time ago."

"Then why so concerned over a kiss?" he said, moving to sit on the couch.

"Because it wasn't just a kiss."

Wolf's face took on that unreadable mask again and she didn't want to imagine what he must be thinking, especially when she saw his fingers tighten on the arm of the couch until his knuckles blanched. She'd seen her brothers perform the gesture often enough to know what it meant. He was angry, and struggling to control the emotion. If Wolf had been one of her brothers, she would have expected a fist fight to erupt at any moment. But Wolf wasn't one of her brothers and she had no idea what to expect. However, as she was the youngest of nine children, and the only girl, if he thought to intimidate her with his gruff manners, he would be sorely disappointed.

"Explain," he said in a tone that brooked no opposition, even as his hand relaxed and colour bled back into his knuckles.

Abby sighed, realising she really would have to tell Wolf

everything. He was like a dog with a bone, and apparently half-truths weren't going to cut it.

He wanted all those nitty-gritty details she'd intended to keep to herself.

"Richard came to town about two weeks ago to take care of some family business, and while he was here he stopped by to see me."

"Is it usual for him to visit you?"

Abby sat on the couch and tucked her feet under her arse. "No, but he said his wife found some of my things when they were cleaning out their garage and he figured while he was here, he'd drop them off." She snorted a hollow laugh and shook her head. "I should have been suspicious right from the start. Richard never does anything without wanting something in return."

"What happened?"

"We sat, we talked, we laughed, and then he kissed me... and I kissed him back."

Abby stared hard at the flames dancing inside the blackened stone hearth as she remembered that cool autumn day. The day she'd been wallowing in self-pity. The day Jane, her dearest friend in the world, had announced her engagement to be married. The day Abby had felt so alone and empty inside that she'd willingly succumbed to her ex-husband's too-smooth ways and kissed him long and deep.

For the briefest moment, she'd felt desirable again, and the constant ache in her heart and the unwavering loneliness that consumed her restless nights had become nothing more than a bad dream.

"But then my brain switched back on and reminded me it was all a lie. I pushed him away and told him to leave, but the look on his face when he left told me he'd be back, and next time...." She looked down at her hands twisting in her lap. "Well, I wasn't sure I'd have the strength to resist him next time."

Wolf turned to look at her. "So, you thought if you got laid, you'd be satisfied enough to resist any future advances from Dick?"

"From Richard, and yes."

"But you cancelled the escort."

"Yes."

"And you had no idea I'd be so irresistible," he said with a sudden and wicked grin.

A grin Abby mirrored. "No, I did not."

"So what was your plan if he did come back?"

Abby's smile faltered, and she shrugged. "I don't know."

Wolf's eyes darkened as he regarded her with a tilt of his head. "Maybe you were looking for an excuse not to resist him, to be with him again."

Abby raised her chin, so very sure of herself this time. "No. I won't let him do that to me. I will not be the other woman. Not again," she said, then bit back a curse, regretting her hasty words.

Wolf's eyes narrowed, his mouth little more than a thin slash across his face. "Again? You've had an affair before?"

"Not knowingly, but yes." When Wolf's frown deepened, she said, "My last boyfriend, Kurt, neglected to mention he was married."

"I see. So earlier today when you begged me to help you forget other men, can I assume you were talking about these two, about Dick and Kurt?" Abby nodded, not bothering to correct Wolf again. Richard was a dick. No point disputing it. "And are there any others I should know about?" he said, but before she could answer, he added, "Because I can't help you if you're not honest with me."

Chapter Five

Several times, Abby opened her mouth to speak only to close it again a moment later, her words fading to nothing before they'd even passed her lips.

Was she wondering how he was going to help her? Was she wondering why? Wolf knew he should probably say something, alleviate that furrowed brow, but he was enjoying her awkwardness too much. This woman had had his gut in knots from the moment they'd met, and he felt a certain degree of satisfaction in knowing he had the same effect on her.

But why had he offered to help her?

He hadn't been lying when he said he didn't need the distraction, but the more he learnt about this woman, the more he wanted to be her knight in shining armour. The more he wanted to be hers, period. Not even his ex-girlfriend, the cause of his year-long self-indulgent case of the fuck-its, had elicited such a visceral reaction from him.

Beth had made him feel many things during their time together—lust, anger, despair—but he'd never been jealous of her previous lovers, had never wanted her as completely as he wanted Abby. His gaze drifted over her, his hands itching to reach out and touch her, to tunnel his fingers through her raven-black hair and pull her to him, to taste her breath and luxuriate in the softness of her lips, to slide his tongue along that full bottom lip and then ravish her mouth.

And the rest of her.

Wolf sighed quietly and cursed his rampant erection. No matter how desperately Abby tempted him, he couldn't afford to give in to her demands for *just sex*.

He needed more than that, wanted more than that, had denied himself more than that for twelve months. No more. Wolf knew beyond a shadow of a doubt that if he denied himself the pleasure of this woman's submission, the distraction he already felt would deepen into pure obsession. Of course, with a woman as distracting as Abby, he ran that risk anyway.

As if to prove the point, he reached for her. With no more than a gentle tug, she tumbled into his arms, her luscious mouth hovering only a hair's breadth beneath his own.

"You do want my help, don't you, Abby?"

Her eyes widened slightly and she gasped. Her warm breath brushed over his lips, and the temptation to lean into her, to close that minuscule distance between them and give in to his desire was near unbearable.

"Or if it makes you more comfortable, we could help each other."

"How?" she whispered, her eyes heavy lidded, her head tilting, readying for his kiss.

"We could make a deal."

She pulled back, her seductive bedroom eyes overshadowed by that all-too-familiar frown. "What sort of deal?"

"You want your ex-husband to leave you alone, correct?" She nodded. "I can help you with that."

"And again I say, how?"

"You said earlier that sex with me gave you the confidence to face him again." He watched her chin lift and her lips purse as she tried to rein in what looked to be a particularly haughty smile. "So, I will have sex with you—if that's what you still want—"

"Yes," she said, her voice breathless as she leaned into him again and slowly tugged his T-shirt free from his pants. Before she could touch his bare flesh and totally destroy his concentration, he grabbed her wrists and pushed her arms behind her, thrusting her breasts forwards and squashing them against his chest. She sucked in a breath with the sudden movement, her eyelids shuttered, her submission instant and gratifying, and Wolf's calm façade gave way to a smug smile of his own.

"And I will also pose as your boyfriend for the duration of my stay."

Her mouth tightened, her eyes narrowed, and she lost all semblance of warmth. "I said no."

"Let's think about this for a moment," Wolf said. "If Dick sees you swaggering around oozing confidence all over the place, do you think he'll be more intrigued by you or less?"

Abby scowled at him for a long moment before grumbling, "More."

"And would I be correct in assuming that the more intrigued he is, the more he'll pursue you?"

She huffed out a sigh. "Yes."

"So, if you want him to leave you alone, it only makes sense that you give him a reason to do so, and you have to admit, a live, in-the-flesh boyfriend is a pretty good reason."

"I thought you said you didn't need the distraction."

"I don't. But you've been distracting me from the moment I saw you, and that, *liebchen*, is where you helping me comes into it."

Abby's face flickered with an assortment of emotions, most notably lust and disbelief; then her look grew curious and suspicion laced her tone once more. "What do you want, Wolf?"

He shifted her in his lap until their lips almost touched, then tightened his grip on her wrists until her eyes fluttered closed, her mouth fell open and her warm breath sawed in and out of her lungs with lustful sighs.

"I want your submission."

If Abby hadn't already been sitting down, she was sure her knees would have given way. Wolf's deep voice and simple confession permeated every corner of her brain and turned it to mush. *Yep, dangerous.* His mouth was so close to her own she could practically taste him. If only he would lean forwards just a little more....

But no. Instinctively, she knew he wouldn't be doing that, just like she knew he'd make her sit there all night until he got the answer he wanted. Until she said yes. And she wanted to say it, could think of no plausible reason not to say it. Except one.

Kurt Haywood.

If Richard was the knife that first sliced open her heart, Kurt was the salt in the wound. She'd dated that bastard for six months before she'd found out he was married, and even then it was only because his wife had tracked her down and told her to stay away from her husband.

Even now Abby's gut wrenched with guilt. Not once

had she twigged to his lies, and she should have, shouldn't she? She should have noticed... *something*, right? But she hadn't. More than once she'd wondered if the signs had been there all along, but not wanting to give up her new-found love, she'd simply chosen to ignore them. But her ignorance had come at a price.

A very high price.

Now she was hyper-vigilant when it came to dealing with men—well, except for her little segue into Idiotsville when she'd kissed her ex, and her more recent burst of spontaneity at the creek. And that just brought her back to all the reasons why she should say yes, but....

"What happens if I say no?" she said quietly.

Wolf exhaled through his nose and then pulled back a little, just far enough that Abby could see the slight frown pulling at his brow.

"If you say no, all of this stops," he said, letting go of her wrists and sitting back against the arm of the couch. Immediately she mourned the loss of his nearness, the removal of his warm body as shocking to her senses as a bucket of cold water. "If you say no, we go about our business as though today never happened. I'll be nothing more to you than your houseguest, and you'll be nothing more to me than my babysitter."

"No sex?" She already knew the answer.

Wolf's mouth twitched, although with amusement or irritation it was hard to tell. "No submission, no pretend boyfriend, and definitely no sex."

So it was all or nothing, huh?

That should have made making a decision easier, but it didn't. She'd been annoyed at herself for letting the opportunity slip past her earlier, and now that she was faced with it again, she was burying herself in ifs and buts.

Abby chewed on her bottom lip. Maybe she was over-thinking it. Wolf wasn't Kurt. She'd known the man for a day and he'd already treated her with more dignity, more respect than her former lover ever had.

The answer was so obvious. Say yes. Submit to the sex god. Have confidence-boosting sex. Rub Richard's nose in it. Have some fun for a change. Lose herself in the moment.

Lose herself....

Abby stared at her potential lover and tried to swallow past the knot of indecision lodged in her throat. "I'm... scared," she said, her voice little more than a whisper, her fingers twisting in the hem of her T-shirt.

Wolf frowned. "Of what?"

She took a deep breath. "The last time I gave myself to a man, he took everything. Every part of me became his to do with as he wished, and somewhere along the way I got lost. I stopped being me."

"And you're afraid that will happen with me?"

Peering up from under her lashes, she nodded. "It's taken me two years to regain even a semblance of my former self, and I just—"

"It's okay," he said. A knowing smile spread across his face. "I understand. And you don't have to worry about that with me."

Narrowing her eyes, she searched his face, hunted for the lie. "Really?"

"Really. I don't want a slave, Abby. I've neither the time nor the patience for that kind of relationship. But what we did today," he said, his gaze dipping to stare at her breasts, a lopsided grin tugging at his lips, "now that's something I'd like to explore."

Abby bit back a grin of her own. "Before I decide, I need to know one thing."

Wolf raised a brow. "Only one?"

"How exactly does my submission help you?"

His grin faltered, and he shifted in his seat. "In much the same way that sex with me helps you."

Her jaw dropped and her eyes widened. "Seriously? *You* lack confidence?"

He lifted his chin and a hard edge crept into his voice. "Is that really so hard to believe?"

"Yes."

He tilted his head slightly, his brow furrowed with a look of genuine curiosity. "Why?"

"Because I've had sex with you," Abby blurted, his prowess in that arena alone rendering all other arguments invalid. "And because I maybe, might have read one or two of your books. Maybe."

A small smile softened his hard face. "And?"

"And they were very good." She offered him a smile of her own. "You're a talented writer, clever, handsome, spectacular in bed—"

"I don't recall making it to an actual bed yet," he said, his smile spreading into a wide grin.

Abby's heart skipped a beat.

Poking him in the stomach, she said, "You know what I mean. So I don't see what *you* have to be insecure about."

"Well, maybe if you're a good girl and say yes to our deal, I'll tell you. Maybe."

Damn him.

Folding her arms over her chest, Abby scowled at the challenge, but she considered Wolf's proposal. Her choices were simple enough. Say yes and pray that Wolf was a man of his word, or say no and spend the next month trying to ignore the man who'd rocked her world twice before lunch.

Oh decisions, decisions....

"Fine," Abby said, letting loose an exaggerated sigh.

Making a point of cupping his hand behind his ear, Wolf leaned closer. "I beg your pardon."

Her answering glare was adorable. "I said fine."

"Fine, what?"

"Fine, I accept your deal," she said, quickly adding, "Sir," when he flashed her a stern look.

Chuckling softly, Wolf hooked a knuckle under her chin, forced her gaze to his. "Fine, as long as you're sure. I don't want you to feel you're being forced to do anything you don't want to do. It's important to me that I have your consent."

Her expression turned sheepish.

Wolf's eyes narrowed. "What?"

"Before Jane arrived this afternoon, it's *possible* I might have been contemplating asking you to help me with this whole... Richard situation."

"You cheeky little.... If you wanted this all along, why were you fighting me?"

She shot him a look that smacked of frustration, then stared down at her hands, pink staining her cheeks. "Because after deciding to trust you, I saw you flirting with Jane and I—"

"Figured I was no better than your husband." It wasn't a question.

Lifting her head, her eyes flashed with irritation. "*Ex-*husband," she growled. "I didn't like it. Seeing you with Jane. I didn't like how it made me feel."

Momentarily shocked into silence, Wolf blinked at Abby. She was jealous, maybe even a little possessive. These were not emotions he typically encouraged in women, especially those who fell into the temporary category as Abby did, but the sudden thumping rhythm of his heart in his chest forced him to admit that the thought of this particular woman wanting him as deeply as he wanted her excited him.

Sliding his hand through her hair and around her nape, he squeezed gently, forcing her to focus all her attention on him. "Tell me, Abby," he said, surprised by the need darkening his voice. "Tell me what you felt."

Her eyes searched his, uncertainty lurking in their dark brown depths. She tried to pull away, so he squeezed her neck harder. Her eyelids fluttered and her mouth fell open, a soft gasp escaping her full lips. Wolf didn't anticipate what seeing her like this would do to him, and a sudden spear of lust ran him through.

He wanted her.

He wanted to be inside her, pounding their bodies together. He wanted to hear those breathless gasps as he pushed the air from her lungs with every thrust of his hips, feel her fingers dig into his muscles, feel her pussy tighten around him and hear her scream his name. He wanted to make her beg for more only to suffer in agony as he withheld her pleasure and drove her to even greater heights.

Focus.

Reining in his desires, he arched a brow and stared at his captive audience. "You chose this, Abby, when you agreed to be mine. Now answer the question. What did you feel?"

Eyes narrowing, she met his stare with a steady gaze of her own, her uncertainty little more than a memory. "I felt angry. Angry and... *jealous,*" she said, spitting the word out like poison.

"Tell me why."

Lifting her chin, she said, "Men have always preferred Jane over me. She's more fun. She's more outgoing. She's more feminine. She's more... *everything*. Everything I'm not. So when I saw her with you, I got angry because I saw you first. You were *mine!*"

Hearing his theory confirmed, Wolf's eyes widened, his nostrils flaring. Abby's simple declaration of possession made his muscles burn with sexual need.

She continued speaking but her voice quietened, became dull and listless. Defeated. And tears glazed her lovely eyes. "Then I felt jealous because I thought of course you'd choose her over me. Men never choose the big girl when they can have the pretty, petite one instead."

Wolf let out a slow, even breath.

Oh, liebchen, *how little you know.*

Staring at Wolf, Abby looked into those warm hazel eyes, eyes that watched her every movement, read her every reaction. Heat prickled up her neck and across her cheeks, her lip quivering as she fought to keep her tears in check. It didn't help when Wolf released her neck to smooth away the few stray tears she hadn't managed to keep at bay.

She could only imagine what he must be thinking about her little outburst—and then she didn't need to. He wrapped his big hands around her waist and positioned her in his lap so her legs straddled his and the hard bulge in his denim jeans pushed against the apex of her thighs.

"First of all, since it seems to have escaped your notice," he said, sliding his hands over her arse and forcing her tighter against his straining cock, "I'm a big man. I like big girls. And second, if I'd known Jane was spoken for, I wouldn't have spared her a second glance. Much to my ex-girlfriend's chagrin, I'm a big believer in monogamy."

"Even when the relationship is fake?" she said.

Wolf rocked her hips against his, slowly grinding their bodies together, mashing her clit against the inside of her shorts and causing a low moan to bubble up her throat. A moan she tried to stifle.

And failed.

His delectable grin was back. "Especially when it's fake."

Abby's lips quirked with a wry smile. "I suppose I can't get too mad at you, since we weren't actually in a relationship at the time, fake or otherwise."

Wolf's humour vanished and his lips twisted in disgust as he said, "No, but Jane was."

Abby's brow furrowed as she studied his stormy expression. "It really bothers you, doesn't it?"

"Yes, it does. And I know she thought I was an escort, but that's no excuse for her behaviour."

Abby grinned at his pompous tone. "Would it help if I told you Jane and her fiancé are swingers?"

His scowl deepened. "No, it wouldn't. Even swingers have protocols," he said, then narrowed his gaze as he studied her in turn. "What about her brother? Is he a swinger too?"

"No," she said with a sigh. "He's just an arsehole."

Wolf snorted a laugh and Abby chuckled too, until her stomach growled with embarrassing volume.

"Someone's hungry."

"And I completely forgot to get dinner started. I hope you like cheese on toast," she said, wriggling backwards to get to her feet. But before she took even one step towards the kitchen, Wolf grabbed her hand and yanked her back, pulling her into his lap with a soft thump.

"Or we could go out to eat," he said, snaking his arm around her middle. She snuggled against his strong chest, soaked up his warmth. "Sally told me about a restaurant in town. Somewhere I can get a little taste of home."

"I assume you mean The Black Forest Café," Abby said, remembering his German heritage. The corners of her mouth lifted in a dreamy smile and she started salivating. The very thought of eating anything off their menu made her dinner plans of cheese on toast seem like gruel on a stick. "It's fantastic, but we may have to go another time," she said. "It's a very small restaurant. They're usually booked out days in advance."

He kissed her temple. "Good thing I called ahead, then."

"You did?" Abby couldn't help but sound surprised. Wolf had called ahead. He'd planned to take her out to dinner tonight regardless of, well, everything.

Or had he?

Her gaze slid sideways. "And would you still be taking me out to dinner had I turned down your proposal?"

"Of course," he said. "What sort of houseguest am I if I don't treat my babysitter to at least one fancy dinner?"

Shuffling her off his lap, Wolf got to his feet and pulled Abby to hers. He bent his head and caught her lips, lingered just long enough to make her crave more, then tossed her over his shoulder in a fireman carry.

Abby squealed and clung on for dear life. "What are you doing?" she demanded.

Wolf twisted one way and then the next, peering down the hallways that led away from the lounge room in opposite directions, making her head spin with the sudden rush of blood to her brain.

"Looking for the bathroom. I thought I'd have that shower now."

"That way," she said, pointing to the left. "And you're taking me with you because...?"

She heard the grin in his deep voice.

"Because you smell, too."

Chapter Six

"Take off your underwear."

Wolf didn't look at Abby as he issued his order, simply turned the page of his morning newspaper and kept reading.

"I beg your pardon?" she said, her words stilted and unsure.

"I believe the proper response is 'yes, Sir'," Wolf said, hiding a grin before flicking a corner of the newspaper down so he could peer over the top and frown at her.

Wide eyes stared back at him across the kitchen table. "I can't work in the forge naked. It's dangerous."

"I'm not asking you to work naked. I'm telling you to take your underwear off." Wolf folded the newspaper and laid it aside, then continued quietly, "Or are you refusing to obey me?"

Her eyes darkened and her throat bobbed. Her sweet pink tongue flicked out to sweep over her bottom lip and she shifted in her seat. "No, Sir. I'm not refusing."

Wolf allowed himself to smile as Abby stood and pulled her T-shirt over her head. As much as his anticipation made him want to fist his hand around his cock, he forced himself to reach for his coffee mug instead.

When she unfastened the hooks on her practical yet uninspiring white cotton bra and set her large breasts free, he growled his approval. The coffee mug amplified the sound. Abby bit her lip and dropped her gaze, but Wolf didn't miss the corners of her mouth twitching up into a grin.

Next she unfastened her jeans and slid them down her long legs, her panties quickly following. Wolf stared at her as she stood there naked and blushing in the middle of her kitchen.

"Lovely," he said, making a motion with his hand, a command for her to turn around. "You are lovely." When she finished turning, he added, "Sit. Finish your breakfast."

She hesitated to comply, a slight frown pulling at her features. "But don't you want to... fuck?"

Wolf grinned and crooked his finger at her. "Do you want to fuck?"

She stood beside his chair and pressed her thighs together, her voice soft but sure, "Yes, Sir."

"And are you wet for me, *liebchen*?"

Abby nodded and squirmed.

"Prove it." When she stared at him, her expression uncertain, he took pity on her. "Touch yourself. Show me how wet you are. Show me how much you want me."

Her lips softened, parted, and he heard her suck in short, sharp breaths. Her hand drifted over her stomach and her smooth, hairless mound.

Wolf was torn between watching her fingers disappear between her thighs and watching the minute changes that danced across her pretty face. Excitement, lust, need.

When she pulled her fingers out, coated in her slick heat, his own arousal ratcheted higher, but he didn't show it.

Abby had to learn.

Wolf was in control.

"Good girl," he murmured and caught her wrist, lifted her fingers to his mouth and sucked them clean, savoured her light, feminine flavour. "Now sit down and finish your breakfast."

She whimpered and shot him a look of frustration, but she sat down and picked up her fork. Her free hand slipped under the table.

"Uh-uh," he warned, keeping his voice low. "You don't touch what's mine unless I tell you to. And your sweet pussy is all mine."

Abby let loose an exasperated sound and squirmed even more in her seat, but her hand reappeared above the table, clenched in a fist.

Wolf chuckled and finished his coffee. "We need to talk about how we're going to proceed. Set some ground rules. Make sure we're on the same page." Abby nodded, indicating she was listening. "All right, we'll start with something simple. What's your safeword?"

She stopped chewing and stared at him then dropped her gaze and reached for her tea cup.

Something tightened in his gut. "You *do* have a safeword, don't you, Abby?"

"No," she said, her voice so quiet Wolf found himself leaning closer just to hear her.

His temper pricked at him. "How many Dominant partners did you have before Kurt?"

Sitting back in her chair, she said, "None." Wolf stared at her, let the silence grow uncomfortable and fill the void between them until Abby huffed out a breath and explained. "After my divorce, I went to a couple of fetish clubs but nothing ever clicked. The few men *brave* enough to approach me did not inspire me to submit."

He didn't miss the disdain she poured into the word 'brave'. "What did they inspire in you?"

"Mostly the urge to punch them in the face."

Wolf could well imagine some wanna-Dom cowering before his little nymph and it made him laugh out loud.

She shrugged. "I think some of them were as new to it as me and didn't know any better, but the others...." She shivered. "They made my skin crawl."

Wolf had met his fair share of snakes over the years, men—and he used the term loosely—who thought control was synonymous with abuse and that submissive women were easy targets. Especially the inexperienced ones. He liked knowing Abby was shrewd enough to tell the difference between the ignorant and the unauthentic.

But some snakes were harder to spot than others.

"Tell me about Kurt."

When she fidgeted in her seat this time she looked uncomfortable for a completely different reason, a mixture of anger and anguish flickering in her eyes.

"I met him at a club one night and he was just... different. He wore tailored suits and silk ties. He was confident, not arrogant, and he didn't try to get inside my panties within thirty seconds of meeting me. He just sat and talked to me. Asked me lots of questions, explained what was going on in the club around us. He was... nice."

Wolf frowned. "But he never discussed a safeword with you?"

Abby shook her head. "I brought it up with him once, when we'd been together for a few weeks."

"And?"

She lowered her gaze. "He said only subs who didn't trust their Doms needed one, and that he was insulted I would even ask."

Sonofabitch.

Wolf's anger itched under his skin, clawed at him until it spilled free in a torrent of violent cursing. When he focused on the woman sitting opposite him with her eyes wide and her mouth slack he cursed at himself.

So much for being in control.

He rubbed the back of his neck. "I apologise, *liebchen*. I'm not angry with you."

He motioned for her to sit in his lap, pleased when she didn't hesitate and wrapped his arms around her middle. Feeling her warm weight nestled against him helped settle his temper, especially when she rested her head on his shoulder, relaxed. Trusting.

"Men like Kurt are an unfortunate and unavoidable part of living an alternative lifestyle. They prey on the inexperienced and exploit their naivety to suit their own ends. You *always* need a safeword. You may never use it, but it's there for *your* safety. I want you to think of one today, okay? No more play until you do." Wolf sighed heavily and his next words were thick with sarcasm. "What other words of wisdom did this arsehole have to share?"

Her fingers gripped his T-shirt, formed a fist against his chest. "That his pleasure was my pleasure," she said, her quiet words tickling his freshly shaved neck. "And only the weak submit."

"There are so many things wrong with what you just said, I'm not even sure where to begin." Wolf's deep voice rumbled through his chest, his disgust evident in the way he practically spat out every word.

It was a sentiment Abby shared. There was a lot wrong with what Kurt had done to her. Not that she'd known that at the time. She'd been so excited to finally meet someone who understood her needs, who with little more than a look made her want to fall to her knees and beg for the honour of sucking his cock.

She'd been so goddamned gullible.

Pressing herself closer, she inhaled Wolf's heady masculine scent, let it fill her lungs and soothe her. She was well aware of the irony of the situation, that she'd succumb to Wolf Adams just as easily as she had Kurt Haywood. But she found that like the previous day when he'd fucked her against the wall, she simply didn't care.

Maybe it was the way he spoke to her, commanding without being condescending. Or maybe it was the way he touched her, his strong hands firm when wanted, gentle when needed, or the honest pleasure that shone in his eyes when he made her come and scream and writhe.

Or maybe she was still a gullible moron and this was another bad idea in a long line of bad ideas.

All Abby really knew for certain was that when Wolf held her and kissed her and pinned her down and fucked her, she felt content and safe. Even without a safeword.

Wolf shifted her in his lap and she felt the huge bulge of his erect cock press against her hip. Her pussy throbbed in response and she squeezed her thighs together.

"Uncomfortable?" he asked.

"Horny," she replied.

His quiet laughter shook her where she sat.

"We had sex an hour ago."

"And you're already hard again," she said, nodding at his crotch.

He sighed and stared at her like she was a simpleton. "Abby, if I fucked you every time you gave me an erection I'd be balls deep in your pussy 24/7."

Her eyes widened and heat crept over her cheeks. She traced her finger around the collar of his T-shirt. "I'd be okay with that."

He smiled and his eyes crinkled in the corners. "Oh you would, would you? Greedy little nymph." And then that smile turned predatory. "I wonder what else you'd like?"

Uh-oh.

Abby gasped as Wolf roughly shoved her legs apart and slid two fingers inside her. She clung to his shoulders and groaned, her pussy instantly clamping down, flooding with her arousal.

His fingers pistoned in and out, urgent and lacking finesse, but when he curled them in just the right spot, she almost arched right off his lap. Wolf was driving her crazy. She was ready to explode.

"Do you like this?"

Was he kidding? Could he not see how much she liked it? Could he not hear the wet slapping noise coming from her pussy every time he thrust his fingers inside her?

"Yes," she moaned. "Dear God yes." She should have known better. As soon as the words slipped from her lips, he stopped. "No!" Abby wriggled and squirmed, her orgasm so close she could taste it. She stared up at Wolf and whimpered, bit her lip. Begged. "Please, Sir."

Wolf held his dripping wet fingers above her mouth. "Suck."

She didn't pause to argue. Abby opened her mouth and he slid his fingers inside. Her own flavour exploded across her tongue and she moaned as she sucked and licked it off him.

"Good girl," Wolf said, slowly slipping the digits out of her mouth and trailing a wet line of saliva down between her breasts, over her tummy, her mound, her clit. He slid them back inside her pussy, gently this time, his rhythm slower but no less erotic. "Look at me, Abby."

She lifted her gaze to his. Intense curiosity burned in his hazel depths and she felt like she was under a microscope, some weird experiment for him to poke and prod at.

"Tell me what else you like," he said, the smooth glide of his fingers keeping her poised on the edge of what felt like an earth-shattering orgasm, holding back just enough to stop her from tipping over. "Tell me and I'll let you come."

She clenched her pussy around him and sucked in a breath. "You mean like spanking, that sort of thing?"

"Yes."

She didn't have to think too hard to remember the things that got her off, the things that made her feel whole. "Well, there's flogging, riding crops, leather straps." Wolf slid his thumb over her clit and she shivered at the jolt of lust that fired through her. "Pinched nipples, biting, being held down and fucked hard." Her buttocks clenched as he nudged her clit again. Her eyelids fluttered closed.

"Look at me, *liebchen*, only me."

Abby opened her eyes and licked her lips, his steady gaze urging her on. "I like leather cuffs, and oral sex, and I like this. I like sitting in your lap, naked, feeling your hands all over me. And...." She dropped her gaze.

"And?"

She took a breath and slowly released it. "I want to sit at your feet," she said, her voice firming as she pinned him with her stare, ignoring the fact his fingers had stopped moving. "I want to rest my head on your thigh and feel you stroking me, petting me, telling me I'm a good girl."

His nostrils flared and his pupils dilated. "Abigail, you are a good girl," he said, tightening the arm he held around her waist, thrusting his fingers into her hard and fast.

Abby didn't just tip over the edge of that orgasmic precipice, she dove off it head first.

Throwing her head back, she screamed as she came. Her body bucked and her legs shook and she clung to the man seated under her so hard she had to be hurting him. But he didn't complain. And when her orgasm died down and she could think clearly again, she noticed him staring at her, watching her, as if he was trying to memorise what she looked like.

"Your face when you come is the most beautiful thing I've ever seen," he said, his voice underpinned with... *awe?* And then he smiled and her breath caught in her chest. He was so handsome. "Don't ever hold back with me, Abby. Don't ever deny me your beauty."

She had no idea how to respond to that, so she said nothing at all. Embarrassed by his praise, she simply curled against him and nestled her head on his shoulder, enjoyed the gentle rhythm of his breathing where his chest rose and fell under her hand.

He kissed her hair. "Time to go to work."

Abby got to her feet and grabbed the edge of the table. "Whoa."

Wolf caught her hips and steadied her. "You okay?"

She waved him off. "I'm fine. Just remembering how to walk, is all."

The big man laughed, the deep sound filling her kitchen. "Get dressed," he said, and swatted her arse. "But no underwear."

71

"Does that rule apply outside of home?"

Wolf pretended to think about it. "No," he said eventually. "You may wear underwear when we go out. But around here, I want to be able to fuck you with as little time wasted as possible."

"And underwear is a waste of time?" she said, pulling her jeans on, jumping on the spot to help tug them up over her full hips.

Wolf grinned. "I couldn't agree more."

Abby pulled her T-shirt over her head, then re-did her ponytail, pulling back all the strands that came loose while she was thrashing around on Wolf's lap. Her breasts sagged under the soft blue cotton and thanks to the heat in the forge she was going to have a wicked case of under-boob sweat come lunchtime, but she enjoyed the idea of following Wolf's command.

A calmness settled over her, a feeling of contentment.

"Do you have any other commands for me?" she asked. "Anything you want me to do?"

Wolf frowned. "You said you like leather cuffs. Do you own any?"

"Yes," she said, a tiny spark of excitement pinballing around inside her.

"What about chains?"

"I think I have some in the forge. Why?"

Wolf crooked his finger at her, grinned and backed out the kitchen doorway. "Follow me."

Chapter Seven

That evening Wolf sat on the couch, Abby on a cushion at his feet with her legs tucked under her big soft arse and her head resting against his thigh. He smiled as he stroked her hair and watched the firelight dance over the silky black strands, and a feeling he hadn't felt in God only knew how long washed over him.

Satisfaction.

Abby was turning out to be even more interesting than expected. After breakfast, when he'd asked her to fetch her leather cuffs she'd sheepishly returned with a small leather case full of all sorts of goodies, and a riding crop clenched between her teeth.

And when he asked her to attach some chains to the rafters in the lounge room, something he could link her cuffs to and use to restrain her, she'd created an entire system of pulleys and chains with a built in failsafe switch for safety purposes. When she'd finished installing it and showed him how everything worked he'd simply stared at her like a dumbstruck fool.

Abby had shrugged and said, "What? Building dungeon

equipment is how I earn ninety percent of my income. Didn't Sally tell you?"

"Must have slipped her mind," he'd grumbled, although he was fairly certain his devious agent hadn't told him on purpose.

Just like she'd neglected to mention her 'spinster aunt' was a young, beautiful submissive with curves for days and a sexual appetite that rivalled his own. While Wolf didn't advertise his sexual predilections, he didn't exactly hide them either. And this new information coupled with Sally's vague descriptions of both himself and Abby, only added fuel to the thought that just maybe he'd been set up. Maybe they both had. A little matchmaking on his agent's part? He grinned as he stared down at Abby because, seriously, there were *plenty* of other places his agent could have sent him for a writer's retreat.

Gaze drifting to the rafters, Wolf's mind drifted back to breakfast and his grin died. If he ever met the fuck-knuckle who fed Abby all those lies about Dominance and submission, he'd rip the little shitstain's arms off.

No safeword!

Who the fuck doesn't use safewords? Abusers, that's who. Abby was a natural submissive, she loved it, needed it, but if her only other experience was with someone like Kurt.... *Fuck.*

No wonder she'd been so resistant, so confused.

When he'd arrived at the house and she'd opened the door, had stared up at him with those big brown eyes, his pulse had raced at an alarming rate and his need to kiss her, to take her, to mark her as his had overwhelmed him.

But after lunch when she'd stomped around the house, trying to avoid him, the look on her face, the conflict....

He could have cut the tension with a knife.

Doubt had crept inside his mind and sent a chill down his spine. He'd thought he'd read her wrong, misjudged her desires. *It wouldn't be the first time.* And the last time he'd read someone wrong, he hadn't been demanding enough, which made him think maybe he'd overcompensated with Abby.

Had pushed too hard, been *too* demanding, and that was why she'd pulled away from him. Of course, she'd made the truth known to him after Jane's little visit—*his foot-in-mouth daughter disaster*—but that had just raised so many more questions. And Wolf wanted answers.

He wanted to know everything.

"Abby."

She nuzzled his thigh. "Yes, Sir?"

"Did you think of a safeword today?"

"Yes, Sir," she said, and turned to rest her chin on his knee. "I chose daisy."

"Daisy," Wolf said, letting the word roll around in his mouth. "It's short, should be easy to say around a ball-gag. Good." He twisted his hand in her hair and forced her gaze to his. "Now, how about we take that rig for a spin?"

Abby's pupils dilated and her fingernails dug into his thigh. "I thought you'd never ask."

Wolf stood and held out his hands for her, pleased when she eagerly complied, and pulled her to her feet. He wrapped each of her wrists in a leather cuff, checked to make sure they weren't too tight then hoisted her up and secured the chains in place.

He stood back and scratched his chin. "Something's missing...," he mused, then he reached into his pocket and pulled out some plastic clothes pegs. "I didn't find any nipple clamps in that little bag of yours, but these will do in a pinch."

Abby snorted. "Bondage jokes. Funny."

Wolf grinned, slid his hand to her nape and bent his head to kiss her. "Tonight is all about you, *liebchen*. Your body, your thoughts, your pleasure. I want to learn all about you, what you like, what you don't like, so we're going to play twenty questions. For every answer you give me," he said as he clipped a peg to Abby's nipple and gently tugged, smiled when she bit her lip and moaned, "you earn a reward. For every answer you refuse, you earn a punishment." With a quick yank he pulled the clothes peg off her nipple. Abby yelped and scowled at him. "Do you understand?"

She moved her body as if trying to ease the sting in her nipple, but nodded. "Yes, Sir."

He stroked her breast, leaned down to suckle her reddened tip. "Good girl," he said, and was awarded with another moan. "Let's begin. What's your favourite colour?"

Abby blinked. "Seriously?"

Wolf cocked one brow. "Do you really want to start off with a punishment?"

"Purple. My favourite colour is purple," Abby blurted, quickly adding a, "Sir," when he narrowed his eyes. He clipped a peg to her left nipple, smiled when she moaned.

"What's your favourite food."

This time she didn't hesitate. "Rare steak and mashed potatoes."

"Good girl," Wolf said and clipped a peg to her right nipple, then he leaned down and blew air across both.

Abby bit her lip and shivered. She wriggled her arse and pressed her thighs together, and when Wolf reached between her legs, he found her already wet.

Responsive little nymph.

He fetched the short leather strap from her toy bag. "How long were you married?"

She shot him a quick glare then looked away. "Five years," she grumbled. "But we were together for eight."

The sound of the leather strap smacking against her bare mound rent the still, warm air around them. Abby cried out, then moaned—*loudly*—and shivered. Another probe with his fingers found him slipping inside her so easily it was all he could do to keep it in his pants and not screw her brains out right then and there.

He took a step back. Found some more clothes pegs. Asked more and more questions. Sometimes they were silly and lighthearted. "Who's your favourite cartoon dog and why?"

Sometimes they were born of curiosity. "What's your middle name?"

And others were more probing and uncomfortable. "How did Kurt punish you?"

Abby gave him answers. Sometimes willingly. "It's a toss-up between Scooby-Doo and Muttley."

Sometimes begrudgingly. "Ulysses," she said, her mouth twisted in irritation. "Don't. Ask." To which he replied, "Oh, *liebchen*, you know I'm gunna ask."

And others were probing and uncomfortable. "Anal sex."

The shitstain is toast.

Abby couldn't hold Wolf's gaze and stared at the floor. Question after question, he asked her so many things, wanted to know about so many things—her brothers and her mother and Jane and the picnic—but when he asked about

Kurt, her gut tightened and her mouth went dry. She hated that even after two years that arsehole could still affect her this much. But Wolf wanted to know, so she told him.

And he was not happy.

"He used anal as a punishment? That goddamned arsehole!"

He paced back and forth across the lounge room, even tossed away the leather strap he'd been teasing her body with as though he didn't trust himself not to use it in anger. And when he stopped in front of her again and his eyes searched hers, he looked stricken, almost fearful.

He cupped her cheeks and stroked his thumb over her lips. "Were you ever non-consenting? Did he ever punish you beyond what you could handle?"

Hot tears gathered in her eyes and her nose itched as she realised what Wolf was really asking. Had Kurt raped her? Kurt may have been a sadistic bastard, may have done a lot of things she hadn't liked and debased her in ways that bordered on inhumane, but he was no rapist.

"No. Never."

Wolf's eyes fluttered shut and his chest rose and fell as he took a deep breath, his relief clearly visible. When he opened his eyes again he smiled at her and wiped away the stray tears leaking down her cheeks, then gently pressed his mouth to hers. His concern for her, the sweet gestures, the softness of his touch all made her crave more, this gentler side of him just as arousing as any of the well placed slaps and smacks he'd peppered her eager body with.

Abby leaned into his kiss, moaned and flicked her tongue against his lips. She felt him smile before opening up and slipping his tongue along the length of hers. One strong hand angled her head to give him better access, the other slid down her back and around her waist and locked her body against his.

The pegs on her nipples rubbed against his strong chest and she whimpered as a delicious bite of pain speared through her breasts and arrowed straight to her clit. Her knees buckled and her body sagged, her weight pulled at the chains.

Wolf moved, leaned back a little and took her weight, his thigh slipped between her legs. If she rocked her hips, Abby could brush her clit over the rough denim of his jeans, but he moved out reach before she could grind herself down and cause enough friction to ease the ache pulsing in her pussy.

She groaned. "You're so mean. You said tonight was about my pleasure."

Wolf chuckled and that wicked grin of his sprang to life again. "It is. But I'm not fucking you. Not yet."

Abby pasted on her most innocent expression. "Are you saying fucking my tight, wet pussy with your big, thick cock wouldn't give me pleasure?"

"Careful, little nymph," he said as he unclipped the pegs from her nipples. The buds swelled with blood, ached so good. "You're dangerously close to topping from the bottom. And by my count, I still have one question left to ask."

Abby was desperate for Wolf to touch her again, to press his muscled thigh against her clit and squeeze her tits in his big strong hands as he bit and sucked and licked her nipples. "What if I beg?"

"I do like hearing you beg," he said, folding his arms across his chest, "but if you answer my question, begging won't be necessary."

Licking her lips in anticipation, Abby nodded. "What do you want to know?"

"Do you think only the weak submit?"

Abby blinked in surprise. That was not the question she'd been expecting. Do you prefer flogging over spanking, or do you like sucking my big fat cock, or what's your favourite breakfast cereal, those were more in line with his previous questions. But no, he was going to make her earn her orgasm with something thoughtful and insightful and now that he knew she was willing to beg for it, he knew she'd answer this question, too.

I hate this game.

"That's what Kurt told me," she said, keeping her voice stiff.

"I know what he told you. I'm asking if you believe him."

She swallowed hard. "Yes."

He tilted his head and his eyes narrowed slightly. "Why?"

"Because I... *want* to submit."

"That's not a bad thing," Wolf said, stroking her hair like he had when she'd been seated at his feet. The rhythm of his strokes calmed her, settled her.

Like a frightened pet.

"But that's not how it's supposed to be."

"No?" He kept stroking her hair and the temptation to lean into his hand, to feel his strength and warmth was too much to resist.

"I'm supposed to be strong, and smart, and independent."

"From what I've seen, you are all those things. You run your own successful business in, what I'm guessing is a male dominated industry. This rig you built is nothing short of genius. And wanting to submit, trusting someone enough to relinquish your control to them, *that* takes strength."

Abby's brow pulled down. "I'm not sure I understand."

"When you first started going to clubs, did you submit to the first person you met?"

"No."

Wolf cocked a brow. "Why?"

"Because I didn't feel he could handle me."

"You needed someone strong because *you* are strong," he said, pulling away to remove his clothes. "You would never submit to someone weaker than you, because you know they'd never give you what you need."

Abby swallowed hard as a now naked Wolf stepped towards her, his powerful body and proud cock a feast for her eyes. "But what if I don't know what I need?"

"You don't have to know," Wolf whispered against her lips as his hand twisted in her hair. Then snarled, "That's my job."

His kiss was brutal, a pure domination of her senses as his tongue stabbed inside her mouth and his teeth clashed with hers. His free hand slid down her back and Abby yelped as he smacked her arse. Hard. Her pussy clenched around nothing and she wished he'd just fuck her already. 'Please," she whispered, the word heavy with her desperation.

Another smack landed in the same spot as the first, the burn adding to the fire already spreading outwards from his palm. Her body quivered with need and she knew her pussy was soaked, could feel it coating her skin where it dripped down her thighs. Wolf must have noticed too because the next thing she knew he was screwing two fingers into her, making her body jump and shake and shiver.

"I'm going to fuck you so hard," he growled. "And don't you dare come before I tell you to. Understand?"

Arousal spiking off the charts, Abby could do no more than nod and whimper, "Yes."

The hand burning a hole in her arse slid down her thigh and lifted her leg around his hip. Wolf pushed forward and nudged her pussy with the head of cock, the thick tip moving through her slick folds with ease. In one quick thrust he was seated inside her, her pussy stretched wide around him and her clit smashed against the rough hairs at the base of his cock. He buried his face against her pulse and she felt his panted breaths caress her throat, felt the heat of his tongue, the sting of his teeth—

Good God the man loves to bite!

Wolf started to move, his pace languid, his thrusts deliberate. "I've wanted to take you like this all day, little nymph," he murmured as he nibbled his way down her neck. "I wrote my fucking arse off today just so I could take my time with you tonight. Just so I could fuck you like this, so I could tell you...."

Abby's breaths were little more than ragged gasps, and even they were requiring way more concentration than she could spare. "Tell me what?"

"That if you *ever* call yourself weak again, I will spank your arse so raw you won't sit down for a fucking week." Then he lifted her other leg around his hips and thrust into her for all he was worth.

Wolf kept his word and fucked her hard and she cried out from the pressure of holding her orgasm back. He lifted his head and watched her, his gaze darting over every feature, watching every emotion she couldn't restrain. It was all there for him to see. The pain, the lust, the need, the desperation.

The submission.

The *freedom*.

"Beautiful," he whispered. "Come for me, Abby. Come now."

The dam wall broke and Abby screamed her release. Her body bucked and her legs spasmed, her pussy clenched and her lover roared. Then she was being held in his arms, crushed against his body as they panted and came down from their high. Her legs still locked around his hips and his cock still buried deep inside her cunt.

Abby nestled against Wolf's sweaty skin as he reached up to unfasten her cuffs, and then he carried her to the couch.

"Don't move," he said, and walked away, gloriously naked and unashamed. He returned a minute later with two glasses of water and pressed one into her hand, then took a seat beside her and gathered her close. "That's my good girl," he said and kissed her sweat-soaked temple. "My sweet, strong girl."

Chapter Eight

Friday morning came around disturbingly fast, and Jane and her bubbly personality arrived at the house disgustingly early.

Abby was barely awake when she heard Jane's Jeep pull up out front, the honking horn shattering what little hope she'd clung to of dozing off to sleep again. Straining her neck to see over the top of Wolf's prone body, she searched for the time. The digital numbers on her clock radio flashed at her with their usual acuity, confirming her suspicions.

It was too damn early.

Flopping against her pillow, she pulled the doona back over her head. She didn't want to go shopping, didn't want to buy a new dress. She already owned one, and as far as she was concerned, it was one too many.

Abby wanted to stay in her nice warm bed, let the soft music and morning news waft to her ears at seven o'clock sharp when her alarm went off. Then she wanted to pretend to still be sleeping when Wolf started kissing her from her navel to her nape before slipping his thick cock

Ceep inside her and waking her up properly, just as he had every morning since his arrival.

As if on cue, he turned to her and slid his big hand between her thighs.

"Good morning," he murmured, pushing her legs apart and thrumming his thumb across her clit.

Abby moaned as the most exquisite sensations unfurled through her body, her limbs trembled, her breathing staggered—

The front door slammed shut.

Groaning in frustration, she heard Jane's lyrical voice call out, "Hurry up and get your butts in gear," and all sexual desire deserted her.

Wolf growled his displeasure at the interruption. "How upset would you be if I strangled your best friend?"

Feeling his hot lips on her throat, the vibration of his voice rumbling against her skin, Abby considered doing the strangling herself. "Given the circumstances?" she said, "Not very. But if we don't get out there soon, she will come looking for us."

Now it was Wolf's turn to flop back against the pillows and groan. "Fine. Go. I'll join you after I take care of this," he said and slid his hand back under the covers. "The last thing I need is to walk around town all day with an erection."

Abby smirked, but it faded quickly as his words sank in. "What do you mean 'walk around town'?" she said, as she slid out of bed and headed to the wardrobe. "You're not coming with us, are you?" She grabbed a clean pair of jeans and a T-shirt and slung them over her arm, then dug through a drawer for clean underwear.

"Yes, I am," he said, a not-so-subtle hint of challenge in his eyes. "Is that a problem?"

She frowned. "But your book, your work is—"

"Ahead of schedule," he said, using the tone of authority she'd quickly come to recognise over the week. The tone that said, "Do as you're told or suffer the consequences." The tone that made her wet without fail. Wolf nodded at his cock. "Now, unless you're going to help me take care of this...."

Pausing by the door, hand on the doorknob, Abby was tempted to do exactly that. Licking her lips, she stared at the sheet tented over her lover's hard cock, watched the fabric move as his fist slid up and down slowly, purposefully. Her pussy pulsed with awareness. She wanted to help. So. Bad... until Jane called out again.

Wolf chuckled, and Abby groaned. "Okay, okay, I'm going."

After a quick shower, Abby entered the kitchen to the sound of a whistling kettle and the smell of bacon frying. *Drool.* For all her faults, Jane could always be counted on for one thing: food. Whether it be an elaborate luncheon for one of her clients or a simple cup of coffee and a hearty breakfast for her best friend, you could rely on Chef Jane to serve it up with style.

"I hope you have your walking shoes on 'cause we are on a mission, baby!" Jane said, sliding a mug of coffee across the table and then snatching the toast from the toaster a second after it popped, cursing quietly as it burned her fingers.

"Wolf's coming with us," Abby said, inhaling the decadent hazelnut aroma wafting from her mug.

Jane shrugged as she slathered the toast with butter. "I know. I invited him."

"You what? Why?"

"Because I want a man's opinion and I can't exactly ask Sam, can I? You know it's bad luck for the groom to see the bride in her gown before the wedding. Besides," she added with a playful grin, "I didn't think you'd mind. Not after what I heard."

Abby stilled, her coffee halfway to her lips. "After you heard what?"

"After I heard from Dieter about the two of you making out like a pair of teenagers in front of The Black Forest the other night. He said it was quite the show. I'm sorry I missed it," she said, laying the rest of their breakfast on the table. She took a seat, then reached for the toast.

Abby clenched her jaw as heat crept up her neck and warmed her cheeks. Pressing her legs together, she tried to halt the familiar feeling of warmth and readiness blooming between her thighs.

Just the thought of that night—or more to the point, how that night ended—had her wishing she was back in bed, naked and restrained, the burn of his hands on her arse and the feel of his cock—

She dragged herself back to the present before she moaned out loud, but she smiled as she remembered Wolf taking her by surprise outside the restaurant, cementing his lips to hers in a toe-curling kiss that had sent a shockwave of lust screaming through her—and firmly planting the idea in the minds of the good citizens of Melville's Cross that he was indeed her boyfriend.

Apparently, the man knew how to use small-town gossip to his advantage, and judging by Jane's comments this morning, it was working.

Abby reached for a slice of buttered toast and then a helping of crispy bacon and scrambled eggs. "Well I hope you're not expecting an encore performance today."

"An encore of what?" Wolf said, strolling into the kitchen. He leaned down to kiss the top of her head, then grabbed a mug.

"Nothing," Jane and Abby chimed together.

Wolf stared at them both with a raised brow but said nothing, just turned away and helped himself to the coffee pot. Abby's blood heated at the mouth-watering sight of his arse-hugging jeans, naked torso, and bare feet, and her eyelids lowered with smug satisfaction at the sight of his tattoos and the memory of his guttural moans and satisfied sighs as she'd traced her tongue over every delectable inch of them.

And like a fan to the flames, that was all it took for her desire to flare back to life and scorch through her once more. Pulse racing like a wild thing, she swallowed hard against the knot of lust in her throat. She itched to touch him, to savour his heat, his strength, to scratch her nails over the hard ridges of his muscles, to soothe the welts with her tongue.

But apparently she wasn't the only one to appreciate the view.

Jane's jaw dropped and her eyes widened to a comical degree. "Oh. My. God!" she mouthed silently before grinning like a lunatic and giving Abby two thumbs up. Abby rolled her eyes, but when she noticed Jane's attention lingering on Wolf's fine physique, appreciating the width of his shoulders, the firmness of his arse, and the strength of his thighs, those same eyes narrowed.

"Jane," she said, unable to hide the underlying menace in her tone. Jane's attention flickered from Wolf's arse to Abby's face. "Mine."

Leaning against the kitchen bench, Wolf stared out the window, grinning from ear to ear over Abby's simple statement of possession. He still couldn't explain why, and he wasn't even sure he wanted to, but the idea of belonging to this woman filled him with more pleasure, more hope than he'd felt in a long time.

Since his timely arrival in this tiny town, Abby had fascinated him with her myriad facets. From the mischievous nymph to the stubborn harpy, from the hammer-wielding blacksmith to the submissive kneeling at his feet, the woman constantly seduced and enthralled him.

Only the day before he'd been mesmerised by the ferocious intensity with which she'd transformed twisted chunks of iron into the most beautiful and intricate creations, all the while swaying her hips in time to the thumping strains of the industrial metal blasting from her stereo. Then in the evening they'd shared a simple meal together before retiring to the lounge room, where she'd stretched out at his feet with a sketch pad and charcoal in hand while the dulcet tones of some long-dead jazz singer played quietly in the background.

Wolf had laid aside the book he'd been reading just so he could watch the way her long fingers danced across the paper, caressing the page with each sure, firm stroke of the pencil. He'd wanted to feel her touch, wanted her to caress his flesh as sensuously as she did the paper. Then he'd seen the reflected firelight dancing in her eyes and the secretive smile playing around the corners of her luscious mouth, and he'd not been able to help himself.

He'd taken her.

Right there on the slightly singed Persian carpet, and without a single word spoken between them. He'd taken her again and again until the fire had died down to little more than embers and the music had faded away to nothing; then he'd carried her, sweaty and smiling to bed, snuggled her close and drifted off to sleep.

He turned to face Abby as the images of the night before continued to play through his mind, of the way she'd stared up at him with those sultry chocolate eyes and touched him with charcoal-covered fingertips leaving dark, smoke-like smudges all over their bodies. By the time he'd taken a seat beside her and helped himself to a plate of bacon and eggs, he was sporting a fresh erection.

After breakfast, Wolf joined the girls as they piled into Jane's old Jeep. He winced as the engine started with a whine. "Will this rust bucket even make it to Brisbane?" he said, strapping himself into the back seat, thankful Jane had remembered to remove the canopy. Being ridiculously tall had its advantages, but sitting hunched over in the back seat of a car for a three-hour round trip was not one of them.

"She'll get us there," Jane shot back at him, then added, "Won't you, baby?" as she lovingly stroked the steering wheel. Wolf wasn't convinced, but then Abby turned in her seat and flashed him a grin and a wink and he ceased to care if the car was roadworthy or not. He was going to enjoy the ride regardless. "Right then. Has everyone gone to the loo?" Abby nodded and Jane stared at him until he did likewise, then flashed him that devilish smile of hers, shoved the Jeep into gear, and they were off.

About half an hour into the trip, Wolf leaned between the front seats so he could talk to the girls without yelling against the wind. "So, what's on today's agenda?"

"Jane has appointments at three different bridal boutiques, and I have to visit a client to discuss an overdue payment," Abby said, her mouth twisting with irritation.

Wolf frowned but before he could say anything, Jane

added, "And we have to find a dress for Abby. That's most important."

"For the wedding?" he asked, still frowning over Abby's comment.

"Well, yes, that too, but mostly for my party. And the picnic."

Wolf's gaze shifted from Jane back to Abby.

Ah, yes.

The picnic.

He leaned back in the seat, smiling as he remembered the way he'd made her squirm nights earlier when he'd asked for all the particulars of the parties they'd be attending.

The picnic was an annual day-long event celebrating the founding of Melville's Cross. Apparently, the whole town turned out to share in a potluck lunch on the neatly clipped lawn of the town square. A tradition, he'd been told as he'd tortured the details out of her during their little game of twenty questions, started by the founders themselves and resurrected by Jane's father when he'd had a turn as the town mayor more than a decade before. The picnic was basically one big birthday party for the town, and this year was the centennial. Citizens past and present were expected to turn out en masse for the big day.

Citizens like Abby's ex, Dick, who was flying in from Sydney for the event—sans wife and kids—and Jane's cousin, a woman who'd delighted in making their teenage years hell and, thanks to her position as principal at the local primary school, was now referred to by both women as ' Debbie the evil witch who snacks on the souls of children".

Abby still wasn't overly enthused about the whole ' ordeal", as she called it, but a phone call from her brothers the previous night had made her slightly more amenable to the idea, as they would be joining the throng of people flocking to the little hinterland township for the anniversary. At least, some of them were. As he'd dug a little deeper into her *unusual* family history, he'd discovered she had eight brothers in total, and no sisters.

"One father, six mothers and nine children. They call us Bennett's Bastards," she'd said.

"They?"

"The people in town."

Wolf had seethed on her behalf, insulted by the narrow-mindedness that would have created such an all-encompassing slur. Abby had laughed it off, said there was no point being insulted by the truth, but Wolf had seen the hurt in her eyes, the subtle twist to her lips, and heard the underlying shame in her voice.

She'd also spoken of her mother, a French-born socialite named Selene who'd met Ulysses Bennett, the eccentric yet enigmatic painter, at an exhibition in Paris and fancied herself in love with him, so much so that she'd run away from home to be with him. But after fourteen months of roughing it in Melville's Cross, she'd turned tail and run all the way home to France, leaving Bennett, his horde of sons and a three-month-old Abby in her wake.

She'd never met her mother, wouldn't even know what she looked like if not for the paintings in her father's studio.

The knowledge made Wolf's head spin. He couldn't imagine not knowing his mother, not knowing the sound of her voice as she scolded him in German, or the scent of her favourite perfume that always seemed to hang in the air wherever she went, or the warmth of her smile, the fierceness of her hugs, the sharpness of her wit.

Abby had none of that with her mother, none of those memories, and it made him sad for her. She'd shrugged off his concerns, saying that instead of one mother, she had eight mother hens, and for everything her brothers didn't know—or didn't want to know—she'd had Jane's mum. She didn't feel like she'd missed out on anything, and she'd given Wolf a glimpse of a woman more extraordinary than she gave herself credit for.

Still, having all those mother hens descend on the town —on him—was an unexpected challenge. One Wolf was determined to face head-on.

Abby had insisted on telling her brothers the truth of their relationship, and he was curious to know how they'd react when he finally met them face-to-face. If someone told him *his* little sister was exchanging sex for submission with a bloke she'd only just met, he'd knock the man's teeth out, and he wasn't so sure Abby's brothers would behave any differently. He certainly didn't think they'd be as enthusiastic about the whole arrangement as she did. But perhaps their unusual upbringing would make them more accepting of the situation.

He guessed he'd find out soon enough.

The morning passed quickly as the trio raced from one bridal boutique to the next, the ladies trying on dress after dress, Wolf ever watchful of Abby and her reactions every time someone mistook him for the groom. He revelled in the boost to his ego when she publicly laid claim to him, and he finally figured out why.

Because no one else ever had.

Wolf had only ever had two serious relationships in his forty years of life, and neither had been common knowledge. The first woman, a fellow teacher, had insisted their relationship remain discrete so as to avoid getting sacked for fraternisation.

The second woman was Beth. She'd been terrified her

ultra-conservative father would find out she was not only dating someone twice her age, but regularly attending fetish clubs where she was summarily stripped, flogged, and fucked in front of a rapt audience. She'd demanded complete secrecy.

Neither woman had scowled and snarled at pretty young shop assistants who made zero attempts to hide their interest in him, or straightened to their full six feet in height, folded their arms across their chests and said, "Touch my boyfriend one more time. I dare you."

Nor had either woman made pretty young shop assistants cry. For a submissive woman, Abby was scary as fuck when she wanted to be, but Wolf also knew it was her he had to thank for his recent explosion in productivity.

For three days running, he'd beaten his personal record for number of words written in a single day. The woman made his imagination soar, and if he kept up his current pace he'd have the book finished with time to spare.

Time he could devote solely to pleasuring his little nymph.

It feels good to have goals again.

After lunch, Jane declared it was time to find Abby a dress for the picnic, a decision Wolf championed wholeheartedly. He for one was sick of the sight of her lovely legs hidden under the impenetrable weave of denim, and he was resolved not to rescue her from the petite redhead this time, no matter how often she threw him a pleading look that screamed, "I'm in hell!"

"You used to have a wardrobe full of dresses," Jane said, passing another frilly thing over the dressing room door. "I'll never understand why you got rid of them all."

Wolf was curious, too. Since moving into her bedroom, he'd seen inside Abby's wardrobe often enough to know the only dress she owned was the one she'd worn the day they'd met, a pale yellow summer one covered in tiny white daisies that had definitely seen better days. When he'd fucked her against the wall, he'd wanted to rip it from her body and use the remnants to bind her wrists.

Maybe next time he would.

The thought made the semi-hardness he'd been sporting on and off since breakfast even more uncomfortable as it pushed against the zipper of his jeans, and it was far beyond time he did something about it.

"Jane," he said, "would you give us some privacy, please?"

Chapter Nine

A bby's shoulders relaxed and she breathed a sigh of relief.

Finally!

Wolf had finally come to her rescue. No more uber-girly monstrosities, no more chiffon getting stuck in zippers, and absolutely no more completely impractical shoes that inched her ever closer to the Guinness Book of Records for the World's Tallest Woman.

"Come out here, *liebchen.*"

She smiled at the sound of his voice, at the rough undertone she'd come to recognise over the last few days. The quiet command that told her Wolf was horny, and she was about to have her wrists bound in soft leather and her body ravished by strong hands and firm, hot lips.

Normally this would have made her horny too, if it weren't for one teeny-tiny problem.

Slowly, she cracked open the dressing room door and peeked out at him. Folding his arms over his broad chest, he raised one brow and stared down at her. Unfortunately, she knew what that look meant, too.

He was daring her to question his command.

"I can't come out," she said so only Wolf could hear her.

"Why not?" he whispered back.

She gnawed on her lip. "I don't want you to see me in this dress. I look ridiculous."

His lips twitched and his eyes sparkled with amusement. "Why don't you let me be the judge of that," he said, and she knew it wasn't a question.

With an icy feeling of dread curling low in her stomach, she opened the door the rest of the way, standing before him in what could only be described as a ruffled handkerchief the colour of frozen yoghurt. *Orange* frozen yoghurt. And it was too tight. It wouldn't even do up in the back.

"I look like a cross between a sea slug and an overstuffed sausage," she grumbled, then folded her arms over her chest in an attempt to cover herself. It didn't help. Wolf's lips pressed together into a thin line, his eyes widened, and his body shook with silent laughter. Angry fire obliterated the ice. "That's it. I'm going to kill Jane."

Wolf pulled her into the open and wrapped his arms around her. "No you're not," he said, still chuckling. "Especially since this godawful dress is the only thing stopping me from dragging you back in there and finishing what we started before breakfast."

Abby faced the mirror again and scowled at her reflection, at the dress so hideous it killed erections.

What the hell was Jane thinking?

The colour, the length, the frills—it was so wrong. On so many levels. Abby was a blacksmith, an artist, and she dressed accordingly in jeans and T-shirts. Even so, Jane was right when she'd said Abby used to have a cupboard full of dresses—until about two years back when she'd discovered her boyfriend was an even bigger arsehole than her ex-husband and she'd gotten rid of almost every girly thing she'd owned in a bid to make herself as unattractive to future arseholes as possible.

Sure, she still felt the *occasional* urge to flaunt her femininity, to don a dress and bake scones and have her brains fucked out by handsome houseguests, but not often enough to warrant owning more than one dress. And yeah, she enjoyed the odd mani-pedi now and again, and owned a vast assortment of expensive scented hand creams, but hey, hand care was important.

The fact of the matter was Abby wasn't a girly girl. Not anymore. Not after—

No.

Won't think about that.

She shook her head to refocus her attention and noticed Wolf frowning at her reflection. "It really is awful, isn't it?" she said as she plucked at the frills with her fingertips as though she were picking up a snotty hanky.

"Yes, it is," he said with a sharp nod. "Now take that thing off and let's get out of here."

With her jeans, boots, and T-shirt back where they belonged, Abby felt far more comfortable. She scooped up the orange froufrou and a half-dozen other crimes against fashion the sales assistant had so helpfully suggested she try on and carried it all out to the sales counter, where she was treated to a showdown between Wolf and Jane as they debated which dresses she should buy as though she had no say in it at all.

Annoyed by their high-handedness, she elbowed her way between them, picked out the only dress she'd actually felt pretty in and shoved the rest to the end of the sales counter.

"This one," she said to the cashier, handing her a floral

halter-neck maxi dress with a red satin waistband. "And I'll take those red wedge sandals and these earrings," she added, choosing a pair of gold hoops from a bowl beside the register.

The cashier nervously flicked her gaze from Jane to Wolf before landing on Abby. "Will there be anything else?"

"No, thank you," she said before anyone else could speak.

Abby handed over her credit card, the cashier rang up the purchase, and Jane made her displeasure known by huffing out an annoyed sigh every few seconds. Wolf, on the other hand, was disturbingly silent. Standing beside her with his hand on the small of her back, he rubbed tiny circles through her T-shirt, creating a warmth that was quite... *soothing*. It only took a moment for her shoulders to relax and the tension knotting her stomach to unravel.

Glancing up at him, she caught the smile playing around his sensual mouth, the rather smug, triumphant-looking one telling her he knew that *she* knew exactly what he'd done. He'd rescued her—again—and this time from her own foul temper.

Of course he'd also rescued Jane from the severe tongue lashing she was practically begging for with every huffy sigh that passed her lips. When Jane threw her hands in the air and stormed outside, Abby had a hunch the opportunity to continue the dress debate would present itself soon enough.

She did not, however, expect it to be in the middle of the Queen Street Mall amidst the Friday afternoon crowds.

"One dress? You only bought *one* dress!"

Abby rolled her eyes. "Exactly how many picnics are we going to that I need more than one dress?"

"That's not the point. Wolf, back me up here, please."

"Leave Wolf out of this," Abby said, almost snarling the words in her frustration.

"No, I won't. I'm tired of leaving men out of the conversation. For pity's sake, Abby, it's been two years already. What are you so afraid of?"

Heat prickled her face and neck, and her hands tightened. "Now is not the time, Jane," she warned through gritted teeth. Turning to walk away, she barely made it three steps before her friend's clear voice rang out over the crowd, halting her escape and stinging her more effectively than a slap to the face.

"Then when, Abby? Would it really kill you to look like a woman every now and again?"

"Stop it," she snapped, glaring at her friend.

Jane walked towards her, her brows drawn and the corners of her mouth pulling down. "To be noticed by men?"

Her body shook. "I mean it, Jane."

"To notice yourself being noticed by men?"

Fuck it.

"I don't want to be noticed!" Abby yelled, the words spilling free before she could stop them, and the shocked faces of passers-by making her wish the earth would swallow her whole.

Wolf watched Abby shake with rage, hands clenched by her sides in fists so tight her knuckles had turned stark white. A more murderous look on a woman's face he'd never seen. But for a woman who didn't want to be noticed, her little outburst was attracting a lot of attention. Attention that was quickly draining the colour from her cheeks as her expression morphed from angry to ashamed.

She wobbled slightly as she stood there on the pavement, her chest heaving, her distress evident to anyone who cared to notice. Wolf rushed forwards, gently taking her by the shoulders. "I've got you, *liebchen*," he said, coaxing her to a bench and sitting her down.

Jane approached them like an apologetic child, her mouth flapping open and shut with no words coming out. Wolf clenched his jaw against his anger at Jane—at himself too, truth be told. He'd seen Abby's agitation, had guessed it wouldn't take much to make her snap, but he hadn't stopped the redhead from pursuing her little crusade.

He shouldn't have let her push Abby so hard, and if it hadn't been for his own stupid curiosity to see where it would lead, he wouldn't have. He did, however, learn one thing.

This was about so much more than a dress.

"Is she all right? Abby, are you okay?"

Wolf relaxed a little when Abby lifted her head and glared at her friend, her embarrassment taking a back seat to her temper once more. Apparently, Jane took that as a good sign too, for a sudden torrent of words spewed from her mouth.

"Abby, I'm so sorry, but you know what I'm like when I'm passionate about something," she said, her voice taking on a wheedling tone. "And you know I'm passionate about you. You're my best friend, and I just want you to be happy. It's been so long since you did anything even remotely girly, and it just makes me so mad because you are so gorgeous and you don't even know it, and my idiot brother deserves to have his face rubbed in it and—"

"Jane," Abby said.

"Shutting up."

Wolf's anger was quickly dispersed by a burst of laughter, but it dissolved into irritation just as fast as Abby's hand landed with a sharp sting on his upper thigh.

"What was that for?" he said, his lip curling back from his teeth as the pain of the slap spread through his leg.

"Don't laugh at her," Abby said, her voice as fierce as a mother protecting her child, her expression as furious as he'd ever seen it.

Wolf opened his mouth to dispute her accusation and then promptly closed it again. To reject the idea that he'd been laughing *at* Jane would have been to tell a lie, a habit he himself had been a victim of and wholly despised. No, he couldn't deny that the spectacle of Jane's animated diatribe and subsequent submission into silence had been as entertaining as it had been interesting, but he also couldn't deny that he'd been in the wrong to laugh at such an inopportune moment.

"I apologise for my inappropriate behaviour," he said, lifting her hand to his mouth and placing a gentle kiss upon her reddened palm.

Her face softened and her scowl disappeared, and the hint of a smile tugged at her lips before she pulled her hand away and frowned again. Wolf grinned at her petulance, but also because he guessed her hand had to be throbbing after the slap she'd given him, which he figured was punishment enough for committing the foolhardy act of hitting him in the first place.

"What are you grinning at?" she said. "I'm still mad at you."

Wolf's eyebrows shot upwards. "What for? I've already apologised."

Abby feigned a look of surprise and pressed a hand to her chest. "Oh, I'm sorry. That must have been the other man I'm sleeping with who was wishing out loud that he could set my jeans on fire."

His grin returned. "Well, I won't lie, they do irritate me, but that's only because it takes so much longer to get you out of them. With a dress I can... well, you know," he said as his grin broadened to a predatory width. He watched with satisfaction as her skin flushed and her pupils dilated, and when her lips parted slightly and he heard her faint gasp of breath, he couldn't help but slip his hand to her nape and pull her in for a kiss.

"Are you still mad at me?" Jane said, sidling closer to where they sat.

Wolf released her and Abby rolled her eyes. "I'm always mad at you."

"I don't know why. You never listen to a damn thing I say anyway."

"Jane, you are my oldest and dearest friend and the closest thing I have to a sister. Of course I listen to you. But that doesn't mean I'll blindly do whatever you say."

Wolf's chest puffed up with pride and he smiled with satisfaction. He liked knowing his woman had a mind of her own. It made her submission more special knowing it was given freely, given because she wanted to share that part of herself with him and not because she felt it was expected of her, or worse, was so needy for attention she'd do anything and everything without question.

Abby was too stubborn to be needy.

"Now, if the pair of you have finished trying to boss me around," she said, getting to her feet again, "I have some business to take care of."

Chapter Ten

"Tell me what you were thinking about today."

Abby blinked at Wolf from behind her fork. "When?"

"When you were staring at yourself in that ugly dress. You drifted off somewhere, and nowhere nice if the expression on your face was any indication."

Abby chewed her steak, relishing the tender, juicy morsel while her brow furrowed in thought. Not that she was giving his question any great consideration, certainly not the full attention Wolf probably thought it deserved.

It was a particularly good steak.

But then her memories slowly reorganised themselves and fragments of images slid into view.

Ugly dress. Mirror.

Ugly dress. Men.

Ugly men. Kurt.

Ugly—

"Abby?"

The chunk of meat got stuck in her throat and she grabbed her wine to wash it down, emptying the glass in the process. Her eyes flicked towards him, but she could tell Wolf, his piercing gaze never leaving her face, had seen the glimmer of recognition she was trying to hide.

"Right there," he said, confirming her fear. "What were you thinking about just now? That's the same look you had in the dress shop."

Abby lowered her eyes, staring at her plate as she pushed a mound of mashed potato through the blood from her steak and watched with more interest than it warranted as it slowly turned pink.

She swallowed a little harder when she heard Wolf's cutlery clatter against his plate, and she looked up again to see he'd laid his knife and fork neatly down and was staring at her, his eyes narrowed and his strong arms folded across his chest.

Her shoulders sagged and she sighed quietly as she recognised the pose for what it was.

A silent command.

Damn it.

Until a moment before, the only thoughts running through her head had been about how much she was enjoying her dinner, and how well her client meeting had transpired before they'd left the city. She'd completed a huge job for a restaurant owner over three months back—an intricate set of wrought-iron gates and a dozen wall sconces for his *très chic* eatery—and until today he'd still refused to pay her the balance she was owed.

It had been almost comical how quickly he'd written out the cheque when he saw Wolf standing behind her—a six-foot-six imposing wall of muscle wrapped in jeans and a T-shirt that did nothing to hide his strength, his arms folded over his broad chest and one brow cocked in a look of displeasure.

Sort of like it was right now.

In an act of defiance she reached for his wine glass, but Wolf shook his head in one slow, deliberate movement. Courage withering under his hazel gaze, her hands retreated to her lap. "I don't want to talk about it."

"Why not?" he said, staring at her, challenging her. But it was a challenge she couldn't meet. Lowering her gaze, she watched him through the veil of her lashes, watched his body relax and his brow crease in curiosity. Leaning towards her, he said, "What could be so bad that you feel you can't tell me about it?"

Wolf's voice reached across the table and wrapped itself around her, warm and soft and gentle, its subtle strength threatening to disarm her. Abby rubbed at her chest, at the hollow feeling welling within her, then blinked hard as she felt a headache taking hold, making her skull feel overfull and throbbing with the exertion of holding everything inside.

Closing her eyes, she pinched the bridge of her nose in a feeble attempt to halt its progression, then gave up and stared wearily at the man sitting opposite her. The man who was still waiting for her to say something, to explain herself.

The man she feared would turn his back on her if he knew the whole truth.

Tears burned behind her eyes, but she wouldn't cry. Not over this. She had no right. "I don't feel well," she said, her voice flat. "I'm going to bed." Sighing quietly, she pushed her chair back.

Wolf rose with her, followed her to the door. "Abby—"

"I'll clean up in the morning," she said, deliberately cutting him off, but as she tried to walk away, Wolf caught her wrist, pulled her into his arms and pressed her back against the unyielding wall of his chest.

"I asked you a question, *liebchen*," he murmured against her ear. "I expect an answer."

Twisting her head to look up at him, she swallowed hard at the sight. The stern, hard eyes, the thinned lips. "I have a headache," she said, her voice stammering.

Wolf's mouth twisted. "You drank your wine too fast," he chided. "But don't think that will save you." Locking her arms to her sides, he frog-marched her out of the kitchen and into the lounge room.

"Save me?" she said, a cold chill sweeping over her skin. "From what?" She tried to wriggle free, but the cage of Wolf's arms only tightened until she winced from the crushing pressure, conceded defeat. But when he stood her in front of the couch and tugged her hands above her head, her tiredness, her misery and even her headache were swept aside by a wave of self-righteous anger.

Just what the hell did he think he was doing?

Wolf wrapped a leather cuff around each of Abby's wrists, attached them to chains dangling from the oaken rafter over their heads, then hoisted her up just enough so her feet weren't flat on the floor. He smirked at her furious expression.

"There's my fierce little nymph," he said. "I was wondering where she'd gone off to." Abby shot him a look of utter malice before turning her face away and pursing her lips. He swatted her arse, grinned when she yelped. "Sulking does not become you, *liebchen*."

"I'm not sulking," she said through gritted teeth.

Running a finger under each of the cuffs, Wolf checked they weren't too tight. "I'm glad to hear it," he said, unzipping her jeans and tugging them down her long, luscious legs. "I loathe dealing with brats."

He hadn't touched her legs since he'd awoken that morning, and the urge to trace his fingers up the strong curve of her calves and along the silky length of her thighs, to squeeze and caress and kiss her bountiful flesh was almost too hard to resist, especially when his eyes drew level with her underwear.

They'd not long gotten home and Abby had not had a chance to get changed, so she was still wearing her pale pink cotton panties with the tiny satin bow at the waist. Such an innocent garment for such a sensual woman.

Exhaling slowly, he chanced a glance at her face. Distinct traces of anger still danced in her lovely brown eyes, and as much as she tried to hide it, so did arousal.

Keeping his gaze fixed on hers, he pressed his thumb against her cotton-covered pussy and rubbed, smiled as her panties soaked through. Sliding his fingers inside the waistband of her underwear, he slowly pulled them down, inch by agonising inch, torturing himself. Torturing her.

Her eyelids shuttered and her teeth sank into her bottom lip, her chest rising and falling with exaggerated breaths.

And her arousal shone slick on her pussy.

Licking his lips, he leaned forwards and licked hers. A quick flick of his tongue against her clit, through her folds. Just a taste of her. A tease. He smiled with satisfaction when her leg quivered and a soft moan reached his ears.

Wolf had never been a Dom who expected sex from his submissives. He found it more annoying than anything, an intrusion into his headspace that often knocked him down from his natural high.

Of course there were always exceptions to the rule, and

in the last year he'd made a lot more exceptions than he cared to admit. On the other hand, sex with Abby felt right, a natural progression in their roles as Dominant and submissive.

But there would be no sex tonight. Not when she was so obviously hiding something from him, avoiding his questions and trying to put distance between them.

The knowledge sobered his mood.

Something was festering inside that vivid imagination of hers, and it was his duty to find out what, to help her if he could. And as much as Abby's anger told him she didn't *want* to deal with it, the guilt and sadness he'd read on her face earlier told him she *needed* to deal with it—whatever it was.

Wolf didn't doubt he'd find out what she was hiding. He'd known her less than half a day before discovering the best way to interrogate her.

Rising to his feet, he gently stroked her cheek. Her eyes narrowed as a look of wariness settled over her features and she held her body rigid. Reaching between her legs, he slid a finger through her wet folds, teased her clit again, probed her pussy, thrust in and out until her body relaxed and she bit her lip, her gaze darting to his mouth, silently begging him to kiss her. Instead, he stepped away from her.

"I hate you," she said, though the words lacked conviction.

"You will tell me what I want to know, *liebchen*."

A light of challenge shone in her eyes as she lifted her chin.

Wolf stepped forwards again. "Stubborn little nymph," he said, sliding his hands under her T-shirt, teasing his fingers under her bra, lifting the garment free. Her voluminous breasts spilled into his hands, their soft, heavy heat pressing against his palms, burning him, tempting him. His erection pushed against the zipper of his jeans. "Always the hard way with you, isn't it?"

"You're one to talk," she said. "If I'm stubborn, what are you?"

He pinched her nipples until angry tears glistened in the corners of her eyes. "I'm determined."

Chapter Eleven

Abby's leg twitched with the urge to kick her lover; only the rattling of the chains above her head cautioned her otherwise. Snarling in frustration, she clenched her hands into fists, tested the thick leather cuffs for weakness. She found none.

Wolf stood there watching her, his face impassive, his hands cupping her breasts, saying nothing as she twisted and turned, the balls of her feet scrabbling for purchase on the Persian rug. His stern gaze was as maddening as it was intoxicating, and it became harder and harder to ignore her traitorous body, to ignore the delicious heat he was inciting in her blood and the slick, velvety warmth between her thighs, making her squirm.

Damn him.

The man was clever—a little too clever for her liking. He had her exactly where he wanted her.

Trapped, and in a state of wanting.

Abby's arousal gave way to curiosity when he released her breasts and walked to the desk. Her curiosity was doused by fear when he returned with a heavy pair of scissors and a wicked grin.

Panic.

"No."

Shaking her head to clear the image forming in her mind, she forced herself to think rationally, calmly, before her anxiety could take hold of her and crush her windpipe.

Wolf wouldn't hurt her. She had to believe that. He wasn't Kurt; he didn't get off on making her cry. He was Wolf, the tender, passionate sex god of her wet dreams, the man who'd made love to her in this very room just the night before.

Obviously sensing her discomfort, Wolf's grin disappeared. He frowned and took a step back, holding the scissors in front of her where she could get a good long look at them, then said, slowly and deliberately, "I will not cut you."

Abby stared at the shiny steel blades, watched the firelight dance along their deadly length, felt hot tears track down her cheeks and drip off her chin, but the truth in his voice cut through the fog clouding her mind. Staring straight ahead and avoiding his gaze, she nodded, lips pursed and trembling.

When she heard the sound of metal shearing through fabric, she hiccupped a laugh of relief. Within moments her T-shirt and bra were in tatters on the floor, leaving her naked but unharmed, and Wolf was putting the scissors away again inside the desk drawer. Safely out of sight.

"Are you okay?" His hazel gaze bored into hers, searching for an explanation, frowning when she didn't offer one.

"Yes. I'm all right."

Wolf stroked her cheek and she leaned into it, the warmth of his palm providing an intrinsic feeling of safety.

"Good. Because once we've settled the issue of you keeping secrets from me, we'll address the issue of your fear just now." Abby tensed. Wolf kissed her forehead. "Don't fret, little nymph. I'm not cruel enough to make you deal with both in one night."

"Thank you," she murmured.

Wolf pulled his hand away and she mourned the loss of his touch, not only the heat of his palm and the safe harbour it provided but because she knew what was coming. That simple gesture, that warm and gentle hand that had soothed her fears would soon be replaced by devious fingers, hot and hungry. Fingers that would tease and tempt her, that would take her to the brink of orgasm only to leave her clinging to the precipice until she spilled her guts and told him what he wanted to know.

She knew his tactics well enough to know that only then would he grant her reprieve, let her climax and put an end to his insidious torture.

But that wasn't the only thing twisting her insides in knots.

She'd kept her sickening secret for two years, hadn't told her brothers or even her best friend, and she didn't want to tell *him* either. She didn't want to see the disgust in his eyes, hear the disappointment in his voice. All she wanted to do was curl up in bed, go to sleep, wake up tomorrow, forget everything. But one look at his set jaw and furrowed brow and she knew.

He wasn't letting her forget anything.

Lightly trailing his fingertips over her skin, Wolf circled her, the captor inspecting his quarry. She shivered in anticipation. Stopping behind her he pressed himself close and buried his face in her hair, sniffing deeply before sweeping her tresses aside and kissing the bare flesh at her nape.

"Du riechst so gut," he murmured.

Abby closed her eyes and breathed him in, a mixture of sandalwood and masculine heat. The scent was purely male, intoxicating, enveloping her senses, distracting her. She tried ignoring him as he moulded his big body to hers and pushed his denim-clad cock, hard and proud, against her arse, but then his hand fisted in her hair, yanking her head to one side. The whimper she'd desperately tried to swallow escaped her, betrayed her as his teeth sank into the muscle curving between her neck and shoulder.

Heated breath whispered over her skin. "That's it, *liebchen.* Don't resist me."

Wolf slid his other hand over her body and cupped her breast. The sting of his fingers pinching her nipple made her cry out, but as he continued to tug at the hardened peak, twisting and releasing in a steady rhythm designed to send bolts of awareness straight to her core, her cry softened to an indulgent moan.

Her resolve weakened.

Abby rested her head on his shoulder, he rubbed his cheek against hers. She knew the tender action was meant to cement her there, to quash the last of what little resistance she'd shown him till now, but the harsh graze of his stubble only sharpened her dulling senses and reminded her of her true situation.

She wasn't chained to the ceiling to luxuriate in the erotic sensations he was exacting from her body. Not this time. This was a battle of wills between Dominant and submissive. His job was to extract information, hers to withhold it.

She only hoped her stubbornness outweighed his determination.

Abby turned her face away from his.

Sighing heavily, Wolf dropped his hands, stepped back and blanked all emotion from his face. He hated what he was about to do, but she was leaving him no choice. The last thing he wanted was to punish her for being sad, but when that sadness emanated from her like the stink of a festering wound, he couldn't sit back and do nothing.

Today wasn't the first time he noticed it, either.

From the day they'd met, he'd seen it banked in her eyes, especially when she thought no one was looking. And he knew it wasn't just from loneliness, the obvious culprit. Wolf was certain she would have admitted to that. This ran deeper, darker.

I will find the cause of it.

Cupping her face in both hands, he said, "I had hoped to avoid this, *liebchen*. I had hoped you would open up to me willingly and save us both from this torment. Please know I take no pleasure in punishing you."

Abby lifted her chin, but the pose lacked her usual haughtiness. "Then don't punish me," she said, her voice wavering. "Let me go."

He walked towards the desk. "Do you remember when I said I can't help you if you're not honest with me?" The rattling of the chains had him casting a sideways glance in her direction. Her eyes darted feverishly from him to the desk and back again. He thinned his lips into a pitiless smile. "I'll take that as a yes."

Wolf watched Abby yank on the chains that held her captive, her face frozen in terror. He knew he was being cruel, taunting her this way, but as he reached inside the desk drawer and pulled out a small black bag instead of the scissors, she ceased her struggles and frowned at him.

"What's that?"

"You're not the only one who did some shopping today," he said, tipping the bag upside down and catching the small black box that fell out of it. He'd seen it in a shop window in town and knew it would come in handy, though he didn't think he'd be using it so soon, or that its first use would be a punishment. Opening the box, he lifted out the small device and the remote control it was attached to. "Do you know what this is?"

She frowned. "It looks like a butterfly."

Wolf bit back a grin. "It's a very special butterfly, designed for a very specific purpose."

Her eyes narrowed. "What purpose?"

"I'm glad you asked."

Crouching in front of her, he lifted her feet one by one through the adjustable bands attached to the device, then slid them up her legs until they sat snug around her hips. The butterfly's body nestled perfectly between her swelling lips, its wings preventing it from slipping inside her completely, and its pointed little beak was positioned directly over her clit. He tapped the device so it knocked against her sensitive nub, allowing himself a small smile at the sound of her shocked gasp.

He stood and brushed her hair from her cheek, let his fingers linger over her warm, soft skin. The heat of the room and the flickering of the fire in the hearth bathed her whole body in a fiery golden glow. Wolf couldn't remember the last time he'd seen a woman so desirable.

Until she bared her teeth and tried to bite him.

"Thank you, Abigail," he said tightly, stepping away from her, "for reminding me why we're here." He turned the dial on the remote control, bringing the butterfly to life, and watched her eyes widen and her mouth fall open. Her legs twitched as the butterfly went to work, humming quietly as it sent vibrations through her nether regions. She bit her lip and moaned, then whimpered when he switched it off.

She lifted her gaze to his, pleading. Forlorn. "Why are you doing this to me?"

Wolf fought the urge to go to her, to unbind her wrists and hold her in his arms, protect her, let her sob on his shoulder until she ran out of tears, but as a Dom he couldn't do that. *Wouldn't* do that. If he let her down, if he didn't finish what he'd started, the opportunity would be lost and he may as well kiss her goodbye. Instinctively he knew there was no way she'd let herself get caught by him again, because underlying all that sorrow he could still see the flare of anger dancing in her eyes.

Anger he could work with.

He turned the dial again, setting it to maximum. Abby squealed, her whole body convulsing. Wolf let her sweat it out, took his time to get comfortable on the couch. Safely out of reach. It was better that way, easier for him to avoid the temptation of touching her, of stroking his hands over her hips and around to her arse, pulling her into him and savouring the feel of her soft curves as she moulded to his body.

He clenched his jaw.

Focus.

"I asked you a question, Abigail, and I want an honest answer. What were you thinking about in the dress shop? Why did you look so sad?"

"Don't call me Abigail!"

Abby didn't know whether to moan or cry.

The butterfly hummed violently over her clit, sending her body into spasm after spasm, pushing her ever closer to that supreme pinnacle of bone-melting, soul-shattering goodness. She'd never felt anything like it.

Such intensity, such raw need.

It was too much... and then it was gone.

Aftershocks trembled along her limbs and she screamed her frustration. Her gut continued to clench as though trying to wring a climax out of her, as if through sheer will she could reach inside her and finish the job, drag her body the rest of the way until it reached the point of transcendence when her endorphins would flow and her brain would shut down and she could simply ride the waves of bliss.

But the chances of that happening without external help were about as likely as Wolf letting her go before she told him what he wanted to hear.

"You asked—no, you *begged* me to help you forget other men, so why are you fighting me, Abigail?"

"I told you not to call me that!"

His eyes narrowed. "Why? Who calls you Abigail? Who makes you hate your own name? Is it Dick?"

Abby glared as Wolf played his guessing game. He had a fifty-fifty shot at guessing correctly, but she wasn't going to help him. Not when he was hell-bent on ruining her evening.

"No, not him," he said slowly, tilting his head and staring her down with his intelligent gaze until something suddenly occurred to him. He looked at the desk and then back to her, his eyes sparking fire, his mouth twisting in disgust. "The other one, then. Kurt."

Abby looked away as the shame of her past made her jaw clench and her skin prickle with unwanted heat. Why couldn't he let this go? Why did he have to know everything about her? Why did he even care? He was only here for a month, a blink in the eye of their lifetimes; then he'd be gone and they'd never see each other again, so why did he have to know?

But she realised as much as she feared his reaction to the truth, if she was ever going to tell anyone, it was Wolf. Something about this man called out to her, told her she could trust him, told her she was safe with him.

What if I'm wrong?

It wouldn't be the first time she'd trusted a man she shouldn't have. It wouldn't even be the second.

"Leave me alone," she whispered, afraid to speak any louder in case her secret came spilling out.

The vibrator whirred to life once more.

Abby's whole lower half bucked as the pleasure built inside her, hitting her faster than before but still not fast enough. She twisted her hips and clenched her buttocks, rubbed her thighs together and shook her legs, although whether in an attempt to dislodge the device and remove the stimulation altogether, or make it work more efficiently, she didn't entirely know. But she did know it was all in vain. Wolf had attached the butterfly with absolute precision. It wasn't going anywhere, and it wasn't doing anything he didn't want it to do.

Growling through clenched teeth, she glared at him. He ignored her, his focus concentrated on inspecting his fingernails. "Let me go."

"No." He dialled the butterfly up another notch and she groaned at the agony of the never-ending pre-orgasm that hummed through her sex. Wolf lifted his gaze to meet hers, his expression bored. "I can do this all night, *liebchen.*"

"Go to hell!"

His eyes narrowed and the butterfly stopped.

Abby took a deep breath, relaxed, only to yelp a moment later as the butterfly sprang into action, incessantly hammering at her clit. "Stop it!" she screamed. "I don't want to talk about it."

"Why?"

"Because it's private. Because it's none of your business."

The vibrator stopped, and Wolf got to his feet and stalked towards her. Abby raised her chin and prepared herself for... what? A slap? Yelling? She clenched her jaw to stop her chin from wobbling, betraying her fear as she realised she had no idea what to expect.

He could beat the shit out her if he wanted to and there wasn't a bloody thing she could do about it. Her home was on the outskirts of town, buried in the scrubland that bordered the Melville State Forest. She had no neighbours to hear her screams, no one to call the cops.

Tears spilled down her cheeks. She was completely at his mercy, and she was all alone.

She felt like an idiot. So naïve. Just because he hadn't hurt her yet didn't mean he wouldn't. Kurt had worked his way up to the really cruel stuff, to the scissors.

Wolf reached out and Abby flinched, but when he did nothing more than push a lock of sweat-soaked hair from her face and stare at her, kindness and curiosity bright in his hazel eyes, she felt like an idiot for a very different reason.

Gently, he pressed his lips to hers and held her there, trapping her against his soft, warm mouth, daring her to resist him, knowing she wouldn't. Couldn't. She moved her lips against his and sighed as he deepened the kiss, sweeping his tongue along hers before pulling back, making her lunge forwards as she tried to recapture his lips, groaning when she missed.

He cupped her cheeks and brushed away her tears. "Your happiness is very much my business, *liebchen*. You agreed to be my submissive, to accept my dominance, and as your Dom it is my duty to take care of you. You're sad. I think you've been sad for a long time, and I want to know why."

"Why?"

"So I can help you not be sad anymore."

Staring at him, her eyes wide, her mouth slack, she couldn't believe what she was hearing. Why was he being so gentle? Why wasn't he yelling at her? Beating her? Cutting her? Didn't he realise she didn't deserve his kindness? That she deserved—*needed*—to be punished?

Of course not, because she hadn't told him her secret yet. Because she couldn't bear the thought of him thinking less of her.

Or worse.

More tears scorched her cheeks. "I can't tell you."

"Why not?"

"You'll despise me," she whispered.

Wolf wiped her tears away, but more took their place. "What makes you say that?"

She hung her head, her shame consuming her. "Because I despise myself."

Chapter Twelve

"You'll despise me."

"*I despise myself.*"

Almost five minutes had passed since she'd made those declarations. Declarations Wolf had seen as a breakthrough, a crack in her armour he could exploit and widen until she opened up to him. But all she'd done since then was stare at the floor and weep silent tears, seemingly oblivious to the butterfly's ministrations no matter which speed he set it to.

Checking his watch, he realised she'd been restrained for close to half an hour. He scrubbed a hand down his face. He honestly hadn't thought it would take this long, had cracked tougher nuts in half the time.

Stubborn nymph.

He eyed her carefully. She looked pale. Stepping closer, he reached up to pinch her fingernail, held it firmly until it turned white and then let it go. When it took too long to turn pink again, he growled. Her blood circulation was beginning to suffer. If he didn't resolve this soon he'd have to let her down regardless or risk causing her an injury.

Turning off the vibrator, he let her body relax.

It was time for a new tactic.

"I tire of this game, Abigail." She flinched at the sound of her full name but didn't lift her head, so he grabbed her chin and forced her to look at him. "You will tell me what I want to know and you will tell me now!"

Her eyes were dull, rimmed in red, her voice hollow. "I can't."

"You can and you will. And since denying your body satisfaction isn't getting us anywhere, let's try something else."

Flicking the dial on the vibrator's remote control, Wolf got the reaction he'd hoped for. Her body jolted, the sudden hammering against her clit a shock to her system even after such a short reprieve. He'd had her teetering on the brink for so long he knew it wouldn't take much to make her come. Modulating the butterfly from gentle tapping to fierce hammering and back again, he watched and waited and listened. When her body jerked and her breathing came in ragged gasps, he knew she was there, ready to explode, and he pushed her over the edge.

Her thighs quivered, her jaw dropped, and her head lolled from side to side, her eyes wide, wild. Above her head, her hands clenched and released, her fingers straining towards the ceiling. "Yes. Yes!" she cried, a small smile warming her tear-stained face.

She was riding high on a wave of release.

But it wouldn't last.

It never did.

And sure enough, the longer her orgasm continued, the less she enjoyed it.

Her body shook with the prolonged pleasure, her brow furrowed, and her cries dulled to mournful moans. She squirmed, rubbing her thighs together as she'd done before, trying to make it stop. But it wouldn't stop. Not until he had what he came for. Not until she gave him the answers he was now desperate to know.

What could possibly make enduring all this worthwhile?

Wolf tucked the remote control into the strap that wrapped around her hip. "Feel like talking yet?" he said, cupping her breasts, squeezing hard. "Because the only way you're getting out of those cuffs is to either tell me what I want to know or use your safeword. And we both know you're too stubborn for the latter."

A spark of defiance flashed in her eyes. "Fuck off," she murmured, her head falling forwards, resting her chin on her chest.

Leaning down, Wolf whispered in her ear, "Tell me what I want to know, Abby. Tell me and all of this will stop." He pinched her nipples hard. "You want it to stop, don't you?"

"Yes," she hissed.

"Then tell me, *liebchen*. Let me help you."

"No one can help me."

"You're safe with me, Abby. You know that. Tell me so I can end this. Tell me so I can hold you the way you want, the way I want."

Lifting her head, she stared at him, her eyes dull, haunted, and it churned his stomach knowing he'd done that, he'd put that expression on her face. "Stop. Please. Make it stop."

He pushed her hair from her face, wiped the tears from her cheeks. "Tell me what I want to know, Abigail. Tell me what you were thinking about in that dress shop. Tell me what made you so sad."

She shook her head so violently he feared she'd hurt herself. Catching her face in his hands, he knew there was only one option left. "Last chance, little nymph." He took a deep breath. "Tell me what I want to know, or I'll release you. Do you understand what that means?"

She sniffed loudly. The pitiful sound tugged at his vitals. Clenching his jaw, he shuttered his emotions.

"You'll let me go. You'll take off the cuffs and let me go."

"More than that," he said, surprised by the hitch in his voice. "If I release you, our deal ends." Her eyes widened and her chin wobbled. "If I release you, *liebchen*," he said, stroking her cheek, savouring the feel of her soft skin against his fingertips, "I will have nothing more to do with you."

Abby's chest felt like it was being crushed by an anvil, and a sob of pure anguish left her lips as she desperately tried to gulp down air.

No. No, no, no!

Wolf carefully removed the butterfly vibrator, in essence stripping her down to nothing, leaving her exposed. The near-constant stimulation left her sex feeling raw, the lack of intimacy left her nerves even more so, and her mind spun with questions and doubts.

Should I tell him?

Will he hate me?

Of course he'd hate her. He was a good man, a decent human being. Too good for the likes of her. Yes, better to keep her secret and bear his displeasure than tell him and drive him away for good.

Wolf reached for her wrists. He was going to let her go—no, he was going to *release* her. And that was far worse. If he ended their deal, she'd have no one to help her, no one to shield her from her ex-husband's taunts and barbs—or his wandering hands.

There'd be no well-spoken, clever, funny, devilishly handsome man by her side as Richard was expecting. And Jane had made sure her brother would be expecting, talking about Wolf every time they spoke on the phone, remarking how good he was for Abby, how well he treated her, how happy she was. Because apparently that was all part of the plan, a plan that Abby seemed to have very little to no say in, and when told to Wolf over lunch today had garnered his full support.

All of which meant if Abby faced her ex-husband without this superhero by her side, if Richard found out she was alone again after all of Jane's hype, she'd be totally and utterly humiliated. And then he'd be back on her doorstep with a bottle of wine and a shoulder to cry on.

Poor old Abbs. Abandoned again.

She'd get drunk. He'd take advantage. She'd wake up with a pounding headache and a bottomless pit in her stomach where unerring remorse churned with a less-than-healthy dose of self-loathing.

The sound of a cuff being unbuckled dragged her mind back to the present.

Remorse and self-loathing.

As her arm fell free of the leather cuff, she experienced the emotions with such ferocity she thought they might crush her. Wolf caught her arm, the limb limp from lack of blood and the tingle of pins and needles coursing along its length, and he lowered it gently to her side.

Massaging the useless limb, the heat of his hands chased the numbness away as they worked their way from her shoulder to her fingertips. He didn't speak while he performed the task. At all. He'd even stopped trying to coerce a confession out of her, his silence damning. He didn't look at her either, preferring instead to focus on her arm.

Abby stared at him as he worked, at the concentrated frown marring his handsome face, and silently willed him to lift his gaze, to look at her. But he didn't. "Please don't do this," she whispered.

A moment passed in silence, and then another. Then he lifted his head and aimed that frown at her, one more ferocious than she'd thought possible from such a patient man. "Give me a reason not to."

She opened her mouth to speak, but no words came out, and he turned his attention back to his task. How could she tell him? Knowing he'd hate her, knowing he'd never touch her again, how was she supposed to tell him what she'd done to deserve her self-imposed exile of the last two years?

If she kept quiet there was a chance—a small, slim, barely-there-but-still-a-chance chance—that he'd reconsider his position. That he'd take her back and they could continue as before. But then Wolf was just as stubborn as she was, more so. He'd already given her a second chance, and Abby very much doubted he'd give her a third.

Even so, knowing she was about to ruin everything, she couldn't bring herself to speak. Her chin quivered and the tears came again as she hung her head. She heard Wolf sigh, felt the heat of his breath caress her skin.

She would miss that, the feel of his big, broad body as he lay on top of her, the warmth of his skin that seemed to melt into her as he stroked his fingertips over her breasts, her stomach, her thighs, leaving tiny trails of fire in their wake. She would miss his mouth and the feel of his lips as they explored every inch of her, making her feel things she hadn't felt in so long she didn't know what to call them anymore.

Would he leave when he released her? Would he go home to Sydney and forget all about her? Or would he simply move out of her bed and into another, tormenting her with his constant presence, reminding her every day he remained under her roof of what she'd given up?

Wolf had given her a glimpse inside his world, a peek at how good the lifestyle could be with the right person.

And she was throwing it back in his face.

Indecision flooded her, leaving her cold and confused. Wolf stopped massaging her arm, reached up to unfasten the other cuff. Abby lifted her chin, determined to hold in the wail of despair she felt rising at the back of her throat, but when his fingers worked over the buckle, her chest constricted, crushing her heart, forcing it to pump harder, her blood rushing through her body so fast she could almost hear it whooshing along her limbs and pounding in her ears. Her decision was made.

Tell him.

She screamed at the ceiling, "She was pregnant!"

Her arm fell to her side and her knees gave way, but the next thing she knew she was slumped on the couch, a blanket draped around her shoulders, and Wolf was easing a glass of water into her hand.

"Who was pregnant?" Wolf said, his voice gentle yet stern. Their deal had ended but he still wanted answers.

Still a Dom, just not *her* Dom.

Dragging her forearm over her eyes, Abby tried to stem the flood of tears that wouldn't stop flowing. She sniffed loudly, wishing she had a tissue, and suddenly a box of Kleenex was being shoved under her nose.

She eyed Wolf cautiously but he didn't do or say

anything, just sat beside her and waited patiently until she'd composed herself. He even removed her snotty tissues to the fireplace when she was done, which started up a whole new stream of tears.

She'd quickly learned that Wolf was all about the little things, things that actually mattered, that made people feel cared for, cherished, but after he knew her secret he wouldn't be picking up her tissues anymore. He wouldn't deign to pick up her germ-ridden anything anymore.

And Abby couldn't blame him.

"Kurt's wife," she said after another round of eye wiping and nose blowing. "She was pregnant."

Wolf's eyes widened, his jaw dropped. "Is that all?"

"You endured an evening of punishment just to tell me your arsehole ex-boyfriend's wife was pregnant? Are you serious?"

Incredulous didn't even begin to cover how Wolf was feeling at that exact moment. He'd had subs tell him some pretty incredible things over the years—and some incredibly stupid things too—but never had he felt so pissed off over something so trivial. He wasn't sure if he wanted to shake Abby for being so silly or spank her for the worry she'd caused him—until her eyes filled with tears and her chin wobbled again.

Wolf winced at the depth of his own stupidity.

I am such an idiot.

He knew her inability to have kids was a sore point for her, but still, he just couldn't reconcile her grief with the innocuous nature of the situation. A woman—Kurt's wife—was pregnant. But for Abby to be so upset, to willingly suffer what he'd just put her through, there had to be more to it than that.

There was something she wasn't telling him.

Shifting in his seat so he faced her, he stretched his arm along the back of the couch, hoping the relaxed position would help relax her too, but when she looked up, he saw fear swimming in those big brown eyes. That was the second time tonight. And he wasn't brandishing a pair of scissors now.

Did she fear his reaction to whatever came next? Or was she afraid of him? Had he simply pushed her too far?

The thought that it might be the latter twisted his stomach. When she pulled the blanket tighter around her body, cocooning herself in its soft layers, shielding herself from him, from his touch, even his gaze, a wave of shame swept through him.

Swallowing hard, he forced himself to relax, to release the breath he didn't realise he'd been holding. He had to tread carefully. He had to forget about ripping that damned blanket away from her, to ignore his need to haul her into his lap, to touch her, hold her, comfort her. He'd helped her reopen an old wound and now he had to help her close it— permanently, if he could—and he couldn't do that by indulging his own selfish needs.

Whether she knew it or not, Abby had spoken up *before* he'd removed the second cuff. She was still his submissive, and he still had a duty of care. He would help her, no matter how troubling her situation turned out to be.

"What aren't you telling me, Abby?"

She closed her eyes and took a deep breath. And then she took another. And when she opened her eyes and looked up at him, he had to grip the back of the couch to anchor himself in his seat, to stop himself from reaching for her.

He'd never seen such intense misery.

"I told you Kurt was married," she said, her voice so low he barely heard it over the crackle of the flames in the hearth. "But I never told you how I found out."

"Go on," he urged, trying not to frown as she pulled the blanket even tighter around herself.

"When I lived in Sydney, I had a great job. I was the assistant curator in a private gallery in Glebe." Her lips thinned in a tight smile. "Kurt and I had been together for about six months when I was coordinating the opening of a new exhibition, a multimedia celebration of local architecture. It was my idea, my baby, and the gallery had let me run with it." She sipped her water before continuing, smiling, a hint of pride in her voice. "On opening night almost every artist sold. I couldn't have been happier. I didn't think anything could bring me down." Her smile dissolved into nothingness. "But then it happened. This woman, this beautiful woman walked up to me and slapped my face."

"She was Kurt's wife?"

Abby nodded, that haunted look he wholly despised and wished he could wipe clean forever coming over her again. "And she was pregnant."

Wolf frowned as he struggled to understand the significance of that one detail. Her boyfriend had lied to her, used her, and made her into the one thing she despised most, the *other woman.*

He'd understand if she'd been disappointed, hurt or even angry, but where did this intense anguish over her ex-douchebag's baby come from?

"My boss called security over, but not before she slapped me again and told me to stay away from her husband." Her look grew determined and she fixed her gaze on his. "I told her she was wrong. I told her I don't date married men, but she showed me a photograph of him, of them, of their children, and they looked so happy." Sadness pulled at the corners of her mouth. "I didn't want to believe it. I couldn't believe it. I... I slapped her. I think I only did it out of shock. But the way she looked at me, horrified... and then she shoved me. She pushed me so hard I stumbled back and knocked over one of the sculptures. It shattered all over the floor, and when she came at me again she... she slipped on the fragments of the broken artwork and she... fell. She fell and she...."

Wolf froze, his fingers clenching the back of the couch so hard it hurt. "What happened when she fell, Abby?"

A gut-wrenching sob escaped her. "Oh God. I close my eyes and I can see it all so clearly."

"Abby?"

"She landed on her stomach. She landed so hard she... she lost her baby," she said, tears streaming down her face. "Oh, Wolf. She lost her baby and it was all my fault."

Sitting very still, Wolf tried desperately to process Abby's story, but one look at her tormented face, her haunted eyes, and he couldn't hold back. His instincts as a man and Dom had finally merged. Reaching for her, he hauled her into his lap. At first he thought she meant to fight him, pushing at his chest and shaking her head, but he held her fast and made her look at him.

"It wasn't your fault."

Her big brown eyes shone with the slightest glimmer of gratitude before overflowing with tears once more.

"But it *was* my fault."

Wolf frowned. "Why?"

Her brow scrunched. "Why?"

"Yes, why? Why was it your fault? Explain it to me."

"Because it was," she said, her voice hardening and her chin tilting up with her usual stubbornness.

"That's not a reason, Abigail."

She scowled at the use of her full name, but a scowl was better than a wince.

"If I hadn't slept with her husband, she'd have had no reason to seek me out."

Wolf raised a brow. "So you *did* know he was married?"

"No!"

"Then tell me how this was your fault."

"I knocked over the sculpture she slipped on."

"She pushed you into that sculpture."

"I slapped her."

"She slapped you first."

"It was my fault!"

Wolf sighed quietly and tucked a lock of hair behind her ear. "No, *liebchen*, it wasn't."

Her shoulders sagged. "Then why does it feel like it was?"

"Because you're a good person," he said, coaxing her into his arms, smiling when she didn't resist. "You have a gentle soul and a kind heart, and you know the pain that comes with the loss of a child."

"But I've never lost a child of my own," she murmured against his chest, hot tears soaking through his T-shirt.

"Haven't you? Some would say your inability to have children is comparable with the loss of a child. You know how painful it is to be denied something precious to you, and you empathise with others when they are forced to face what you endure every day."

She lifted her head and stared at him, her face a study

of bewilderment as though the thought had never occurred to her, and he realised it probably never had.

Stroking his knuckles over the softness of her cheek, he savoured the warmth of her skin, warmth he'd craved during their battle of wills.

A battle he'd come perilously close to losing.

Snorting a laugh, he smiled. "You really don't know just how strong you are, do you?"

She shook her head. "I'm not strong."

Gripping her chin, Wolf forced her to look at him. "Yes, you are. And I am so very proud of you."

Chapter Thirteen

A satisfying hiss met Abby's ears as she quenched the hot metal blade she'd been pounding on for the better part of an hour. She watched the steam rise from the surface of the water barrel, curling up and away into the cool morning air before pulling the blade free and balancing it in her gloved hand, testing its weight.

"That looks deadly."

Wolf's sleep-roughened voice teased a smile from her lips.

"Did I wake you?" she said, knowing full well that she had. She'd gone out of her way to ensure it.

It served him right too, stopping in the middle of the previous night's foreplay to scribble down notes for his book. As it was, scribbling had turned to typing, and Abby had fallen asleep waiting for him to come back to bed. After a restless night, she'd awoken to find him quietly snoring on the couch, his laptop balanced precariously on his stomach.

The urge to let the offending device fall to the floor, possibly smashing into a dozen pieces, had been keen, but the look of serenity on his face, the easy way his chest rose and fell with every slumberous breath he took, told her he'd accomplished something of importance with the damned thing.

"You're angry with me," he said, pulling a hand-stitched quilt around his naked shoulders. The same quilt she'd draped over him after rescuing his laptop from certain doom.

"No, not angry, exactly. Just—" She sighed and turned back to the fire. "—unsatisfied."

Now there was a word she'd never thought to associate with the man.

Since meeting him two weeks before, Wolf Adams had proven himself to be an amazing lover, attentive, inventive, strong. Honestly, the things the man could do with his hands, his tongue... it made her wet just thinking about it.

But last night....

Wolf had been torturing her, running the tip of his tongue along the sensitive flesh of her inner thigh, forbidding her to touch him—no matter how often she begged to be allowed otherwise—sliding his big hands under her arse, spreading her legs far apart.

The closer his mouth had come to latching over the apex of her thighs, the higher her anticipation had soared. So for him to suddenly sit back on his heels, a look of unexpected realisation shifting his focus to some faraway place before leaping off the bed with a mumbled apology and a vague promise to return, had been extremely frustrating.

And downright rude.

Wolf rested his hands on her shoulders. Abby shoved the blade back in the forge with more force than was really necessary.

"You *are* angry with me," he murmured, his hands falling away and his mouth twisting in the smallest of pouts.

He looked like a gigantic puppy who'd been scolded for chewing her favourite slippers.

"Maybe," she conceded. "A bit."

That pout morphed into a dangerous smile, sensual and enticing, and he lifted his gaze to hers. "Maybe I can make it up to you," he said, stepping close again, sliding his hands to her hips and pulling her into the line of his body.

"I'm kinda busy right now," she said, ignoring him as best she could while poking at the coals with an iron bar. Then she felt his warm lips against throat.

Suddenly, ignoring him wasn't an option.

Loosening the ties on her leather apron, Wolf wasted no time twisting one hand in her ponytail while sliding the other under her T-shirt. His mouth was soft and wet, trailing open-mouthed kisses down her neck, his hand seeking and finding her nipple.

Abby moaned as he plucked and pulled, bent her to his will. Her eyelids fluttered and her mouth fell open, her breasts feeling full, her pussy wet, and when he turned her in his arms and his mouth fell on hers, she was lost to the moment. Wolf took her away from the dark heat of the forge and transported her somewhere filled with light, with passion and sex and endless kissing.

Until she heard a loud *pop*.

"Shit!" Eyes snapping open, she jerked from his grip. Not an easy task considering where his hands were. She twisted and shoved away from him before snatching the blade from the coals and holding it up to examine the metal, pitted and scarred and glowing white. With a string of expletives, she hurled the offending waste of time across the forge, watched it bounce off the wall and fall to the sandy floor with a soft thump. "Fuck!"

Wolf stared at her like she was nuts. "Abby?"

"*Now* I'm angry," she said, storming past him and out into the garden.

Dark clouds rolled through the sky, reflecting her mood and chilling the air. It would rain soon, and she still had so much to do. There was cooking to be done for the picnic tomorrow, beds to be made for her brothers. Working the metal was her way of relieving tension, of settling her mind and organising her thoughts, preparing her for the day ahead. Something she'd desperately needed after the previous night's disappointing conclusion.

Wolf followed her into the garden. "Talk to me, Abby. What just happened?"

"What happened," she said through gritted teeth, "is two days of work just went up in smoke. Literally."

"Abby—"

"What just happened is I told you I was busy and you persisted in distracting me anyway. Do you have any idea how hard it is to make a blade? How much time it takes to fold metal by hand? No, of course you don't. Why would you?" she said and gave him her back. "You wouldn't understand."

"I think I do," Wolf said quietly. "And I am sorry."

Something in his voice made Abby turn and face him. One glance at him standing there, looking rather pathetic in bare feet and a blanket, and the anger rushed out of her on an exhale of breath. She nodded in acknowledgement of his apology and then removed her heavy leather apron, slinging it over the back of a queening throne she was halfway through constructing.

"Are you hungry?" she said, anchoring her hands on her hips.

"Always," he said, his timbre husky again.

Abby frowned, then noticed the direction of his gaze.

Removing her apron had pulled down the front of her ratty old T-shirt, revealing a generous amount of cleavage.

Rolling her eyes at him, she strode towards the back door. "Hungry for breakfast, you overgrown pervert."

He fell in step beside her. "That'd be nice, too."

Wolf watched Abby buzz around the kitchen. "Can I help?"

"You've helped enough for one morning, thanks."

Shuffling his feet, he said, "I really am sorry, *liebchen*. I behaved like a dick."

"Yes, you did." And then after a pause, she added, "But thank you for saying so."

A few minutes later, she indicated for him to sit and served up a plate of French toast with bacon and maple syrup, a cup of strong tea on the side. One of his favourites. His eyes narrowed slightly. If she was trying to make him feel guilty—*more* guilty—she was laying it on a bit thick.

And it was working.

Taking the seat opposite him, she looked him in the eyes before focussing on her breakfast. "I'm sorry I lost my temper."

Tension eased from his shoulders, and Wolf relaxed as he realised he wasn't the only one feeling guilty this morning. "It was my fault."

"No. Well, yes, actually it was your fault, but that's not the whole of it." She laid aside her fork and sighed. "All my life I've been surrounded by art. My dad, my brothers—"

"Even the lawyer?"

She smiled. "Rafe can be very creative with the law when he needs to be," she said. Her smile faded. "But with the artists came the naysayers. The people who think what I do is less important, that it doesn't matter. That I don't matter."

"*Liebchen.*" Wolf reached across the table but she pulled away and placed her hands in her lap. His jaw clenched.

"Both Richard and Kurt saw my art as a hobby, a meaningless diversion that would never lead anywhere. They always encouraged me to be practical, rational, to keep my *real* job. But as much as I loved working in the gallery, it wasn't what I truly wanted to do."

"What did you want to do?"

"I wanted to be an artist. Like Dad. But not a painter like him, a sculptor. I love building things, using my hands." Her smile returned, almost wistful. "To have my art displayed in a gallery somewhere would be amazing. And I don't care if I never win awards or make a ton of cash, at least my work would be out there for people to see, for someone to connect to." She looked up from under her lashes. "I'm not a radical. I don't have an agenda or anything profound to say. And I know it sounds naïve, but I look at the world and see so much hate, so much ugliness, and all I want is to make the place more beautiful."

Wolf rose from his seat and reached across the table, taking her face in his hands and pulling her to him. "You already do," he whispered over her lips, then pressed his mouth against hers, fast, hard. A little moan escaped her before she pulled back.

"Stop sucking up," she said, scowling. "But why are we always talking about me? Why can't we talk about you for a change? Or is that against the rules?"

"Depends. What would you like to know?" he said, grinning as he sat down again.

Eyeing him cautiously, she bit her lip. "Why has it taken you so long to finish your book?"

Wolf closed his eyes as he thought about his answer. He'd known she would ask him sooner or later, but what was he supposed to say? His confidence had taken a severe beating? Beth's betrayal had pushed him to the brink?

Everything he'd understood about himself, everything he'd been proud to say was intrinsically *him* had been yanked out from under him like the proverbial rug, and for close to a year he'd lost his footing, depression, anger, and vengeful resentment filling the void she'd left in his chest, choking the creativity out of him?

"Wolf?"

He opened his eyes and saw her watching him, her gaze questioning, her eyes so dark and beautiful but full of promise too. His body relaxed, the anxiety of his past flowing out of him until only clarity remained. He was such an idiot. If anyone would understand what he'd been through, it was her.

"I suppose for the same reason most men do something stupid."

Abby's mouth twisted slightly. "A woman."

Wolf's mouth quirked at one corner. Perceptive little nymph. "Yes. A woman." He took a deep breath. "Her name was Beth, and I met her at Sydney University. She was a literature student, and I was doing a series of guest lectures on popular fiction. She came to me one day after class, asking to pick my brain for a paper she was writing. At first I was hesitant. She was a student, she was a lot younger than me, and it was fairly obvious from her demeanour that my books were the last thing she wanted to talk about."

"So why'd you change your mind?"

Wolf grinned. "Well I won't lie. She was cute. I was flattered, and intrigued. So I thought why not? I hadn't been with anyone in a long time, work always coming first. And I admit I was... lonely."

Her brow furrowed. "Lonely? Didn't you have a submissive?"

"I had a couple, but none I took home. I didn't have that kind of relationship with them."

"But you saw yourself taking Beth home, having that kind of relationship with her?"

"I saw the possibility. I saw...." He sighed and swirled his now-tepid tea around in his cup. "I saw what I wanted to see. That was the problem. I was so blinded by my loneliness that I didn't see her for who—*what*—she truly was."

"And what was she?"

"A masochist."

Abby's mouth fell open. "But you're not—"

"A sadist. I know."

"What happened?"

Wolf clenched his jaw as he remembered, his anger not as virulent as it once was though remnants still remained. "A friend of mine owns a fetish club in the city. He'd invited an internationally renowned Dominant—a sadist—to visit Australia for a couple of weeks and give demonstrations, lessons, that sort of thing. I was supposed to take Beth to one of the demonstrations, but my muse was on a roll that day and she ended up going by herself. My friend warned me to keep an eye on her, that he'd noticed her interest in this other man."

Realisation lit Abby's face. "She cheated on you."

"Yes," he said. "Apparently, she'd been unhappy for a while, my style of Dominance not enough for her, too passive, too...." He grimaced. "Gentle."

Abby stood and cleared the table. "Didn't feel gentle the other night," she scoffed. "My arse is still sore."

Wolf barked a laugh and she smiled at him, the warmth of it heartening despite his current mood. "When Beth left, she took everything I'd ever believed of myself and crushed it like it was nothing. I felt trampled, useless, and I doubted everything I did, professionally and socially. Truth be told, I felt like a fucking idiot. I'm a Dom. A damned good one, too. Reading people is what I do, so how could I have misjudged her so completely?"

Abby laid her hand on his shoulder, the heat of her palm on his skin as soothing to his soul as it was exciting to the rest of him. "How did I miss all the signs my husband was cheating on me? How did I not know my boyfriend already had a wife? Some people are just better than others at hiding who they truly are."

Wolf tugged her into his lap and wrapped his arms around her hips. "Thank you, Abigail."

"For what?"

"For making me feel like less of an idiot. If it weren't for you, I'd still be wallowing in self-pity."

"Glad I could help," she said, sliding her arms around his shoulders, flashing him a coy little smile. "But may I ask you something else?"

Wolf cocked one brow. "Hmm?"

"Is Wolf short for Wolfgang?"

A rumble of laughter worked its way through him, jostling her in his lap. "I thought you were going to ask me to stop calling you Abigail again."

"I'm getting used to it," she said, twisting her lips. "Slowly. But stop changing the subject."

Wolf sighed, an exaggerated sound. "It's short for Wolfram," he said. "Wolfram Ulrich Adams."

Abby's gaze dipped to his lips and back again. "Wolfram. I like that."

He shifted her in his lap. "Does that mean you're not angry with me anymore?"

"Maybe."

"Does that mean I can make it up to you now?"

She slid her hand down his chest until her fingers rested on the waistband of his jeans. "Depends. What did you have in mind?"

Standing in one fluid movement, he deposited Abby on the kitchen table. "What I have in mind," he said, tugging her T-shirt over her head to reveal her big, soft breasts, "is to finish what we started last night." He pulled her hips forwards, unzipped her jeans. "To make sure you are thoroughly." He kissed her lips. "And completely." He kissed her again. "Satisfied."

Wolf yanked her jeans down her legs, grinned when she giggled, pleased she'd stopped trying to hide her more feminine side from him. Even more pleased she was still following his order to ditch her underwear when they were at home. His grin broadened when she leaned back on her hands and spread her legs in blatant invitation.

Lowering himself into a chair, he slid his hands along her thighs, savoured every soft and supple inch. He knew well their pillowy warmth was the perfect cradle for his hips, and his cock twitched with expectation.

But his cock would have to wait.

Lifting his gaze, he studied her face, saw the reflected lust in her dark brown eyes, watched her eyelids shutter and her gaze turn languid. Her mouth curved in a sensuous smile, her lips full and ripe and tempting. And just a little bit smug. Cheeky little nymph. But he knew he deserved it, so he let it go and leaned forwards instead, pressing his lips against her belly, grinning as he felt it rise and fall, each breath measured and deliberate.

Not as confident as she'd like me to think.

Good. He liked keeping her guessing.

He grazed his lips over her flesh in a leisurely downwards path and enjoyed the minute shivers he felt ripple through her body. The closer he came to his goal, the more erratic those shivers became. She rested her hand on his nape, encouraging him in his journey south, and he was happy to oblige, his fingers and mouth converging on her pussy to the sound of her breathy gasps.

She felt so wet around his fingers as he slid them deep inside her. Wet and tight and willing. He gently parted her silken folds and ran his tongue between them, tasting her sweet and salty flavour as he flicked the tip of his tongue over her clit, the sensitive nub growing harder under his careful ministrations. Abby moaned and pressed her hips forwards, forcing his tongue deeper. "Fuck me," she said as her grip tightened in his hair. "Please."

Wolf pulled back and eased her hand from his head. He grinned up at her and her impatience. "You're an eager little nymph," he said, "but you have to wait."

She pouted. "I hate waiting."

He laughed. "I know." And then he gripped her thighs and buried himself between them, thrusting with his fingers, stabbing with his tongue, laving her with all the attention he should have given her the night before, and would have had his stupid muse not had the worst timing in history.

Wolf inwardly grimaced as the little minx reared her head again, dangling plot points and character dialogue in front of him on the ends of intangible threads, begging him to chase them, to capture them, to weave them together.

Not now, he silently ground out from between gritted teeth, and then all thought fled him as a succession of noise, of moans and sighs and gasps of breath met his ears. The sounds of a woman—*his woman*—as she inched ever closer towards orgasm.

He felt the twitch of her flesh under his fingertips, the telltale tightening of her muscles as they clamped down on her bones, and he resisted the urge to pull back, to tease her, to use her body's reactions against her and make her wait for that sweet release. He owed her that much at least—his own impatience to bury himself deep inside her had nothing to do with it. And then she was there. Screaming, moaning, cursing. Coming.

Thrusting her hips against his face so violently she looked like a woman possessed.

And Wolf revelled in every moment of it.

Abby's chest rose and fell with exaggerated purpose as she sucked the air back into her lungs. Wolf was still between her thighs, his smug face grinning up at her and speaking volumes. His deep voice rumbled through her mind: *Not so unsatisfied now, are you*, liebchen?

She opened her mouth to speak only to have her words die on her tongue as he stroked the pad of his thumb across her clit, the oversensitive nub sending a shock wave of plea-sure-pain rippling through her, jerking her hips and making her gasp. Her elbows gave way under her sated weight and she collapsed against the table top with a heavy thud.

"Ouch," she grumbled as she rubbed her head.

She heard the kitchen chair scrape across the floor as Wolf got to his feet, and she lifted her head to look at him.

His hazel eyes were heavy lidded, his grin gone, the corners of his mouth barely lifted in the most carnal of smiles.

Predatory. She felt her body flush with renewed warmth and watched with intense interest as he unzipped his jeans.

"Come here," he said as he held out his hand, his timbre low and smooth.

Abby took his hand and he pulled her upright. He nestled himself between her legs once more, the table at just the right height for him to push his rock-hard erection firmly into the apex of her thighs, but he made no move to enter her. He slowly ran his hands up her arms and over her shoulders, his palms warm in the cool kitchen air, and then he leaned down and placed a kiss on her neck, his hot lips branding her as surely as his teeth when they sank into her flesh a moment later.

Abby gasped his name and clung to his shoulders, her fingers curling into his muscles, her fingernails leaving weals in his flesh. Wolf growled and bit down harder. Abby's hips jerked forwards, pressing her body even tighter against Wolf's cock.

She bit her lip and moaned as he rocked his hips, teasing her, taunting her, rubbing his hot flesh against her mound when all she wanted was for him to be inside her, fucking her senseless, making her scream. And he knew it too, judging by the feel of his mouth, smiling against her skin as he kissed his way from her shoulder to her earlobe before sucking it between his lips and gently nibbling with his teeth.

"Please," she whispered on a ragged breath. "Please, Wolf."

A sharp sting assailed her earlobe. "Please, who?"

"Sir," she gasped as Wolf traced his tongue around the shell of her ear. "Please, Sir. Please fuck me."

Wolf stood to his full height and gazed down at her, his face blank of all emotion.

Save one.

Lust. Pure, simple, hungry.

Even the sensual smile she'd witnessed earlier had disappeared. "I do love it when you beg," he growled as he took his cock in his hand and eased himself into her, inch by glorious inch until he was buried to the hilt.

Abby closed her eyes and sucked in a breath, moaned as her head lolled on her shoulder.

"And I love all the little noises you make when we fuck," he said as he cupped her arse with bruising intensity, his big strong hands pulling her forwards to meet him thrust for thrust.

His raw words made her blush and she ducked her head so he wouldn't see.

"No," he said. "I've told you before, Abigail. Don't hold back, don't hide from me."

Abby's blush deepened three shades darker, but she lifted her chin until she met his gaze square on.

His stare was intense, commanding.

Frightening. And the longer he stared at her, scrutinising every emotion that flashed across her features, watching every nervous lick of her lips and bob of her throat, the more Abby had to fight the urge to fidget, to shy away from him and retreat inside herself.

To shut him out.

As if reading her thoughts, his eyes narrowed, challenging her to try it if she dared. Infuriating man. He always had to have his own way, even when he was the one apologising. Abby clenched her jaw and lifted her chin higher.

She would not be intimidated.

She would not retreat.

No matter how exposed she felt under his penetrating stare.

"There you are," he whispered with a smile. "Little nymph." And his mouth found hers with unerring precision.

Abby squeaked at the sudden assault on her mouth, her eyes wide with shock, but the moment his tongue swept over her lips and pressed for entry, she opened up and let him in. How could she not?

Here was a man who had gone out of his way to help her regain the confidence she'd lost so long before. A man who understood her wants, her needs, and her desires. A man who knew exactly how she felt because he'd experienced the same things she'd been through, had been cheated on, used and then abandoned to the yawning abyss called loneliness.

Was she still mad about the ruined blade? Of course.

Was it the end of the world? Not really.

But she wasn't telling him that. Not while he was determined to make it up to her with toe-curling kisses and table sex.

Wolf thrust into her with increasing force, narrowing her thoughts to the immediate here and now and the orgasm building inside her. She broke their kiss and stared up at him. The colour of his eyes had darkened, the hazel almost obliterated by the black of his pupils.

He gripped her arse tighter and Abby's eyes rolled back, her pleasure heightened by the pain of his fingers digging into her flesh. She wrapped her legs around his hips, her arms around his waist, and moaned long and loud at the feel of his cock sinking even deeper inside her. She leaned forwards and took his nipple in her mouth, sucking and licking. Biting.

"Liebchen."

The word sounded strangled, guttural. Abby smiled against his chest and swirled her tongue over the hardened nub, only to have her head ripped back and her mouth claimed once more. She clung to Wolf as he pounded into her, her breathing ragged, her whole body flushed with delicious heat. And then she was there. Her body stiffened, her muscles tightened—she was coming. And with one final thrust of his hips and a deep, throaty groan, so was he.

Abby sagged in Wolf's arms, her ear pressed to his chest. She could hear the rhythm of his heartbeat as it slowed, could feel his panted breath as it mussed her hair, and watched as her own breath gently stirred the hairs on his chest.

"So, am I forgiven for my thoughtlessness?"

In answer, she stretched up and kissed him, a languid exploration of his neck, his jaw, his lips—so very different from their earlier urgency.

"What do you think?" Abby purred.

"I think we need to take this somewhere more comfortable," he said, brushing his knuckles over her nipples. She moaned when he bent his head and took one between his teeth. But before they could go anywhere, the front door of the house crashed open and a line of men marched past the kitchen doorway, talking, laughing, dripping water all over her nice clean floor.

"What the hell!"

Abby squealed as Wolf yanked her into his embrace, shielding her from the intrusion with his broad back. She peered over his shoulder just as Tobias ducked his head through the doorway.

"Get dressed," he said quietly as his bright blue gaze flicked over them. "Now."

"Your brothers?" Wolf asked as they quickly dressed.

"Yep."

He took her hand, pressed her fingers to his lips and then stepped aside. "After you."

Abby led Wolf through to the lounge room, where she promptly forgot about him as her eyes danced from one hulking brute of a brother to the next, sprawling on the furniture, stoking the fire, and touching things they shouldn't.

"Ollie, put that down," she said, unable to hide the panic in her voice as he picked up the small black box containing the butterfly vibrator, then held it up to his ear and shook it. Abby lunged across the desk to snatch it away but he held it high in the air, out of even her long reach, and grinned at her frustration.

Rafe stood at the far end of the room, stabbing an iron poker into the coals and stirring the fire back to roaring life before he toed off his boots and shook the water out of his hair like a dog. The fire hissed in protest at the impromptu shower.

Then Charlie strolled into the room with nothing but a bath sheet slung around his hips, tossing a towel to each of the others before facing the fireplace and drying himself off, giving the entire room a view of his muscular arse and ridiculously long legs.

Abby hid her face behind her palm. "Charlie! Is that really necessary?"

"I'm cold and wet, so yes, it is." She lowered her hand and glared at him. "What?" he said, turning to level a challenging stare at her as he dried himself off.

She pursed her lips. "Why are you all so wet?"

Oliver stared at her like she was an idiot, his hands falling to his sides, bringing the vibrator within reach. "I guess you were too busy to notice it's been raining," he said, lifting his arm in the air again as Abby tried to wrestle the box free of his grasp.

She stopped fighting him just long enough to look out the window and see the sky was clearing, shafts of golden sunlight cutting through the thinning clouds. Tobias was in the garden, digging the toe of his work boot into the muddy ground.

The storm had come and gone and she hadn't even noticed.

She chanced a glance at Wolf, who was standing in the doorway observing her family reunion from afar, his hands in his pockets and a barely concealed grin on his face. Her eyes narrowed. His grin widened.

She folded her arms over her chest and tried not to pout like a petulant child. "Well, why are you here so early? You weren't supposed to be here until after lunch."

"I blame Ollie," Rafe said.

Oliver tossed the box to Paul and picked up a towel. "How is this my fault?"

"It doesn't matter," Abby snapped, her temper and her panic rising as Paul examined the box. "You could have at least knocked before barging in here. You didn't even give us a chance to get dressed."

Paul, the second eldest of all her brothers and the eldest in the room, was sitting on the couch, his shirt a soggy mess on the floor and his towel wrapped around his head like a turban. He opened the box just enough to peek inside. His brow rose and he flicked his steely blue gaze from Abby to Wolf and back again. Her cheeks flamed with heat and she wished the floor would swallow her whole.

"Considering how long we were left to stand in the rain, you should be thankful we waited as long as we did."

Her arms tightened across her chest and she lifted her chin. "Oh please, you can't have been waiting more than a few minutes or so."

"That's not something I'd brag about," Charlie said with a grin, the bath sheet anchored around his hips once more.

Abby ignored him and focussed on Paul—and the little black box he still held in his hand. She swallowed hard as he rose to his feet and turned to face her lover.

"So, you must be the big bad Wolf," he said, handing him the vibrator. "Or do you prefer 'oh God, don't stop'?"

Chapter Fourteen

Wolf's eyes slowly blinked open, allowing the smallest crack of light to reach his brain and shake it loose from its dream state.

Only the dream didn't seem to be ending.

In his dream, Abby's soft, full lips and wet tongue were gliding over his painfully erect cock. His hands were fisted in her hair, guiding her, encouraging her. His breath caught in his throat, pleasure exploding through him as her teeth gently scraped his flesh, only to release on a moan a moment later as she snaked her tongue around his hard length.

"Liebchen."

Her hair tickled him, every bob of her head spreading the soft strands across the expanse of his hips and between his thighs. Her hands were hot against his skin, pushing his legs farther apart as she settled herself between them, then cupping his sack and gently kneading. His eyes rolled back and his hand tightened in her hair.

Oh yeah.

His eyes opened a little farther and he groaned at the welcome sight. She looked up and caught his stare, her molten chocolate gaze so dark and decadent. Wicked. Slowly, ever so slowly, she slid her mouth up and off his shaft with a wet *pop*. He grinned down at her and the cheeky gleam in her bedroom eyes.

"Did I tell you to stop?"

She reflected his grin. "No, Sir," she said, and then she licked him from base to tip before enveloping him with her warm mouth once again.

He held her gaze as she worked him, as she sucked and licked and bit him. His chest rose and fell, his breathing ragged. His little nymph had talent, knew exactly how to please him. He fought the wave of jealousy surging inside him—an emotion he was becoming all too familiar with since arriving in this place—as he wondered who exactly had taught her such wondrous tricks.

But then her cheeks hollowed out as she sucked him hard and deep and all conscious thought fled, replaced by something urgent and primal. He thrust his hips hard and fast, single-mindedly seeking the warmth of her. More warmth than her mouth could offer him.

He yanked on her hair, pulling her off his cock, and enjoyed the vicious look in her eyes, the slight snarl of her upper lip. She leaned her head towards his hand to lessen the pain in her scalp. He twisted his fingers to increase the strain.

"Fuck me," he said, and watched with concealed delight as her eyelids lowered and her lips smoothed out.

Her resulting smile was almost predatory.

Slowly she crept up his body, kissing here, biting there, and always she watched him, her dark eyes shuttered by lowered lids and long lashes, eyes that still held a hint of venom as he held his grip on her hair. She took her time, straddling his thighs and leaning forwards, moaning as she brushed her pussy against the head of his cock.

He brought her head down so her lips hovered a mere hair's breadth from his own. She tried to kiss him but he held her back, teasing her with his kiss just as she was teasing him with her pussy.

"I gave you a command," he growled.

Her tongue whipped out and flicked across his lips —*cheeky nymph*—and then she reached between their bodies and wrapped her hand around his shaft, rubbed herself against him once, twice, and then sank down, enveloping him in silky heat and wetness.

Wolf's moan echoed Abby's. He relaxed his grip and slid his hand around her nape, pulling her in for a slow-burning kiss, a languid exploration of her lips. She tried to lean into him, to force a deeper connection. He squeezed the back of her neck, causing her shoulders to hunch and her lips to purse. Reminding her who was in control. He held her gaze for a long moment, until she lowered her eyes in surrender, and then relaxed his hold and gently rubbed away the ache he'd caused.

"Sit up, Abigail. Let me look at you."

Abby obeyed immediately, her eyes rolling back in her head as the movement forced his cock deeper inside her. Her hair fell over her shoulders and covered her breasts, her dark pink nipples poking through the long raven strands, erect and proud.

Wolf reached up and brushed her hair aside so he could cup those beautiful mounds and feel their heavy weight, so soft and warm against his palms. He licked his lips, hungry for a taste, and Abby squealed and laughed as he sat up, scrambling for a hold on him so she didn't topple backwards.

"Hmm...." Wolf took his time, deliberating which breast he should devour first.

Abby grinned down at him. "Eeny, meeny, miney, oh!"

Wolf latched his mouth around one pert little nipple and sucked hard. Abby gasped and clung to him tighter, almost suffocating him in the pillow of her breast. He bit her nipple and made her recoil just enough that he could breathe again.

"Sorry," she said with a bashful smile that made his heart race and his blood burn.

Wolf swirled his tongue around the reddened nub and gave it another, longer, gentler pull. At the same time, he slid his hands down her back and cupped her bottom, encouraging her and the slow rocking rhythm of her hips that was driving him wild. He could feel her fingers dig into his back, could hear the moan that vibrated up her throat, and it was music to his ears.

Abby's surprise blow job had put Wolf in a languid state of mind. He wanted to go slow, to savour every moment, to touch and taste and tease her. To draw out their pleasure until they were gasping for release. But his mind and his body were at war. His body didn't care for slow, didn't want to tease. His body had more urgent plans.

His body wanted to fuck. Hard and fast.

And before he could stop himself, he had her on her back, wrists pinned above her head, teeth sinking into the muscle connecting her shoulder to her neck, his hips thrusting to their own demented rhythm, taking, giving.

Fucking.

Wolf could hear Abby's struggle as she tried to rein in the sounds of her passion, her brothers' presence in her house making her cautious to further censure. But Wolf didn't care what they thought. Abby was his. He would make her come and he would hear her scream. He needed it. Like an addict jonesing for a fix. He needed to hear her cry of surrender as her body succumbed to his, as she let go of her inhibitions and gave free rein to her hunger and lust.

There was no sound sweeter.

He lifted his head and saw her teeth sink into her bottom lip. If she bit down any harder she'd draw blood.

"Don't hold it in. Don't hold back."

"They'll hear us," she whispered, shooting a furtive glance at the door.

He grinned. "So?"

Her eyes narrowed. "You're evil." Wolf pumped his hips, slamming home again and again until her eyelids fluttered and her mouth fell open on a moan. "*Soooo* evil."

Wolf released her wrist to squeeze her breast, to pluck her nipple between his thumb and finger and twist. He nuzzled her throat. "Come for me, Abby," he murmured against her flesh. "Scream for me."

Her legs tightened around his hips and her fingernails raked across his back, vicious and painful. He shook off her claws and pushed himself up on his arms so he could stare down at her, at the writhing sex goddess tangled in the bed sheets beneath him. He watched in awe as she gave him everything she had, her dark eyes wild, her raven hair a matted curtain strewn across the pillows, screaming his name as her body shook in completion, her lusty cries drowning out the sounds of Wolf's own satisfaction.

Collapsing on the mattress, a sheen of sweat and the smell of sex clinging to their skin, Wolf buried his head in the crook of her neck, kissed her hammering pulse and whispered, "That's my girl."

The time for the picnic had arrived. Abby took about five steps across the village green before she realised the wedge-heeled shoes she'd bought were an ankle-snapping mistake and stopped to take them off. While kneeling, she took the time to look around, to seek out friends—and foes.

She spotted Jane and her parents, watched as they deposited an array of dishes on the buffet tables set up across the northern end of the green, under a row of white marquees, but she didn't see Richard with them.

She grinned as she saw Wolf nick a blueberry pikelet and quickly shove it in his mouth just as the Melvilles approached and introduced themselves, and she rolled her eyes and sighed with sisterly affection as she watched her brothers fend off the first of what would undoubtedly be a near-continuous wave of women.

Eligible bachelors were a scarcity in this tiny town, and as much as the Bennett family was denigrated for its bohemian ways, there was no denying the facts: the Bennett brothers were a devilishly handsome bunch of men, single and moneyed. A tick in all the right boxes for all the wrong women, though she doubted any of the local girls would get very far.

Paul, an ex-model and now photographer, generally spoke to everyone outside their immediate family with a distinct air of disdain—when he deigned to speak to anyone at all. More often than not he was downright rude. The women buzzing around him now, however, seemed to either not notice or not care.

Twins Tobias and Charlie were as different as chalk and cheese. At six feet and eight inches tall, Toby was a gentle giant. Painfully shy but as quick-witted as they come, he really only spoke when he had something worth saying. The ever-so-slightly shorter Charlie, on the other hand, was a complete show-off, as intelligent as he was ripped and not afraid to use either to his advantage.

Rafe, the Bennett family lawyer, was exacting in everything he did, from tying his shoes to dominating in the courtroom. He was a serious sort, but then having your heart broken would do that to a man.

And then there was Oliver: tall, witty, muscles on his muscles and spent most of his life dressed as a Viking, travelling the world from one medieval festival to the next, demonstrating the ancient art of blacksmithing to all and sundry. Thirty-five years old and yet to have a serious relationship, Ollie was a man-child of unrivalled proportions.

As tempting as she knew her brothers would find the local ladies for a quick roll in the hay, none of them would stoop so low as to encourage them in their amorous pursuits. They knew the women wanted something they just weren't willing to give them—commitment.

Shoes in hand, Abby made her way to the table her brothers had laid claim to and tossed the sandals under a chair. Wolf was yet to return, and she cast her gaze around as she searched for him.

People were filing in at a steady rate, adding to the collection of dishes already weighing down the buffet tables. Families were settling in, some choosing to sit at the beautifully decorated tables while others chose to utilise the more traditional picnic blankets that dotted the grass. Rope after rope of fairy lights and a rainbow of coloured paper lanterns were strung between the trees that surrounded the green, ready to light up the evening sky and extend the festivities well after dark.

A burst of masculine laughter caught her attention, directing her gaze to the newly erected gazebo, and there was Wolf, talking and shaking hands with the current mayor of Melville's Cross.

So that's where he got to.

He looked so tall, much taller than usual. She supposed it didn't help that Mayor Rose was almost a foot shorter than him, her greying bouffant barely reaching his shoulder. Abby grinned to see the usually puffed-up older woman so demure, almost shy.

"Wonders will never cease to amaze," she murmured to herself as she watched the mayor blush like a schoolgirl before moving on to welcome more people to the celebration.

"He calls you Abigail."

Toby's quiet observation pulled Abby's attention away from Wolf for a moment.

"He calls me a lot of things," she said absently with a dismissive wave of her hand.

"He calls you Abigail," he said again, "and you don't flinch."

Abby turned back towards their table and frowned as she was met by five pairs of curious eyes. She sighed. She'd wondered when the interrogation would begin. "He thinks it's wrong that I hate my own name, so he keeps saying it over and over in an attempt to make me like it again." She wrinkled her nose. "It's quite annoying, really."

Paul smirked and cocked one perfect eyebrow. "Uh-huh. And what did he say to get you to wear a dress?"

"Yeah, you look weird," Rafe said.

"You look like... a girl," Ollie added with a shudder.

"You can talk," Abby snorted, nodding at the thick blond braid that fell halfway down his back.

"Don't listen to them, kiddo," Toby said, his quiet manners silencing his brothers. "You look beautiful."

"Yes, she does."

Abby spun around to see Wolf leaning against the old oak that shaded their table. He was smiling.

Sneaky bugger, she thought, quickly followed by, *Oh crap!*

Had he heard her say he was annoying? Was that why he was smiling so serenely, because he was imagining new ways to punish her? New and exciting ways to bind her wrists and spank her arse until it burned, until she burned from the inside out as sexual need and wanton desire careened through her body, freeing her from all restraint and lifting her to a place where she could just... *float*.

She took a step towards Wolf, itching to tear his shirt open and slide her hands over his chest, to feel the strength of his muscles as they bunched and flexed under her fingertips, to do something wicked, something—

"Does anyone else feel *really* awkward right now?"

"No more awkward than this morning."

"They were going at it like rabbits."

"Very noisy rabbits."

Abby rounded on her brothers. "Just because I'm dressed like a girl doesn't mean I punch like one."

"*Now* she looks like our sister," Paul said. "Let's eat!"

As they joined the mass of people already circling the buffet tables, Abby kept an eye out for Richard. She hadn't seen him yet, but that didn't mean he wasn't lurking about somewhere.

Wolf was getting along with her brothers better than expected, although she was a little suspicious they hadn't grilled either of them about their deal, besides noting that Wolf called her Abigail, which they all knew she hated. Thankfully no one had said anything about the chains wrapped around the rafters in the lounge room.

Currently her lover was chatting with Toby about poisonous plants, picking her horticulturist brother's brain as a form of book research. She wondered what he'd think of Richard when they finally met. Her brothers had spent half the previous night regaling him with tales of her ex-husband's douchebaggery. They'd painted a picture of arrogance so pure and complete that Richard himself would have been impressed.

Speaking of people who find themselves impressive...

"I didn't know *you* were coming today."

Jane's cousin, Debra Melville, spoke from the other side of the table, her plate piled high with an assortment of cakes, cheeses and American-style ribs.

"Why wouldn't I be?" Abby said as she scanned the table for the ribs, then licked her lips when she found them.

"You do know Richard is here, don't you?" she said, her lips pursed in a smug little smile as she reached for a token piece of lettuce in an attempt to balance out the edible heart-attack on her plate.

"And what does that have to do with anything?"

"You don't think it'll be awkward?" The look on her face screamed volumes.

She knew.

She knew about Richard's last visit. The bastard probably rang Debra the moment he was out the front door, boasting about his achievement to humiliate her.

As a teenager, Abby had never known why he'd always defended Bitch Face, as she and Jane were calling her back then. Yes, they were cousins and of a similar age, and yes they were often unavoidably thrown together at family events, but it wasn't until after Abby's divorce at the ripe old age of twenty-eight that she'd realised just how alike her husband and his cousin were.

Debra had always gone out of her way to make Abby feel like an outcast, as though she'd never be good enough. And when they'd discovered she couldn't have kids, so had Richard. Oh, he was subtle about it at first, and then he wasn't, so she wasn't completely shocked when he'd announced he was leaving her. The fact that he already had a girlfriend, however, came as a surprise. That girlfriend also being a friend of Debra's... well, no surprises there.

Before she could answer, Wolf bent his head to her ear. "I'm not sure which is more delectable, this banquet or you in that dress." And then he nuzzled her throat, bringing a smile to her face.

"Wait a minute, *he's* here with *you*?"

Wolf raised his brow at her disbelieving tone. "Who else would I be here with?"

"You haven't left Toby's side the whole time you've been here. I naturally assumed...."

Toby sighed heavily. "For the last time, Debra, I'm not gay," he drawled as he scooped potato salad onto his plate. "I'd just rather cut my dick off than ever let it anywhere near you." And then he turned and walked back to their table.

"Bastards," she spat amid a sea of muffled snickering. "Every last one of you." And then she took her plate and left in the opposite direction.

"What was that all about?" Wolf asked when they got back to the table. Her brothers were already devouring their meals with their usual gusto but stopped long enough to share a conspiratorial look before diving into an explanation.

"Many years ago," Rafe began, "Debra made it *very* clear she was interested in Toby. And Toby made it very clear he was *not* interested in her."

"He turned her down flat," Abby continued.

"In public," Charlie added.

"So she told everyone he must be gay," Ollie said.

Toby grunted. "Pass the salt." Abby grinned at his disinterest.

Wolf indicated to the rest of her brothers with his fork. "Was she ever interested in anyone else?"

Charlie laughed. "Only Oliver."

"Was she successful?"

Ollie shrugged his broad shoulders. "She got me drunk."

"And you lack standards," Paul said.

"And there's that," Ollie agreed with a sudden grin.

"How long did you two date?"

"If by 'date' you mean fucked, then I guess... I don't know, a couple of hours, maybe?"

"You're so disgusting," Abby said with a shake of her head.

Oliver replied by belching. Loudly.

The conversation continued as their meals slowly vanished. Abby hadn't seen so many Bennetts in one place at one time for so long, and she was enjoying the familiar banter and easy camaraderie between her siblings, but she was also acutely aware of the man sitting next to her. A man who by all accounts was a virtual stranger, but one who had melded with her life, her family, with such ease she could almost forget that his presence in her world was only temporary.

She felt his knee brush against her leg and a jolt of awareness lanced through her. She squeezed her thighs together and squirmed in her seat, but as she looked up at him, her renewed desire vanished, for while the smile on his face told her he was enjoying himself, the distant look in his eyes told her something very different.

She laid her hand on his forearm. "Wolf? Are you all right?" she asked quietly.

He placed his hand over hers and gave it a squeeze. "I'm fine," he said. "I was just thinking about my sister."

"You have siblings?" Paul asked.

"Just the one. My younger sister, Kristin," he said as he picked at his food. "And she's not talking to me."

"What did you do?" Charlie asked with a broad grin.

Wolf sighed. "It's a long story."

"You miss her," Abby said.

"Yes."

"So why don't you call her?"

"Communications blackout, remember? Sally's orders. No phone calls or internet while on retreat."

Abby frowned. She could see the excuse for what it was: he was avoiding a confrontation with his sister. She almost laughed. The big bad Dom was afraid of his little sister. Or maybe he was just afraid of losing her altogether. Abby couldn't imagine life without her brothers always being there for her, how lost she'd be without them.

"We won't tell Sally if you don't," Charlie said.

Wolf smiled and tipped his head to her brother. "Thanks, but it's fine. I'll call her when I get home."

"I'll hold you to that," Abby said, then felt her cheeks heat as she realised the implications of her words. As if there was a future to which she could hold him.

Apparently she *could* forget he was only temporary.

Wolf tilted his head and stared at her for what felt like an eternity, but that faraway look had disappeared from his eyes and his mouth curved in a slow smile. She was about to ask him what he was thinking when he turned back to her brothers and changed the subject.

"So, there's three more of you, correct?"

Rafe answered first. "Yes. Henry, Crispin and Avery. Cris is visiting his mum in London. Avery's in Tokyo, I think, at some jeweller's trade show thing, and Henry... well, he doesn't get out much."

"And Sally is Henry's daughter?"

"Yeah," Charlie said, frowning. "Didn't Sally tell you any of this?"

Wolf shook his head. "She keeps pretty quiet about her personal life. Obviously I know about the leg thing, and I know she's an only child, and she mentioned once that her mum died of breast cancer, but before she demanded I sequester myself at The Forge, I had no idea she had such a large family."

The boys talked about Sally for a while, regaling Wolf with stories about all the mischief she used to get up to as a kid. And Abby watched them all, her gaze flicking from one brother to the next, gauging their reactions to her lover and wondering how they'd feel if he were to become a more permanent fixture in her life.

She knew it was stupid to think that way, that she was just setting herself up for disappointment—*temporary, remember?*—but she couldn't help but wonder: what would sharing her life with Wolf Adams look like?

She shifted her gaze to the big man sitting beside her and bit back a sigh as he tipped up a bottle of water and drank long and deep. She couldn't explain why but the sight of his strong throat working to swallow down the cool liquid did all sorts of naughty, wicked things to her.

Her teeth sank into her bottom lip and the urge to lick that sensual column of flesh was quickly overriding her common sense. But as she leaned closer, someone kicked her under the table. Looking at the obvious culprit, she mouthed the word, "What?" Ollie raised one brow then slowly shook his head. Abby poked out her tongue at him.

Either not noticing her interaction with her brother or choosing to ignore it, Wolf asked, "Do any of you have kids?"

"I have a daughter," Paul said, his stern face softening with fatherly pride. "Sophie."

"And I have thirteen-year-old twin girls," Charlie said. "Josie and Diana. They're as tall as Abby and still growing." He laughed. "Their mothers are tearing their hair out keeping them in clothes that fit."

Wolf arched a brow. "Mothers?"

Charlie grinned. "Yeah, my best friend, Amy, and her girlfriend, Jess, couldn't afford IVF treatments so they asked if I'd be willing to donate my sperm. The old-fashioned way."

Wolf looked confused. "The old-fashioned way?"

"Jess is bisexual." Charlie winked. "Knocked her up on the first try."

Abby was acutely aware that all eyes were on Wolf, everyone waiting to see his reaction to Charlie's story. When he didn't bat an eyelid and continued the conversation, she released the breath she didn't realise she'd been holding.

"Cool. What about you, Oliver? Any kids?"

"Nope. Not a one."

Toby snorted. "That you know of."

"For all you know," Rafe said, "you could have a laundry list of illegitimate offspring longer than Ulysses Bennett's."

"Doubtful," Ollie replied, waggling a sausage between his fingers. "Unlike dear old Dad, I know what condoms are for."

After lunch Abby watched her brothers drift off in different directions. Several people came by the table and stopped to chat, all interested in Abby's new man—or more accurately, in having something new to gossip about.

Jane waved to her from the other side of the village green.

"I'm going to go mingle for a while. You wanna come?"

Wolf slid his aviators up his nose. "I think I'll just people-watch for a little while."

Abby frowned, his sombre mood niggling at her. "Are you sure you're okay? Charlie's right, you know. What Sally doesn't know won't hurt her. Call your sister."

Wolf took her hand, pulled her into his lap and kissed her long and deep. "I'm fine. I promise," he said, and even crossed his heart. Then he smiled, all wickedness and delight as he whispered a command in her ear.

A command that left her squirming all over again.

Chapter Fifteen

Wolf leaned his elbows back on the picnic table and watched the celebration with an air of contentment. It was a feeling he hadn't enjoyed in a long time. Of course, before he'd been forced to go on retreat, he hadn't enjoyed a lot of things in a long time: good food, good conversation, the good graces of a good woman.

He breathed deeply, sucking in the crisp, cleansing air of the hinterland. The scent of roses and barbequed sausages tripped over his senses and made him smile. He felt so at peace here. So at home.

Odd, considering he'd never really liked the country; he was a city boy through and through. Then again, his previous experiences with country life—school excursions consisting of long, boring bus rides, crusty biology teachers and whinging city kids navigating a minefield of cowpats—were vastly different to actually living in a place like Melville's Cross.

Perhaps it was just the difference between his teenage self and now. Maybe maturity was the key to appreciating a town that placed value on a slower way of life, a more relaxed state of being. His smile grew lazy as he watched and observed, his mind humming with ideas.

Life excited him again.

"I'll hold you to that."

He wasn't sure who had been more surprised when those words had left her mouth, him or Abby, but the presumption was clear. Consciously or not she saw a future with him. When he'd held her gaze afterward it had been so easy to imagine her in his house, to see her sitting on the couch in his office or pottering around out the back in the tiny wasteland he generously referred to as a garden. Or kneeling at his feet, naked, her knees spread and her pretty pussy on display.

Or maybe I can live here with her.

"Wolf."

Wolf stood up and turned towards the man who'd called his name. Abby's brothers strolled towards him from across the village green, the eldest of the group, Paul, leading the way. "Mind if we have a few words?" he said as they approached.

"Of course not," Wolf said, only to find himself suddenly surrounded by Bennetts, each and every one of them as tall and imposing as him—Tobias even more so. His peaceful state of mind slipped away, and for the first time in his adult life, he actually felt intimidated.

"We can't help noticing the way you look at our little sister," Paul said. "Our one and *only* little sister."

"And the way she looks at you," Charlie added. "Makes us think you might be playing with something more than just her body."

Playing?

The word carried a certain connotation that set Wolf's

teeth on edge. He clenched his jaw so hard it ached under the pressure, but he willed himself to stay calm, to give Abby's brothers the benefit of the doubt and hear them out, even though he had a pretty good idea where this discussion was headed.

"Don't get us wrong," Rafe said. "We dig that you're helping her out and making her face her fears, but...." He shrugged.

The unspoken statement was as blunt as Abby's anvil. "But if I hurt her, you'll hurt me?"

He understood their need to protect their sister from would-be arseholes, had done it himself more than once in the past when guys he didn't approve of had shown just a little too much interest in *his* sister. But it still grated his nerves that they were even having this conversation.

With no obvious ringleader, he stared down each of them in turn. "So, is this the part where you threaten to smash my kneecaps?" he said.

The brothers moved closer, like a pack of hungry dingoes surrounding their prey, sly grins making their handsome faces more than sinister, almost demonic. "Kneecaps," Paul scoffed, his voice dropping to little more than a whisper. "We won't bother with your kneecaps, Mr Writer."

"Abby has eight brothers," Oliver said.

"And you have eight fingers," Rafe added.

Charlie leaned close, whispered, "You do the math."

Wolf's calm slipped. His eyes narrowed and he gritted his teeth against the urge to punch someone. His hands drew into fists so tight his fingernails bit into the soft flesh of his palms. He would never hurt Abby, would never hurt the woman who in such a short amount of time had gifted him with so much joy and life and laughter, the woman he'd come to care for.

The woman he was *falling for*.

And suddenly the explanation, the *why*, he'd been searching for hit him with such clarity it made his head spin. When he was with Abby he could just be *himself*.

He didn't have to be the leather-clad Dominant in the fetish club sifting through the ocean of wanna-subs who'd read a kinky best-seller and thought they knew exactly what he wanted, and missed the mark by a mile.

And he didn't have to be the Famous Author, the bloke on the hardcover dust-jacket with the enigmatic smile who wore a suit and did book tours and gave talks to literature students.

Abby didn't care about his fame in the book world, or his infamy in the lifestyle. She didn't expect anything more or less of him than what she'd already seen. The jeans and T-shirt wearing, motorcycle riding, free-balling, scruffy-haired, often grumpy introverted ex-teacher. And she submitted to that man, wholly and willingly.

Perfectly.

She was perfect for him.

A burst of excitement pulsed under his skin, as though his heart and mind had shared this epiphany and wanted —*needed*—to spread the word to every cell in his body, every fibre of his being. He wanted to find her, to kiss her long and deep, to show her with his body how much he desired her, to tell her with his words how much she meant to him—but there was another, more pressing urge underlying that one.

The urge to prove himself worthy of her, and her heart.

He lifted his chin as any intimidation he'd felt was swept away by his determination. "Let me make myself very clear," he said. "Abby is *my* woman. She's *mine* to protect. And if you ever insinuate otherwise again, you and I will be sharing more than words. I'll rip your fucking heads off."

A slap on his shoulder almost knocked him off balance, and a bark of laughter met his ears. "I told you he was in love."

From the corner of his eye, Wolf saw the usually stoic Tobias, a grin splitting his face, his body shaking with laughter, laughter that all at once surrounded him as the others joined in. Wolf closed his eyes and clenched his jaw as he felt the telltale heat of a blush rise up his cheeks, wincing at the depth of his embarrassment.

"And just what is going on over here?"

Wolf's eyes popped open at the sound of Jane's voice, for once a welcome intrusion. He spied her standing beyond the wall of Bennett brothers, a tray of pink-frosted cupcakes in one hand, a jug of something cold in the other.

"Janie!" the brothers cried in unison.

The wall split apart and quickly reformed around the diminutive redhead—most of it, anyway. Wolf watched with a raised brow as Rafe turned on his heel and stalked away from the rowdy gathering. His brothers eventually drifted after him, but not before waggling their thumbs at Wolf and casually reminding him of the amazing advancements in speech-to-text software.

He flipped them off, sending them into another round of hearty snickering.

"Lemonade?" Jane asked, holding up the jug.

"Sure," he said, still scowling, and grabbed a cup from the table.

"May I ask you something?" Jane said as she poured.

Wolf took a sip of the old-fashioned lemonade and immediately sucked in his cheeks at the paralysing tartness. "Sure," he said as he smacked his lips together and frowned at the plastic cup. "Unless you intend to threaten me, too."

"Ah, so that's what they wanted," she said, inclining her

head towards the brothers and the bevy of women suddenly buzzing around them with endless trays of finger foods and come-hither smiles. "And no. If I was going to threaten you, I would have done so long before now."

"Okay, so what do you want to know, then?"

"Are you in love with Abby?"

Wolf choked down the last of the lemonade. "Wow," he said with a cough as he banged his fist on his chest. "You countryfolk don't beat around the bush, do you?"

She shrugged as she deposited the cake tray and jug on the picnic table. "I find it saves time. But you do, don't you?" she said. "And the boys must think you do too, or they'd never have threatened you."

Wolf groaned and stared down at his boots. "Am I really that obvious?" he said quietly, glancing sideways at her.

Jane flashed him that smug smile of hers and peeled a cupcake. "A little bit, yeah."

He shoved a hand in his pocket and shuffled his feet. Jane's simple observation made him feel as awkward as he had the first time his mother busted him reading *Playboy*. "Do you think Abby suspects anything?"

"Possibly. Cake?"

He shook his head, then sought out Abby in the crowd. A serene smile touched his lips when he finally saw her, kneeling to help a young boy tie his shoelaces. The mere sight of her calmed his nerves and yet, as she stood up, the silhouette she cast with all those luscious curves, all those soft hills and deep valleys and knowing he'd had his hands, his mouth, on every single inch of her made his heart race with unparalleled lust. "Do you think she feels the same way about me?"

Jane sucked a glob of frosting off her thumb. "Probably."

Wolf straightened to his full height, new confidence

puffing out his chest, making his smile broaden—a smile that faltered as he caught sight of a man matching Richard's description sidling up to her, reminding him of their deal that, as far as Abby was concerned, their relationship was temporary. A safeguard for her vulnerable heart.

His chest deflated. "Do you think she'll ever admit it?"

"Wolfie, baby," Jane said, slapping her small hand against his shoulder. "Not a chance in Hell."

Abby inwardly groaned as she spied Rich—Dick, sauntering towards her. Her lips thinned as she pasted on a wan smile to greet him.

"What are you smirking about?" he said, one brow raised.

"Nothing."

"Uh-huh. So, who's the Neanderthal?"

Abby followed Richard's gaze to the other side of the village green where she saw Jane licking the icing off a cupcake, her tongue moving slowly, deliberately through the bright pink frosting. She was obviously teasing someone with the salacious display, and a quick glance over Richard's shoulder revealed Rafe scowling in Jane's direction.

Abby rolled her eyes and shook her head as she turned her attention to the man standing beside her best friend, who, with his tattoos and biker boots, probably did look like a Neanderthal to someone like Richard, a man who looked like he'd just stepped out of a menswear catalogue with his perfectly pressed camel-coloured chinos and expensive crisp white shirt. Even his fine woollen scarf was perfectly styled.

Wolf, on the other hand, was the epitome of cool in his

faded blue jeans and aviators. Abby watched as he folded his arms over his broad chest, the movement pulling his shirt tight across his biceps, his tattoos shifting as the muscles in his forearm tensed. She found herself undressing him with her eyes, fantasising about those long, strong legs and that muscular arse.

Could bounce a coin off that arse.

"Earth to Abby."

Richard stroked his hand down her arm. A cold chill ran down her spine but she repressed the urge to shudder. She stepped away from Richard's grasp and studied him in a new light. He was still as handsome as ever with his pale blue eyes and full lips, scruffy ginger-blond locks and the shadow of a beard lining his jaw, but the sight of him no longer elicited the pleasurable response it once had.

And his voice....

"Abbs?"

His voice was so *irritating*. How had she never noticed that before? She'd always thought his voice was soothing, gentle, the perfect pitch for a doctor who needed to calm and reassure his patients. But Abby didn't need soothing. She didn't want gentle. She wanted deep and sonorous and rough. She wanted sexy. She wanted Wolf. Richard's placid timbre sounded almost whiny by comparison.

"Don't call me that. And he's not a Neanderthal. He's an author."

"Author," he said with a *tsk*. "Code for unemployed."

"What do you want, Richard?"

"I wanted to see how you are, how you've been," he said, his eyes shuttering, his lips softening, his voice dipping seductively. At least, she would have found it seductive a month before. He moved closer, invading her personal space. She wrinkled her nose. He smelled like he'd bathed in a mixture of heavy cologne and hospital-grade disinfectant, the cloying scent of one used in an attempt to disguise the stringent smell of the other. The toxic combination clung to him like a second skin, and she tried very hard not to gag. "You look amazing in that dress."

Abby ground her teeth and offered him another tight-lipped smile. "Thank you, and I'm fine. How are Laura and the kids?"

Richard cleared his throat and mirrored her expression. "Fine. They're all fine."

"Pity they couldn't make the trip and fly up with you," she said, trying desperately not to smirk as he took a step back. "I know your parents are disappointed. They'd hoped to spend some time with their grandkids."

His jaw visibly clenched and his skin paled. "Yes, well...."

Abby could practically see the cogs turning in his mind, no doubt trying to invent an adequate lie to explain his family's absence, but just as he was about to spew his untruths, Wolf appeared by her side and slid his arm around her waist. He pulled her into the hard line of his body and she instantly relaxed, wrapping her arms around his middle and snuggling into his warmth, the action as natural to her as breathing.

"Abby, *liebchen*, who's your friend?"

Richard immediately stuck his hand out. "I'm Abby's ex-husband, Doctor Richard Melville."

Wolf relinquished his hold on Abby to shake the proffered hand. "I'm Abby's future husband, Author Adam Wolfe."

Abby's eyes widened and she pursed her lips, although whether it was to contain her shock at Wolf's bold statement or to stop herself from laughing outright at Richard's boggled expression, she didn't quite know. It was a full ten seconds before her ex-husband was able to form a coherent sentence.

"Future husband?" he spluttered. "But I thought you'd only just met."

"Sometimes you just know," Wolf said, his voice soft as he wrapped his arm around Abby once more and pressed a kiss to her temple. She breathed in deep, almost sighing out loud as her lover's natural masculine scent filled her nostrils and enticed her to snuggle closer. For just a moment she could almost forget where they were. And who they were talking to.

Until he spoke.

"Adam Wolfe?" Richard said the name twice more before adding with a frown, "Why do I know that name?"

"Perhaps you've read one of my books," Wolf said dismissively as he turned his full focus to her and slid his hand down her back to cup her bottom. "The last one sold over one million copies worldwide." Then he bowed his head and pressed smiling lips against her ear. "You're not wearing any panties," he whispered, his roughened voice sending a shiver of excitement through her. "Naughty little nymph."

Abby pressed her face into the side of his neck to hide her blush. The command Wolf had given her when he'd pulled her into his lap and kissed her hard: go commando for the rest of the day, or wear the butterfly for the rest of the night. She'd hidden in the public bathroom for a good ten minutes before finally obeying. She still wasn't sure if the potential reward outweighed the potential embarrassment if discovered, but it was definitely better than the pain of another never-ending, clitoris-obliterating orgasm.

Oh how I loathe that butterfly.

Richard cleared his throat. "And what brings a world-famous author to Melville's Cross of all places?"

Abby's eyes narrowed at his tone, derision mixed with venom. "And what's wrong with Melville's Cross?"

Richard shrugged. "Nothing, I suppose, if you enjoy having no privacy."

"I'm on retreat," Wolf said. "It's a working holiday of sorts, and my agent assured me that Melville's Cross was exactly what I needed."

"To make you appreciate the big city?" Richard laughed at his own joke.

"Something like that. But now that I've had time to see the place and meet the people, I wouldn't mind making a permanent home of it."

Richard's expression sobered. "You're kidding."

"Not at all. From the moment I arrived I was made to feel right at home. Why would I want to leave when I can't think of a single reason not to stay?"

As Richard stumbled for a reply, Wolf took Abby's hand. His large fingers squeezed hers, the warmth emanating from him a gentle reminder that he was there for her. That he was watching over her, protecting her.

Defending her and the town she loved.

An irresistible urge to show him her gratitude had her sliding her hands over his chest and fisting her fingers in his shirt collar. He looked down at her, his expression curious, but she simply smiled. Smiled because this wondrous man had kept his promise and kept her safe. Surely that was worth a small token of her appreciation?

"If you'll excuse us, Dick," she said, her eyes never leaving Wolf's, "but I need to tear this man's clothes off."

Chapter Sixteen

A bby pottered around the house, sighing quietly as she picked up after her brothers. Thankfully she was down to two, Charlie, Toby, and Rafe having scarpered after breakfast Sunday morning. They claimed to have a lunchtime engagement in the city that they just had to get back for, but Abby had a hunch the twins were actually spiriting Rafe away from Jane Melville before he could do something stupid.

Well, more stupid.

They'd all seen Jane storm out of Rafe's bedroom Saturday night. Though why they felt the need to lie about it she'd never know. It wasn't as if it hadn't happened before. But at any rate, that left her with only Paul and Ollie to contend with.

Paul was happy to take his camera and go exploring every day, leaving the house after breakfast and not returning until late afternoon. Ollie, on the other hand, was harder to get rid of. He was a blacksmith, like her, and loved nothing more than being knee deep in metal and fire and soot.

Currently he was helping her clear her backlog of odd jobs, fixing old garden gates, replicating ancient door hinges and so on, so she couldn't really complain about him being underfoot, but his constant presence had taken the spontaneity out of her and Wolf's sex life.

Speaking of Wolf, the man had been head down, bum up over his laptop every day since the picnic, his long, strong fingers flying over the keys with such dexterity she was almost jealous of the keyboard.

But every now and then, she'd catch him looking at her with such a heated expression that it made her blush, made her think that maybe he also resented her brothers' continued presence and the interruption of their daily sexathons.

Still, each night he stroked her hair as she sat on the cushion at his feet and read books while she sketched. And he still peppered her with questions about her past experiences, including circling back to her fear of the scissors the night he'd strung her up and forced a confession out of her.

Abby had hoped he would forget all about it, but the man had a mind like a steel trap.

And a protective streak a mile wide.

She'd told him the details of what had instigated her fear, that Kurt had made fun of her, had said that since she would never bear children, would never know the simple joy of breastfeeding her child, that her nipples were as useless as her womb and threatened to cut them off. The sick prick had even gone so far as to press the opened blades to her skin and lightly squeeze, drawing blood and scaring the shit out of her that he would actually go through with it.

Wolf had been livid. He'd sworn retribution. Had vowed to find the sonofabitch and have him banned from every kink club across the country, after he'd had ten minutes alone with the evil sack of shit, of course.

And then he'd kissed Abby's breasts. He'd laved her with so much attention, so much tenderness, had licked and sucked her flesh until she was a whimpering, needy mess in his arms and Kurt's humiliations were nothing more than a distant memory....

"What's on your mind, little nymph?"

Wolf's deep voice snapped her out of her reverie and she suddenly realised she was staring at his mouth, imagining his warm tongue licking her nipples, teasing them into hard little peaks, and she fumbled the dirty coffee mugs she'd been clearing off the mantle, dropped one on the hearth.

The cup shattered on impact and she swore as she dropped to her knees and cleared away the broken shards.

Wolf appeared by her side and helped her clean up the mess.

"Shit," he said a moment later, pulling his hand away.

"What?"

"I cut my finger."

"Let me see," Abby said as she took his hand in hers. A tiny sliver of glazed ceramic stuck out of his finger, blood welling at the sliver's base.

Abby quickly pulled it out, then stuck his finger in her mouth to suck the wound clean. She was about to let go of him when she looked up and caught his gaze. His dark hazel eyes held nothing but lust, pure and hungry. She swallowed hard as he slowly removed his finger from her mouth and slid his hand to her nape.

He pulled her to him, his lips soft yet demanding, his tongue delving past her lips and sweeping against her tongue as his lust took over and he tumbled her to the floor.

Abby moaned against his mouth and their hands took on a flurry of action, tugging at T-shirts and yanking on zippers. Not a word passed between them as he flipped her over and bent her forwards over the couch cushions, his knee knocking her legs apart as his hand fisted in her hair and his mouth latched over her earlobe. She sighed softly as his hot lips worked their way down her neck, gasped as his teeth found their mark.

"I want you," he growled by her ear as he pushed his erection hard against her bottom. Her heart raced with anticipation as he slid his free hand inside her jeans and cupped her heated flesh. As he pushed a thick finger into her, she cursed her jeans to Hell, swearing to the heavens that she would wear more dresses, but then he said something she did not want to hear. "I want to fuck your arse."

Abby froze. "What?"

What!

He wanted to fuck her *what?*

No! No, no, no.

She struggled to free herself from his grasp only to have his hand tighten in her hair, the pain it caused no longer pleasurable. She then realised Wolf had bent her over the couch for one very good reason: so she couldn't escape.

"I know your brain just imploded, Abby," he said with a soft chuckle as he rested his forehead on her back, "but let me explain."

"No explanations necessary," she snarled back at him. "You're a sadist." She tried again to struggle out of his hold but he was so damned heavy. All he had to do was press his weight down on her and she couldn't move.

"I'm no sadist, Abigail," he said, his voice hard and tinged with hurt. "Trust me, you'd know if I was." And then his weight lifted off her and he stood there, staring down at her, his hand held out to help her to her feet. She eyed him cautiously before accepting his help, and when she stood in front of him, he huffed out an irritated sigh. "This isn't exactly how I wanted to broach the subject with you," he said, "but our limited privacy is driving me crazy." He leaned his forehead against hers. "I'm so fucking horny."

His declaration coupled with the look of sheer frustration on his face made Abby burst out laughing, and any annoyance she'd felt melted away to nothing.

"Poor Sir," she said, grinning broadly. Wolf grabbed her arse and pulled her into him, mashing their groins together.

"It'll be poor sub if you're not careful, *liebchen*." Wolf sighed and relaxed his grip. "I know you said Kurt hurt you, that he used anal sex as a form of punishment, and I know the very thought of it scares the hell out of you. But I also know how wonderful it can be, how truly intimate and sensual it can be. And that is something I'd like to share with you, if you'll let me."

Abby chewed the inside of her cheek as she fought the urge to run. She wanted so desperately to be the brave person Wolf believed her to be, but she had so many bad memories, had experienced so much pain. And not the fun kind.

How could anyone find *that* pleasurable?

But then, this was Wolf. This was the man who had vowed to help her in any way he could before they parted ways. Maybe he could help erase her old pain. Maybe he would help her make new memories, better ones. Maybe....

"Can I think about it for a day or two?"

Wolf nodded. "Of course, but just today. I don't want you getting anxious from overthinking it."

Abby looked away. "And if I decide that I truly don't want to do it?"

Wolf lifted her chin and stroked her cheek, his fingers warm and smelling faintly of her lust. "It's my job to help you heal your hurts, not create new ones. If you decide this is a hard limit, that you truly don't wish to proceed, we won't."

Abby measured the tone of his voice for the truth of his words. She believed him. But that didn't alleviate her fear.

"Ollie?" Abby watched her brother dunk his head in the water barrel outside the forge and then flick his long blond hair back over his shoulders, spraying her with big fat droplets in the process.

"Hmm? Did you say something?"

Abby wiped the water from her face. "You got a minute?"

"Sure," he said as he pulled his hair back into a soggy man-bun and strolled back into the heat of the forge. "Hey, I see you've almost finished that throne... chair... thing."

"Queening throne," she corrected.

"Queening throne." Oliver screwed up his face. "What the fuck is a queening throne?"

Abby grinned. "A tool for teaching subs to respect their Mistress through the liberal application of their tongues."

"What?"

"You're an intelligent man, Ollie. I'm sure you'll figure it out."

Oliver looked back out to the chair, his brow scrunched and his lips moving silently. Abby knew the exact moment his brain pieced the clues together because a wry smile dawned on his handsome face.

"You could've just said it's used for oral sex," he said, rolling his eyes.

Abby shrugged. "Where's the fun in that?" she said, pulling on her leather gloves, then she picked up the twisted iron rod Ollie had been working on, mostly for something to focus on while she tried to figure out how to casually drop anal sex into the conversation. "What's this for?"

Ollie stoked the fire and stuck another iron in. He eyed her with a curious tilt of his brow. "I'm making a few outdoor kitchen sets to sell at the Abbey Tourney in July," he said as she put the rod back on the workbench with a collection of S hooks and various Viking-style knives, "but you've seen me make these before. So what's really going on?"

"Well...."

Oliver huffed, impatient. "Come on. Out with it. I have shit to do."

Her mouth opened and shut as she struggled to find the right words. "I was wondering if you ever... ah... in your infi-nite experience with such matters, would ever have... um...."

"I assume there's a question coming sometime today."

"Fuck it," Abby said, her shoulders hunching forwards in defeat. "There is absolutely no way to ask this delicately."

"Ask what?"

"Have you ever had anal sex?"

Ollie's mouth fell open and his brow scrunched as he wrestled with his response. "Wow. You're right, that was not delicate."

"But have you?"

"Has Wolf asked *you* to?"

Abby nodded and picked up a knife. "Yes."

"You know you don't have to do it if you don't want to, right?"

She heard the concern in his voice, saw it in his clear blue eyes. "I know."

His expression grew stern, protective. "And Wolf knows that too, right?"

Abby smiled. "Yes, he knows."

"Good. I like Wolf. I'd hate to have to break his jaw."

"Will you please just answer the question?"

Ollie pulled the iron from the fire and twisted it into shape. "Yeah, I've had anal sex. I've never been on the receiving end, mind you, so I don't know what insights you think I have to share, despite my 'infinite experience'."

"Well, was it, I don't know, pleasurable? For the women?"

Her brother set aside his work and wiped the sweat from his brow, leaving a black sooty smudge across his face, and turned his full attention to her.

"I never heard any complaints. One woman I was with a few years back wanted nothing but anal sex. Kept spouting some nonsense about staying a virgin until she got married."

Abby screwed up her face. "What?"

Ollie laughed. "I know, right?"

"But she liked it?"

"Yeah, she liked it. Does that help?"

Abby chewed at her bottom lip. "Maybe." Then she threw her hands in the air. "I don't know. I mean, I like the man, but do I really want to go *there* with him?"

"Why not?"

"Because he's temporary. And anal sex, the way he describes it anyway, seems a little too intimate for someone who's only temporary."

Ollie shoved the iron back in the coals. "Who says he's temporary?"

Abby scowled at her brother. "I do."

"Why?"

"Because I'm happy on my own," she said, sticking her chin out, defiant.

"Bullshit," Ollie said as he worked the metal. "If you're happy, I'm celibate."

Abby tsked and rolled her eyes. "I don't know why I bother talking to you. You never take me seriously."

Ollie tossed his hammer on the workbench and speared the searing metal rod into the water barrel by his feet, causing it to splutter and hiss.

"You want serious?" he said as he pinned her with an irritated stare. "Fine, I'll be serious. Wolf is the best thing that ever happened to you and you're fucking it up. I get it, Abbs, I do. You've been hurt and you don't want to get hurt again, but you can't just close yourself off from the world and hope for the best."

Abby gaped at her brother's sudden outburst. "I am not closed off."

"Yes you are. You've barely left the house for two years. You push everyone away, keep everyone at arm's length—"

"I don't have to listen to this," she said as she made for the door.

Ollie grabbed her by the shoulders and forced her to look at him. "Yes you do. The others won't say anything because they don't want to upset you, but I'm sick of handling you with kid gloves. I'm sorry Richard and Kurt hurt you so bad, but you know what? Fuck them! The whole point of this little side arrangement between you and Wolf was to purge those arseholes from your life once and for all, to stop letting them dictate how you live your life. Now, either Wolf isn't up to the task, or you haven't been paying attention, because from where I sit, sister, you're still letting them win."

Abby couldn't speak, and she didn't know what she'd say even if she could. Oliver's words were like a slap to the face. Several slaps, in fact. And each one fell with the weight of truth.

Her chest felt tight and she couldn't breathe, and then great sobs were shaking her body and her brother's arms came around her, guiding her to a stool.

She felt so stupid. So weak.

She stared up at Ollie, at the concern etched across his smudged face. "I'm scared," she admitted, her voice barely above a whisper.

"I know," he said as he wiped the tears from her face.

"Everything between us since the day he arrived has been so easy, so wonderful. He gets me, you know? He totally gets me. But in the back of my mind, I keep waiting for the other shoe to drop, for everything to go sideways and I keep thinking, 'Thank God he's not staying, because if he did....'" She shook her head and covered her face with her hands.

"What?"

She let her hands fall to her lap in defeat. "If he stays, there's a very real chance I'll fall in love with him. And I can't do that. I won't allow myself to do that."

Ollie took her hands in his and gave her fingers a gentle squeeze. "Why not?"

"You know why not," she said, fresh tears falling down her face. "What if he turns out to be exactly like Kurt? Lulling me into a false sense of security before going all psycho on me. I can't go through that again. Not with him."

Her brother sighed heavily as he tucked a stray lock of hair behind her ear. "You are such an idiot."

Abby sniffed loudly. "Why? Because I want to protect myself?"

"Because you're not protecting shit," he said with a laugh, making her feel even more stupid than she already did. "Anyone with a half a brain can tell Wolf's a good man, and you're already half in love with him or you wouldn't be this upset at the thought of falling in love with him. And if you'd pull your head out of your arse for more than five seconds, you'd realise he's falling in love with you, too. So why don't you do us all a favour and stop holding back. Wolf deserves better. And so do you."

Abby stood in the doorway and watched Wolf as he stared at his laptop, his chin in his hands and his lips moving silently as he read through his work.

Oliver's words whispered through her mind: *"He's falling in love with you, too."*

Was he really? And more to the point, was she?

The physical attraction between them was obvious—they'd barely kept their hands off each other from the moment they'd met—but was there anything more to it than that?

Could she see herself spending her life with this person? Sharing her days and nights, her ups and downs, opening herself up to him completely, trusting him entirely? Her breath caught in her throat as she realised that yes, she could.

Because she already had.

The knowledge shocked her to her core.

After so long alone, she'd forgotten what it felt like to trust someone new, and the fact that it had happened so quickly, so unknowingly, only demonstrated exactly how dangerous Wolf Adams truly was.

"I know you're there, *liebchen*," Wolf said, casting his gaze in her direction. His glasses sat halfway down his nose and he watched her over the top of them as she stepped into the light of the room. His grin vanished. "What's wrong?" he demanded as he pushed to his feet and crossed the room. "Are you hurt?"

Abby stared up at him as he ran his hands over her, searching for whatever had caused her to look so pale and fragile. The heat of his hands where he touched her, of his gaze as it skated over her, and the depth of his concern evident in his voice and in the tight moue of his lips, made her think that maybe Ollie was right. Maybe Wolf did love her. Her heart fluttered at the thought, but she wasn't about to throw all her caution to the wind.

Not again. Not with him. Not yet.

So instead she slid her hands up his chest, feeling the hard muscle beneath his T-shirt, the gentle rise and fall of his breathing, the soft, springy rustle of his chest hair. Then she wrapped her arms around his waist and snuggled against him, inhaling his scent as he rested his chin on the top of her head and held her close.

"Are you all right?"

Abby nodded but still said nothing, and when Wolf leaned back and stared at her, his brow pulled down in curiosity, she simply smiled at him. Ollie was right. It was time she stopped holding back.

Wolf wasn't Richard, and he most certainly wasn't Kurt.

"I'm sorry I called you a sadist," she said, ducking her head from his gaze as her smile faltered.

She felt his lips press against her hair. "And I'm sorry I was so blunt about such a delicate subject."

Abby lifted her head to stare at him, her new resolve helping to cut down the tendril of fear trying to creep back up inside her. "Then would you like to ask me again in a less blunt manner?"

Wolf cocked one brow. "Are you sure?"

"No," she said. "But ask me anyway."

"Okay." A slow smile stretched across his face and he cupped her cheeks in his warm palms. Gentle, as always. "Abigail, will you allow me the honour of reintroducing you to anal sex?"

Abby swallowed hard and forced herself to nod. "Yes, Sir. I will."

Chapter Seventeen

Wolf pretended not to watch Abby as she lounged in the bathtub. Her raven hair was piled on top of her head and skewered in place with an old paintbrush, steam curling stray tendrils of black at her nape. Her skin was blushed by the heat of the water, and she wore a sensual smile as she bathed, one that told him she was completely aware of his little game and she was determined to win.

He bit back a grin as she slid the washcloth along each of her long limbs, starting at her fingertips before trailing up to her shoulder and across her big breasts, down her belly and between her thighs, and then all the way along her leg to her sweet little toes. The endless glide of movement was effortless. And deeply arousing.

She looked up at him, those dark brown pools veiled by long black lashes, and his heartbeat skipped. But instead of throwing away every last ounce of self-control he owned and climbing into the tub with her, he let loose a disinterested sigh, flicked to the next page in his book and continued reading, steadfastly ignoring the erection growing painfully inside his jeans—until she flicked water at him, wetting the page and making him lose his place.

Not that he was actually reading.

He glanced over the top of the book, his glasses perched on the end of his nose. "Yes?"

"There's room in here for two, you know," she said as she slung her leg over the edge of the tub and opened herself up to his gaze. Her hand slipped beneath the water, but he could see well enough where it went. She moaned softly as she played with herself.

He closed the book with a snap. "Time to hop out, I think."

Abby pouted at him for a moment before hauling herself out of the tub, slopping soapy water all over the scrubbed timber floor. Wolf leaned back in his chair and admired the view, one reminiscent of the first time he'd seen her with all her glistening wet curves and soft-looking flesh.

His lovely little water nymph.

He set aside his book and glasses, watching her with a lazy smile as she dried herself off, dragging the fluffy pink towel over and around her voluptuous curves until every last inch of her was warm and dry. Then he coaxed her over to him, bade her stand between his knees, and with one quick tug the towel she'd wrapped around herself fell to the floor.

Her skin was clean and pink, and she smelled of rose-scented soap and female arousal. It was all he could do not to yank her down into his lap and sate his desire for her right then and there, but somehow, with teeth gritted and hands fisted, he resisted the urge.

It helped knowing something better awaited them in the other room, so he shook the tension from his hands and rested them on Abby's hips. He felt the warmth of her body radiate into his palms, the fullness of her flesh between his spread fingers as he slowly rotated her until he was staring at her luscious arse.

He moistened his suddenly dry lips. "Lean forwards," he said, his voice almost choking on his lust. He cleared his throat. "Touch your toes, *liebchen*."

She complied without a word. The paintbrush slid free from her hair and clattered to the floor, allowing her raven locks to cascade down and pool at her feet. She shivered a little as she stood there in all her naked splendour, her pretty pink pussy on full display and so tantalisingly close to his mouth.

Focus.

"Cold?" he asked as he ran the pad of his thumb along the length of her glistening, wet slit.

"A little," she said, her voice shaky, uncertain.

He spread her cheeks apart and rubbed the moistened pad of his thumb against her arsehole, but didn't penetrate. Not yet. "Afraid?"

He heard her suck in a breath and then slowly release it. "A little."

Since the night of her punishment, Wolf had made a point of digging deeper into her past relationships, of revealing every disgusting, despicable thing Dick and Kurt had put her through. The lies, the cheating, the abuse, the scissors—emotionally and physically, they had brought her low and then kicked her while she was down.

Wolf still couldn't decide which of the two was worse; he only knew that every wound they'd inflicted needed healing, and every time he helped her heal a little, her trust in him deepened.

It was an exhilarating feeling.

He slid his hands over her rounded flesh, feeling every

lump, every dimple, tracing his fingertips over the roadmap of silvery stretch marks that curled over her hips and down the backs of her thighs. He adored every one of them, each one a sign that this was a woman full of life, a woman deserving of respect and love.

Love.

There was that word again, speeding through his mind so quick and easy that he had to bite his tongue to stop it slipping past his lips and into the realm of no return. Not that he would take it back if it did slip out, but until he was sure of Abby's feelings, he would keep his to himself. The last thing he wanted to do was scare her off, or open himself up to more hurt.

Abby fidgeted.

"Don't move." He slapped her rump just hard enough to sting, grinned as her bottom quivered and clenched. "Relax, little nymph."

Abby made a growling sound low in her throat.

Wolf laughed. "That's an order."

She breathed deep. "Yes, Sir," she said, and when the tension in her buttocks finally eased, he leaned forwards and sank his teeth into one perfect, fleshy orb.

She cried out at the sharp contact, but as he worked on her with his teeth and tongue, her cries morphed into moans. Moans that were music to his ears. Her arse continued to clench and release, clench and release as he bit and licked and squeezed and spanked, and her moans became drawn-out sighs of pleasure, filling the bathroom with sounds of sexual anticipation, driving his own carnal need to a near-frenzied state.

Wolf pulled away and took a deep breath to calm himself. "Come with me," he said as he stood and held out his hand. Abby took it without hesitation, all fear wiped from her expression by the lust that had replaced it.

He led her through the house to their bedroom and quickly fastened a pair of leather cuffs to her wrists, checking for mobility before attaching them to the chains she'd installed on their bed at his insistence.

"What are you grinning at?" she asked as he snapped the chains in place.

"Nothing," he said with a slight shake of his head.

"Tell me," she insisted.

He cocked one eyebrow at her.

She lowered her gaze. "Please tell me, Sir."

Wolf chuckled. "I was just thinking how sexy you look handling power tools," he said and waggled his eyebrows. Abby laughed, a full-body laugh that shook the bed and rattled her chains and jiggled her body in a way that drove him crazy. He smiled and sighed quietly, content. "God, you're beautiful."

Abby looked away and shied her smile but it didn't vanish completely. "Shut up."

Wolf took her nipple between his fingers and gave it a gentle tug. "I beg your pardon?"

Emboldened by his threat, she looked him straight in the eyes as she said, "Shut up, Sir."

He barked a laugh as he stroked her breast. "Are you ready, brat?"

"As ready as I'll ever be."

Abby took a deep breath and slowly exhaled as Wolf stood at the foot of the bed, then took another and held it as he pulled his T-shirt over his head and discarded it on the floor.

"Breathe, Abby," he said with a lopsided grin.

She blushed under the intensity of his stare, then swallowed hard and wet her lips. It still amazed her how quickly this man could change the mood in the room just by taking his shirt off, and how quickly her lustful infatuation became an insatiable hunger for his body.

Her gaze roamed over him, drinking in every glorious, powerful, tattooed inch of him, and her chains rattled as she reached for him, the involuntary and ineffectual action causing his grin to broaden.

Smug bastard.

He knew he had her exactly where he wanted her.

Exactly where she wanted to be.

Wolf spread her legs and slid his hands along their length. The bed dipped under his weight as he knelt between them, and the faded denim of his jeans pulled taut across his muscular thighs. "There are three things you must remember during anal sex," he said as he popped the button at his waist. "First, when I push in, you breathe out. That will relax your muscles and make penetration easier. For both of us."

Abby nodded, her nerves making her fidget. "Second?"

"Anal sex is supposed to be pleasurable for *both* parties. If it becomes too uncomfortable, more than you can bear, I want you to use your safeword. Do you understand?"

"Yes, Sir."

"I mean it, Abby. If I find out you allowed me to put you in true pain because you feared the consequences of not following through, I will spank your arse raw. And not in the fun way."

Abby blinked up at Wolf, at the fierce expression

pulling at his brow. He was deadly serious. He did not want to hurt her. And the thought of her allowing him to hurt her actually hurt him. She took a breath and her nervousness eased a little. "I understand, Sir."

"What do you understand?"

"If it becomes too much for me, I will use my safeword." She offered him a tentative smile. "I promise." When she saw the tension leave his face, she ventured to ask, "And third?"

A grin of pure wickedness chased away the lingering shadow of his frown as he pulled a blue and white tube from his pocket and held it aloft. "There is no such thing as too much lube."

Abby shook with laughter and the last of her nerves dissipated.

"Now you're ready," Wolf said, and he set the tube aside.

Abby watched as he crawled up the bed and covered her body with his, as he nestled himself between her thighs and rocked his hips against her. The feel of his worn denim jeans and thick, hard arousal pushing against her clit sent a shiver of awareness through every part of her and made her skin prickle with anticipation.

The feel of his lips as he slowly grazed them across her collarbone and up the length of her neck made her breath catch. His teeth nibbled along the edge of her jaw, his tongue slipping around the shell of her ear and his hot breath mussing her hair, and her breath exhaled on a whimper.

"I'm going to enjoy taking your arse, little nymph," he whispered before sinking his teeth into her earlobe. "You make me so fucking hard."

Abby tried to focus on Wolf's voice, on the richness of his timbre and the eagerness underlying his words. And she absolutely tried not to think about the last time she'd had a cock shoved up her arse, about the pain and the humiliation, the taunting as she'd cried and begged.

That was the last thing she needed to think about.

But the more she tried not thinking about it, the more it intruded into her thoughts, and the more it intruded, the more uncertain she became.

Bit by bit she retreated from Wolf's tenderness. Her limbs felt heavy and her muscles grew taut. A lead weight settled in her stomach. Her breath sawed in and out of her lungs.

Panic settled in.

Wolf stilled above her. "Look at me, *liebchen*." The command was no less potent for the quietness of his voice, but she couldn't drag her eyes away from the chains securing her to the bed. She tugged at her restraints. His hand slipped around her throat, his palm warm, his grip firm yet gentle. "Look at me."

Her anxiety made her mouth run dry, and she licked her lips as her gaze shifted to his. His eyes were narrowed, but not in anger. He was staring at her with a look of intense concentration, and it made her squirm knowing he studied her so thoroughly. "Say my name."

Abby blinked. "What?"

His hand tightened slightly, reminding her that he was in control. "Say my name."

"Wolf," she whispered, her uncertainty making her breathless.

"Again," he said. She hesitated. "Say. My. Name."

Her eyes widened at his sharpened tone. "Wolf."

"And do you trust me?"

She swallowed hard against her nervousness. "In theory."

The hand around her throat relaxed and he stroked the pad of his thumb against her pulse. "Let me put it another way. How many times have we fucked?"

Abby's mind scrambled for an answer even as her brow pulled down in confusion. "I don't know. A lot. I wasn't keeping count."

"And in all those times, have I done anything to hurt you, truly and honestly hurt you?"

"No, you haven't."

His gaze softened, his voice, too. "Do you want to use your safeword, Abby?"

She relaxed a little as she realised what he was doing.

He was giving her an out.

If she wanted it.

He wasn't judging her, wasn't forcing her, and then she suddenly realised that he'd even stopped calling her Abigail, deferring to Abby or one of his pet names instead. He'd been doing everything possible to make sure she felt safe, to remind her who was in her bed with her.

And it wasn't Kurt.

It was Wolf. Kind, gentle, and yes, trustworthy.

Her anxiety settled, the heaviness in her body eased, and she took a deep, calming breath. "No, Sir. I don't want to use my safeword."

"Then do you trust me?"

She bit her lip and nodded. "Yes, Sir. I do."

His lips tipped up at the corners in that predatory way of his. "I'm going to kiss you now."

She exhaled a shuddering sigh. "Okay."

His lips met hers, firm and hot and demanding, and she met his tongue thrust for thrust as the kiss deepened and swept away every last doubt still swimming around inside her. Her neck arched as Wolf's lips left hers to travel along her jaw and down her throat, and an excited gasp left her lungs as his tongue retraced the path and plunged once more inside her eager mouth.

The taste of him.

The feel of him.

The smell of him.

Abby tugged at her restraints, but not in panic. Not this time. This time it was need coursing through her. The need to touch him, to feel all that hard muscle encased in soft skin, to rake her fingernails over his biceps, his pecs, his thighs, that arse. The need to hold him to her, to wrap her arms around him as he thrust his cock deep inside her, hard and fast, slow and gentle, taking, giving.

Fucking.

Wolf pulled away, making her chase him as she tried to recapture his lips, and then her eyelids fluttered closed as he continued his sensual assault. His kisses were feather-light as he explored her body, a tantalising tease against her throat, an erotic exploration of her breasts, her stomach, lower.

She sucked in a breath as his lips latched around her clit and gave it a gentle pull. She moaned as she felt his tongue slide over the tiny bundle of nerves, and she thrust her hips upwards as his fingers slipped inside her, filling her pussy but not enough.

Abby wrapped her fingers around her chains as her back arched and her head fell against the pillow. The sound of the lid popping off the tube of lubricant barely registered in her lust-addled brain, but the feel of Wolf's finger as he worked it inside her arse was harder to ignore. She yelped, more from the shock of the cold gel than the intrusion into her arse.

"Relax, Abby. Let me in."

She took a deep breath, and remembering Wolf's earlier instructions, she breathed out slowly, relaxing her body and giving him time to push his finger deeper.

"Good girl," he said, his voice low and rough, and then he returned to licking and fingering her pussy.

It was odd, feeling his fingers filling her from both sides. Even more odd was the fact that it wasn't hurting her. Far from it. She broke out in gooseflesh and moaned long and loud as Wolf's actions caused a weird flutter low in her belly. It was a more insistent feeling than usual, more intense, more... *everything*. And it certainly didn't feel anything like her past had led her to believe it should feel.

Her belly quivered as the pleasure built inside her. Her breathing came in ragged gasps, and she thought she would run out of air long before she could come. But then she came. Her whole body felt alive, like electricity was shooting through her, igniting every nerve ending and setting them ablaze. Every muscle in her body clamped down tight as her orgasm careened out of control, leaving her writhing in ecstasy and screaming Wolf's name.

Wolf continued licking and sucking and fingering, pistoning his fingers in and out of her arse and pussy in an alternating rhythm until she thought she might pass out, but then he slowed and her orgasm subsided. Aftershocks still trembled through her though, even as her muscles relaxed, and as she lay there, hands chained, legs spread, replete in her afterglow, she couldn't keep the goofy, blissed-out smile from her face.

"Oh, wow...."

More intense.

More intense had been an understatement. What she'd just experienced had been overwhelming. Extraordinary. Awesome in every sense of the word.

And that was using only his fingers.

What would it be like with his cock?

"I think you liked that," he said, the humour evident in his voice.

"I have no idea what you're talking about," she said, feigning ignorance.

"Your body doesn't lie, *liebchen*." He held up his fingers, the ones he'd used to fuck her pussy. "You're wetter than usual," he said, then slid his fingers in his mouth and licked them clean.

Abby's heartbeat kicked up a notch and her lust thundered in her ears. It was a good thing she was restrained; watching him suck her come from his fingers had her wanting to do all kinds of wicked things to him. She lifted her gaze to his and yanked on her restraints, but he just slid off the end of the bed and walked to the dresser, returning a moment later with—

No.

The butterfly vibrator.

Her blood ran cold at the sight of it and her smile died. "What is *that* thing doing here?"

He was all innocence. "It's here to help."

"No. Hell no. That thing doesn't help. It hurts." If she could have crossed her arms over her chest she would have.

Damned chains.

Wolf dangled the plastic butterfly from his fingers. "Its usual job is to bring pleasure."

Abby scowled at the thing and her jaw tightened. "That hasn't been my experience."

"It was your own stubbornness that turned it into a torture device," he said as he slipped it over her legs and moved it into place. "But I promise you, I will only wield its power for good. This time."

Abby's eyes narrowed. "I hate you," she grumbled.

He flashed her his signature grin. "We'll see. Lift your arse." And when she refused to comply, he added quietly, "I thought you were going to trust me."

With her lips pursed and her eyes still narrowed, she planted her feet and raised her hips so Wolf could finish positioning the vibrator.

He smirked at her the entire time.

Smug bastard.

Her mood quickly changed when Wolf unzipped his jeans and released his raging hard-on. With a quick shove, the denim slid down his legs and he kicked the clothing to the side. As always, he wore no underwear. He crawled back up the bed until he was propped over her, one hand plucking at her nipple as he leaned down and nuzzled her throat. A sharp sting made her gasp.

The man did love to bite.

Not that she minded. Not at all. She loved all the little ways he marked her flesh. The biting and the spanking and the hickeys on her body in places only she would see. She loved the feel of them, the sudden shock of adrenaline followed by the slow burn of his big hand landing on her arse. The tiny indentations he left behind in her skin when he bit her and the feel of his tongue as he ran it across the overly sensitive flesh. And the way his stubble tickled when he lay between her legs and sucked on her thighs....

Wonderful.

Abby understood why people didn't *get* bondage, why they couldn't believe that anything that caused pain could possibly be pleasurable. With so much hurt in the world, why would anyone go looking for it on purpose—and get off on it, no less?

But she'd always known she was different.

When Jane had gushed to her about losing her virginity, Abby had been excited for her turn to come. But when it had, it'd felt so lacklustre. She'd been incredibly disappointed. Then she thought it was just because she was new at it, that surely it would get better with time. But even as she got older and got a little more experience under her belt, she still didn't get what all the fuss was about. Sure, it was enjoyable, but so was cold pizza.

Where was the heat she'd been promised?

The passion?

Then she'd seen a documentary about the kink scene in Sydney and it had lit up a giant neon sign inside her brain.

Ta-da!

She'd known right then that *that* was what she needed. It had taken three goes to find the right partner, to find Wolf. He'd said it was her confidence that made him stop his bike that day by the creek, but that wasn't confidence so much as it was false bravado. In truth, it was his dominance that gave her the confidence to finally be who she truly was, and as his lips caressed her neck and made her shiver with desire, she said, "I need you."

And she knew right down to her core it was true.

Wolf took Abby's mouth in a passionate kiss, and he wasn't gentle about it.

"*I need you.*"

The woman had no idea how much those words affected him, because he needed her, too.

Like he needed air to breathe.

He heard her squeak and felt her body tense at his roughness, then felt her soften and heard her moan as she returned his passion in kind. He pulled away, just far enough to make her lean up and try to recapture his mouth, and then he slammed his lips against hers once more and devoured her mewl of submission.

He loved making her chase his kisses, loved knowing she wanted him as much as he wanted her. Almost as much as he loved marking her body, leaving small signs of his presence all over her. And he knew damned well that if she wasn't restrained right now, she'd be biting the fuck out of him, too.

His groin tightened at the thought and he pressed his mouth down harder. He would have been happy to spend the rest of the day like this, teasing her body with his fingers and kissing her senseless, but he also knew if they were going to do this thing, have anal sex she would enjoy and hopefully want to have again, then he had to strike while the iron was hot, while she was still riding high on her last orgasm.

He bent his head towards her ear. "Tell me what you want." She turned her head and caught his earlobe between her teeth, nipping him sharply. He pulled back, his teeth bared in a snarl, but the way she stared up at him with her velvety brown eyes heavy lidded and darkened with lust made him smile.

She is so ready for this.

And so was he.

"Fuck me."

He plucked at her nipple, gently at first, then added a sharp twist. Her eyes closed and she bit down hard on her bottom lip. Her chest thrust upwards, pressing her breast into his hand, and a soft moan escaped her.

"Fuck me, what?"

She opened her eyes, and he watched her gaze dart to his mouth and back again. "Sir. Please fuck me, Sir. Please."

"Well, since you begged me so sweetly," he said, and then he moved to kneel between her legs.

A quick check of the butterfly ensured the small vibrator was exactly where it needed to be. He put it on the lowest setting and tucked the remote control into the band wrapped around her hip. Just like the time before, she sucked in a gasp of air and her hips bucked as the device whirred into action. And just like that time, he thoroughly enjoyed watching the look of ecstasy on her face as the little machine did its job.

Wolf sat back on his haunches and took his cock in his hand, stroked himself as he enjoyed the vision of his lover spreadeagled before him.

He watched as her fingers tightened around the chains that held her captive, listened to the staccato of her breathing as she sucked air into her lungs and immediately pushed it out again, and his heart warmed at the sight of the smile that teased at the corners of her mouth, the one that promised so much more than she could ever put into words.

"Please."

Her quiet plea was music to his ears.

Wolf slid his hands under her thighs and tugged her closer, lifted her legs round his hips, then slid his cock deep inside her pussy. Abby's eyed widened, silently questioning him, but he just let his head fall back and enjoyed the tremors the vibrator sent shivering through her, clenching her pussy around him like a vice.

Slowly he moved in her, thrusting deep, taking the time to make sure she was as aroused as possible. He knew fucking her pussy would help relax her physically and emotionally, would make taking her arse that much easier for them both.

He listened to her sighs and moans, and when he thought she was ready, he rubbed more lube where she needed it most, pulled out of her pussy and pressed the head of his cock against her arse.

"Breathe, *liebchen*. Don't forget to breathe." To her credit, she didn't flinch when he pushed forwards and breeched her tight little opening. Her hands tightened around those chains though, and her breathing became very controlled.

He felt so proud of her in that moment that he wouldn't have cared if she'd used her safeword. She'd tried, she'd overcome her fears and she'd tried. That was all that mattered to him. They could always try again later.

Because there would be a later.

I'll make sure of it.

"You're doing well, Abby."

She nodded with sharp, jerky movements and he could see the focus, the concentration in her eyes, in the way her teeth sank into the pillow of her bottom lip. He pushed forwards again, all the way into her. Her head fell back and a guttural groan escaped her. Wolf waited for a few agonisingly long moments to allow her body time to adjust, then moved his hips and slowly thrust into her.

Her arse was glorious—tight and hot and soft. She felt incredible as he slid in and out of her, and he wasn't sure he'd last long. But he had to try.

For her, he'd try.

From the corner of his eye, Wolf saw a flicker of movement.

Paul and Oliver had promised they'd be in town for the whole afternoon, giving him the time and privacy he needed to spend with Abby. Had they come home early for some reason? Or was it Jane, come to discuss the engagement party preparations?

Keeping his movements steady and his thrusts even, he tilted his head towards the distraction.

Shit! Dick was pacing outside the window, just beyond the rose bushes.

What the fuck was he doing there?

How long had he been there?

And more importantly, how much had he seen?

His gaze flicked to Abby. Her eyes were shut and her mouth hung open, her breathy moans filling the air around them, but if she knew her ex was outside their bedroom window she'd panic, which was not ideal while he was still buried to the hilt in her arse. She'd already tried to wrench herself free of the chains once, her anxiety getting the better of her. If she tried that again, she'd most likely cause them both an injury.

He looked towards the window. Richard was staring right at them, arms crossed over his chest and a murderous look twisting his pretty face.

Wolf couldn't help himself.

He smiled at the prick.

If ever her ex-husband needed proof that he wasn't man enough to handle a woman like Abigail Bennett, this was it. She was his woman now, and there was no reason to hide it. He felt no shame for the lifestyle he led, and neither should Abby.

He looked down at her, at his woman laid out before him. Sweat beaded on her breasts and neck and he longed to lick her skin, to trace the column of her neck with his tongue and suckle her dark pink nipples. Her hair was strewn across the pillow in wondrous disarray, a black curtain that shifted and swayed every time she arched her back or turned her head. Her mouth, her lips, so plump and red from biting them, called to him, begged him to taste them, to drink her in.

In that moment he chose to ignore the peeping Dick at the window. Fuck him and his narrow-minded views. Fuck his attempts to intimidate and embarrass them. If Abby saw him, so be it. They'd cross that bridge if they came to it. But here and now, the world outside their bedroom didn't exist.

Abby rocked her body in time with his thrusts, her fingers flexing around the chains holding her captive. "Please. Harder. Please, fuck me harder." She lifted her gaze to his, her dark chocolate irises molten heat, and he knew he wouldn't—*couldn't*—deny her.

He gave her what she wanted.

He fucked her harder.

Wolf gritted his teeth and pumped his hips, the feel of her tight arse milking his cock threatening to undo him with every thrust, but he couldn't come yet. Not yet.

Abby's moans grew louder, her breath sawing in and out. She was close. So close. She stared up at him, a wicked grin spread across her face, and he laughed as he watched her fingers fist around her chains and hold on.

"Wolf?" Her grin died and her mouth fell slack. Her neck arched and her body tensed.

She was coming.

Wolf watched her every reaction as it flitted across her face. The look of shock at the intensity of her orgasm and the tears that flowed down her cheeks, the look of joy that overtook her shock and filled her gaze with wonder, and the aftershock that had her eyes rolling back in ecstasy as her body shook and trembled.

His heart pounded in his chest, and he was both

amused and aroused as he listened to her scream at him, "Fuck me hard, you dirty old cunt. Fuck me. Harder. *Please*." And as he felt her body, her perfect body, tighten around his own, clamping down on his cock with crushing force, he roared as he came.

The potency of his orgasm had him jerking against her bottom for what seemed like an age until finally, sweaty and sated, the urge to collapse on top of her, to pull her close and fall asleep in her arms was foremost in his thoughts. Until he remembered the creeper outside. He turned his head and looked out the window, but Richard was gone.

"What is it?" Abby's quiet question drew his attention back to where it should be.

He looked down at her tear-stained cheeks. "It was nothing. How do you feel?"

A lazy smile slowly stretched across her face. "You're a writer. What word means more amazing than amazing, and yet at the same time utterly delicious?"

Wolf laughed. "I think the word you're searching for is sublime."

"My legs feel like jelly," she said with a satisfied sigh.

"Then my work here is done," he said with a grin, then removed the butterfly, unfastened the leather cuffs and helped her to her feet. "I'm proud of you, Abby."

She wrapped her arms around him and rested her head in the crook of his neck. "Thank you, Sir."

Wolf held her close and rubbed his hands up and down her sweat-slicked back, giving her the comfort she needed, but his mind drifted. The appearance of Richard at the window bothered him. Should he tell Abby what happened, that her ex had seen her chained to a bed and writhing in ecstasy? Or would the knowledge only serve to humiliate her, to shatter her confidence and send her scuttling back into hiding?

The thought of lying to her, even a lie of omission, didn't sit well with him.

Abby pressed her lips against his neck, and he smiled as he felt her tongue flick against his pulse.

He had to tell her, and he would, but *after* the party. He wanted her to face her ex with her head held high and unafraid, not cringing in embarrassment every time Dick glanced in her direction.

He pressed a kiss to her temple. "Let's get you cleaned up."

Chapter Eighteen

Abby held Wolf's hand as they ascended the steps into the recently refurbished town hall. The smell of fresh paint still clung to the timber weatherboards, and the sound of eighties rock music and cheerful conversation drifted through the open doors.

People milled about on the veranda and just inside the vestibule with drinks in hand. Some waved to her and Wolf as they passed, some called out to her brothers. Some stared at her as though she'd grown a second head, their eyes lingering on her as she walked by.

She tugged at her blouse. "I look ridiculous," she murmured.

"You look amazing," Wolf said, and she found herself being pulled into a dimly lit corner and well kissed.

He'd made the same comment as she'd dressed, the outfit he'd chosen for her one she'd not worn since leaving Sydney more than two years before. She was a little amazed it still fit. The black leather-like skinny jeans, sequinned blouse and tailored leather coat were remnants of her old life, a throwback to a time when she'd had exhibition openings to attend and people to schmooze, when looking her best at all times was just a part of her job.

She'd worn fashion like a soldier wore armour. After two years of little more than denim jeans and T-shirts, wearing these clothes felt strange, but she supposed if ever there was a time she needed armour, it was now.

The sound of a throat clearing broke their kiss apart, and when they faced their intruders they were met with an abundance of smiles, handshakes, and introductions.

"You haven't worn that outfit in forever," Jane gushed. "You look fantastic!" And then to Wolf, she added, "Couldn't convince her to wear a dress, huh?" Abby laughed.

"Sam Lyndon, good to meet you." Jane's fiancé grasped Wolf's hand. "Sorry I missed you at the picnic but I've been away with work. Abby, looking hot!" She pressed against Wolf's side a little tighter. The way Sam's eyes lingered on her ample chest made her uncomfortable.

"Wolf, it's lovely to see you again." Jane's mum, Mary Melville, leaned up to peck his cheek. "And Abby, darling, don't you look beautiful this evening?" The older woman hugged her tightly and murmured by her ear, "I don't care what my son says, Wolf's good for you."

Abby frowned. "Richard said something to you about Wolf?"

Mary patted her hand. "Don't pay him any attention," she said quietly. "I know it's bad form for a mother to say so, but you were always too good for him. You know that, don't you?"

Wolf slid his arm around her waist. "I'll be sure to remind her if she ever forgets."

Mary's gaze trailed over him, and an appreciative tilt of her mouth adorned her face. "Oh, I'm sure you will."

Abby's cheeks heated at the salacious insinuation. 'Mary!"

Her friend's mother laughed and moved on to greet more guests while Wolf checked Abby's coat, then ushered her through to the main hall.

Tables lined one wall, laden with all sorts of delicious treats, a grand three-tiered chocolate cake taking pride of place. A single file of people worked their way along the table, filling paper plates and plastic cups with food and drink. People danced in the middle of the hall, and Abby heard Richard's obnoxious laughter spew from the middle of the couples swirling around the room in time to the music. Debra was nowhere to be seen.

"Would you like a drink or something?"

Wolf grinned. "Or something." Suddenly she found herself being twirled around the floor, dancing and laughing in Wolf's strong arms. He bent his head and whispered in her ear, "As soon as we get home tonight, your arse is mine." He emphasised his point by sliding his hands down her back, cupping her bottom and pulling her tightly against him.

She smirked as her lover's sizeable erection pushed against her lower belly. He'd been particularly handsy since the previous afternoon when she'd submitted herself to the pleasures of anal sex.

And it had been a very great pleasure.

She still couldn't quite believe what had happened, how overwhelmed she'd felt by the onslaught of sensation Wolf had wrought upon her with his hands, his mouth, his cock, that bloody butterfly.... She'd come so hard she'd cried. Hell, she'd come so hard she'd screamed at him, not just his name but screamed *at* him.

She'd called him a dirty old cunt and begged him to fuck her harder.

And he had.

He'd pounded into her body like a man possessed, and Abby had just... *let go*. She'd surrendered her control so completely, had felt so free that she'd cried, had sobbed her release until her body was utterly devoid of everything but blissful indolence, and then she'd stared up at him, had drunk in his masculine beauty with a sigh in her throat and a smile on her lips.

Happy.

She'd felt totally and completely happy.

"You look so goddamned sexy," Wolf said, pulling her from her thoughts. "You have no idea how hard I'm trying not to drag you out of here and fuck you senseless."

She rocked her hips against him and watched his eyelids shutter in pleasure. "Maybe not," she said, biting her lip. "But I'd like to."

Wolf growled and they stopped dancing so abruptly that another couple ran into them. Then they were cutting a path through the room, headed towards an empty corner of the hall, one draped in shadows that gave the illusion of privacy.

He took her hands in his and stared down at her, desire casting a warm glow in his hazel eyes. "I was going to wait until after the party to tell you this, but I finished my book today."

Abby tensed. "Finished? But that means...."

He'll be leaving. One week early.

"I know that look on your face, *liebchen*," he said as he leaned his forehead against hers. "And I'm not going anywhere. Not for a week, at least."

She released the breath she didn't realise she was holding. "You're staying?"

"Yes. I will have to go back as scheduled, but when I do...." He took a breath. "Come with me."

She swallowed hard. "To Sydney?"

"Yes."

"The city I vowed never to return to?"

"Yes."

"Even if the world was drowning in piss and Sydney was the only lifeboat?"

Wolf's body shook with laughter. "That's the one."

Before her mind could drown itself in indecision and doubt, Abby said, "Okay."

Wolf frowned. "Okay? Just... okay?"

"Yep."

He leaned back and scratched his chin. "To be honest, I was expecting more resistance. You're usually much more stubborn."

Abby shrugged. "I can argue if it'll make you feel better."

"No, no, I'll take the win," he said, then leaned forwards to kiss her. "But I'm curious to know *why* it was so easy."

Abby stared at his broad chest and frowned in concentration as she traced a finger around his shirt buttons. 'Sydney is... Hell for me. It's the end of my marriage, it's Kurt's abuse... Kurt's wife. I haven't been back in over two years, not when Jane nagged me to go on a girls-only weekend, or when Dad had an exhibition there last year. Not even to visit Sally. I just... couldn't. I was afraid. Every time I thought about it, I'd find myself drowning in a nightmare.

"But you, you made me shine a light on all those places I wanted to forget, made me dig up the memories I'd tried to bury, and I hated it. I hated every single second of it. But I never hated you for doing it, and afterwards... I felt less afraid. I felt stronger. So yes, I will go to Sydney with you, because I want to be strong again. I'm tired of living alone in the dark."

She lifted her eyes to look at Wolf and bit her lip as a wave of uncertainty washed over her. He was looking at her oddly, staring at her as though stunned into silence. She wasn't even sure he was breathing he stood so still. Then his arms came around her and she was being crushed against the solid wall of his chest.

"I am so proud of you."

"You are?"

"Yes I am. I'm also flattered." He pressed a kiss to her temple and chuckled. "You're a little too good at stroking my ego, you know that?"

Feeling his still-rampant erection pressing into her belly, she slid her hand between them and cupped his hard length. "Speaking of stroking...."

Wolf moaned. "Naughty little nymph."

"Oh my God, you pair are so sweet I think I'm gunna puke." Jane. "Honestly, I'd tell you to get a room but I need your help."

Wolf groaned and positioned himself behind Abby, his arms wrapped loosely around her waist, his chin resting on her shoulder. The spicy scent of his cologne made her mouth water, but she forced herself to concentrate. "What's up, Janie?"

"Uncle Simon had to duck home to grab, I don't know, *something* Aunty Relle forgot and absolutely can't live without. Debra is doing an excellent impersonation of someone who's *not* a member of our family and ignoring every request for help, and Mum's got her hands full in the kitchen because the two local kids I asked to help out never showed up. Richard and Sam are nowhere to be found, Dad needs help putting out more chairs and—"

"Say no more," Wolf said, his deep, commanding voice silencing Jane's hysteria. "I'll help your dad, and Abby...?"

"I'll help Mary in the kitchen."

"Thanks. I'll grab the empty trays and meet you in there," Jane said and moved off in the direction of the food tables. She looked frazzled, tired. Not her usual self. Abby made a mental note to take her out for brunch the following day, have some one-on-one girl time.

"I'll go find Dad and do what I can out here," Wolf said and kissed her cheek.

"And I'll come find you once everything has calmed down."

Wolf growled by her ear again, a primal, carnal sound. "You better. Given the choice between making small talk with strangers or making love to my woman, I know which one I prefer."

"You're incorrigible."

Wolf winked. "You have no idea."

Abby shooed Mary out of the kitchen, then sent Jane off to find Paul and Oliver. By the time they got back, she'd unwrapped another half-dozen platters of finger food and uncorked three more bottles of champagne.

Like riding a bike, she thought, remembering all the exhibition openings she'd organised and directed from behind the scenes.

"Ollie, I need you to do a rubbish run and clear away any used plates and cups, then come back and grab these," she said, indicating the bottles. "Paul, help Jane set out the fresh platters and check if we need any more cups, napkins, plates, et cetera. Jane, once these platters go out, you don't come back in." She took her friend by the shoulders and smiled down at her. "This is supposed to be your engagement party. Go find Sam, relax and enjoy yourself."

"But—"

"No buts. It's my turn to boss you around," she said as she handed Jane a platter loaded with small triangular sandwiches. "Now bugger off."

Jane smiled and visibly relaxed. "Thanks, Abbs."

Paul and Ollie came and went until she ran out of things for them to do. Then she sent them out to enjoy the party while she finished up, and lost herself in a sensual daydream.

She imagined standing in Wolf's kitchen, helping him do the dishes, maybe splashing him with dish water and earning herself a session over his knee, his big strong hands delivering a sound spanking that would get them both so hot and bothered that he'd take her on the kitchen table and fuck her senseless.

Her pussy grew wet just thinking about it.

Behind her, the sound of the kitchen door slowly creaking open lifted the corners of her mouth in a mischievous grin. Maybe she wouldn't have to wait until they were in Wolf's kitchen. Maybe any kitchen would do.

She held her breath as she heard him approach.

"Hello, Abby."

Richard's soft voice sent the hairs on the back of her neck into high alert. Spinning around to face him with her lips pursed, she exhaled sharply through her nose, making her irritation as obvious as possible.

"Dick."

His eyes narrowed slightly. "That's not my name."

"Assuming I was calling you by name."

"Wow." He looked taken aback. "Hostile much?"

"Any reason I shouldn't be?"

His smile was disarmingly handsome as he stroked his fingers down her arm. "I can think of one or two."

Goosebumps broke out all over her flesh and she had to force herself not to shudder. She slapped his hand away and busied herself with wiping down the benches. "What have you been telling Mary about Wolf?"

His smile faded. "Why, what did she say?"

She tossed the cloth in the sink. "That she doesn't care what you think, that she thinks Wolf is good for me."

"She's senile."

"And you're an arse."

Richard moved closer, his expression tight, his voice low. "I see enough domestic abuse cases come through my ER to know what he's doing to you is wrong."

Abby felt like he'd punched her in the gut and the air rushed from her in a harsh laugh, but she stood her ground and stared him down.

"You still don't get it, do you? You never understood me and you never will, and statements like that only show how ignorant you truly are. Wolf doesn't abuse me. He challenges me, helps me, infuriates me. He makes me laugh until my sides hurt, he makes me cry in frustration and he is —*oh my God*—the best sex I've ever had in my life. He makes me feel things I thought I'd never feel again, but he never—*never*—hurts me. Everything we do is one hundred percent consensual, and not to be rude, but what Wolf and I do in the privacy of our bedroom is none of your fucking business."

"Abby—"

"Go home, Richard. Go home to your wife and your

kids and your patients. Go be with the people who actually need you."

Richard opened his mouth to speak but she'd heard enough. She shoved her way through the kitchen door and back out into the hall, hoping to lose him in the noise of the party.

She failed.

"Abbs, wait. Don't walk away from me."

"Don't call me Abbs," she snapped as she tried to cut around the edge of the dance floor. "And stop following me."

"Abby, come on. I'm just looking out for you."

"You're looking out for me?" she said, stopping to stare at him, brows raised. "You couldn't be bothered when we were married, but *now* you're looking out for me?"

Richard stared at her from under his ginger-blond lashes. "I still care for you."

"Yeah right."

His mouth twisted and his tone darkened. "You're being unreasonable."

"Unreasonable?" Abby was too pissed off to be dumbfounded. "No, Richard, unreasonable is you thinking you have any say in my life after you cheated on me and then left me for another woman."

His jaw tightened. "But you're being reckless. Think about it, Abby. What do you really know about this guy, huh? And yet here you are, just letting him live in your house and do whatever he wants with you." He laid his hand on her shoulder. Abby slapped it away. He met the action with a heavy sigh and pinched the bridge of his nose. "How do you know he's not exactly like your last boyfriend?"

"How the hell do you know about Kurt?"

"I know a lot of things," he said.

She paused to stare at her ex but when he avoided her gaze, she scoffed, "You don't know shit."

"I know this Wolf bloke is dangerous."

Abby bit back a sudden urge to grin.

Dangerous.

How many times had she wondered that over the past few weeks? Abby knew Wolf was dangerous—in more ways than one—and as her gaze found him in the crowded hall, she was finally willing to admit to falling victim to the biggest danger of all.

She was in love with him.

Why else would she agree to return to Sydney of all places?

She focused on the man on the other side of the room, the man who towered over everyone but looked so at ease with that fact. He'd borrowed clothes from Oliver for the evening; dark grey trousers and a crisp black shirt.

She smiled as she drank him in, as her eyes followed the contours of his body and the way the clothes hugged him in all the right places. He was effortlessly sexy with his shirt sleeves rolled up to reveal strong forearms and his collar unbuttoned, displaying the oh-so-lickable column of his neck. His casual appearance barely masked the raw masculinity that radiated from him.

And he's all mine.

"Oh shit," Richard said as he shook his head.

"I know that look on your face." She caught Wolf's eye and he flashed her a quick wink, making her smile broaden, but it didn't last long as Richard persisted. "Don't do it, Abby. He's no good for you."

"And you are?" she spat at him.

"What? I didn't mean—"

"What do you want, Richard? Tell me. Why did you come to my house that day? Why did you kiss me?"

"You kissed me back!" he countered with a degree of smugness that made her stomach lurch with sudden sickness.

"Yes, I did. Because I was lonely and vulnerable. What was your excuse?"

"Is everything okay over here?" Abby was so focussed on her argument with Richard that she hadn't noticed Wolf cross the room, or the numerous pairs of curious eyes that had turned to watch them. "Why don't we take this some-where more private?"

"Why?" Richard said, his lip curling back in a snarl. "So you can tell her what to say?"

Wolf grabbed Richard around his upper arm and forcibly led him out through the French doors to the deck beyond. "Don't ever speak about Abigail in that tone of voice again," he said, his voice low and menacing. "Am I understood?"

Richard wrenched his arm free of Wolf's grip and rubbed his bicep. "I was talking about you."

Wolf's eyebrows arched into his hairline. "Really? Because it sounded more like you don't trust Abby to think for herself?"

"It's you I don't trust."

Abby shot a nervous glance inside and saw the mob of people edging closer to the doors, trying for all they were worth to look casual while eavesdropping on what was prob-ably the best gossip of the year.

Well, she'd be damned if she was going to be the evening's entertainment.

"Wolf," she said as she laid her hand on his arm. "I'd like to go home now, please."

Wolf's face softened as he shifted his gaze from Richard to her. "Are you sure? Jane and Sam haven't cut their cake yet. You know she'll be upset if you're not here for that."

Another glance at the curious crowd inside and she said, "She'll get over it. Let's go."

Wolf smiled and slid his arm around her shoulders, the warmth of both aiding to soothe her nerves. "Let's get your coat, then," he said, and pressed a kiss to her temple. But before they could take even a single step and put an end to this lunacy, Richard spoke up.

"I know what you've been doing up there at The Forge," he said, his voice layered with disgust. "I know how you've been treating her."

"Wolf has been nothing but a gentleman," Abby said, painfully aware of how people in this tiny town would view them both if they knew the truth of their relation-ship. People who were well within earshot of their conversation.

"A gentleman?" Richard scoffed, his voice raised. "Is that what he is when he chains you to the bed and fucks you like a whore?"

Abby froze to the spot, mortified, as a collective gasp rose from inside the hall. Her arms felt heavy, her knees weak. Her eyes shot wide and her jaw fell slack. Ice ran over her skin and she shivered with the shock of it.

"What did you say?" The words barely escaped her rapidly tightening throat.

"I saw what he did to you, Abby. I saw everything. And he knows I saw you, too. Made a real good show of it, didn't you, you bastard?"

Abby swallowed hard, her brain scrambling to accom-modate this new information and coming up with nothing but static. She was so confused, but only for a moment, because then her confusion gave way to a whole other emotion.

Anger.

"You knew he was there?" she said slowly, unable to look her lover in the face, her words as shaky as the legs she was standing on.

"Yes," he replied without even a hint of an apology in his deep voice.

Abby thought her head would implode. Richard saw her? He saw her in her most vulnerable and exposed state, and Wolf—

Wolf had known about it, had let it happen.

He'd exposed her to ridicule and humiliation. He was just like them, like Richard and Kurt. Always taking, never truly giving. Only this time he'd taken more than Abby felt she could ever possibly hope to regain.

It wasn't just her trust that Wolf Adams had broken.

She clutched at her chest as a sharp pang stabbed through her, as though her heart had splintered into a thousand pieces and the shards were piercing her, stabbing their way through her veins and slicing them to ribbons.

"Abby." Richard reached for her, but Abby slapped his hands away. "I only wanted to protect you," he said.

"Don't you dare." She spoke quietly through gritted teeth, her eyes narrowed on his pretty face as her hands balled into fists. "Don't you *dare* try playing the hero with me, you self-righteous prick! You can scorn me and my sex life all you want, but how long did you stand there, watching me like some kind of... *deviant?*"

Richard pointed at Wolf. "He chains you up and beats you but *I'm* the deviant?"

Wolf ignored Richard and took her hand in his. "I'm taking you home," he said, his voice calm and commanding.

She turned on him next. "No. You're not," she said, yanking her hand back. "You are no longer welcome in my home."

"Abby—"

"No, Wolf. You don't have any say in my life. Not anymore. And you," she said as she spied Richard directing a smug smile at her former lover, "don't call me, don't drop by the house anytime you're feeling sentimental, and don't you *ever* touch me again, or I swear to God you will live to regret it."

The smile died from Richard's face and he reached for her. Abby dropped her gaze and let it linger on his fingers as they tightened around her upper arm, and then she pulled her free arm back and slammed her fist into Richard's nose.

A satisfying crunch met her ears even as the pain of the impact shot straight through the full length of her arm. Richard stumbled back, clutching at his face while blood dripped from beneath his hand. And Abby felt... strange, a sort of haziness settling over her, replacing her satisfaction with something darker, confounding.

"You bitch!"

She saw Richard raise his hand to strike her but she never felt it land. Wolf caught his arm and used it to spin him into the wall, pulling the offending limb behind Richard's back and twisting it until the smaller man cried out in pain.

"Unless you want a broken arm to go with that broken nose, I suggest you calm down."

Abby could hear Wolf's voice but it sounded wrong, distant. Everything sounded distorted, like she was trying to listen through static.

"What the hell is going on out here?" Jane. "What did

you do?" She was angry, but her anger wasn't directed at Abby.

"I have to go," she said to no one in particular, her voice like an echo inside her mind. Did she even speak out loud? She didn't know. She just wanted to leave, to be alone, away from the static and the hollow feeling inside her chest where her heart used to be. She looked around the scene without really seeing and then pushed her way through the onlooking crowd, their murmurs and whispers only adding to the white noise buzzing through her head.

"Abigail! Wait!"

But she didn't wait. She couldn't. She pushed her way clear of the party and out the front door, stopping for a moment as the evening air hit her full in the face, its cool caress making her realise just how flushed she was from the heat of the crush inside. She reached up to touch her cheeks and found them wet with tears. She was so numb she hadn't even realised she'd been crying.

"Abby!"

Wolf.

She couldn't face him. Not without saying something they'd both regret. She fished her keys out of her purse as she ran to the car, paying no heed to the man thundering down the front steps of the town hall. She shoved the key in the ignition and the engine roared to life.

A quick glance in the rear-view mirror revealed Wolf's anguished face as he stalked across the carpark, twisting the knife of guilt in her stomach as she took the coward's way out and sped away from the man she loved.

Wolf skidded to a halt as Abby peeled out of the

carpark, leaving him in a cloud of dust. Furious anger pulsed through him, flushing his body with heat, pushing the air from his lungs until it escaped on a roar and hate—blinding, white-hot hate—filled him.

Hands clenched into fists, he turned back towards the historic town hall, his boots crunching the gravel beneath each purposeful footfall, and his chest rising and falling with every measured breath he took.

Paul and Oliver appeared on the front veranda with their hands held in front of them, but if they were hoping to placate him, they would be sorely disappointed.

"Where is he?" Wolf snarled as he climbed the stairs.

"Think this through, Wolf," Paul said. "He's not worth it."

"Oh yeah?"

Oliver angled himself between Wolf and the door. "Trust us, mate, we know exactly what you're going through."

Wolf's lip curled. "Then you should know what I'm gunna do to the little fucker." He pushed his way past them.

Startled party guests scurried out of his way as he stalked into the main hall. His sharp gaze scanned the crowd and landed on Jane's parents. Lines of tension marred their faces and their smiles looked forced. No doubt they were being good hosts and trying to down play the earlier excitement, trying to salvage what they could of their daughter's special evening.

Another scan of the room told him Jane and her fiancé were nowhere to be seen, nor Richard. Wolf took a deep breath and some of the venom coursing through his veins left him, but not enough to stay his hand.

Not this time.

Where is the little pissant?

"I believe the person you're looking for is in the kitchen."

Wolf turned around to find Debra Melville standing behind him, sipping champagne and looking thoroughly bored. The obscenely low-cut neckline of her dress left nothing to the imagination, and the overpowering aroma of cigarettes and heavy perfume choked the air between them.

He crinkled his nose. "Thanks." But as he tried to step around her, she grabbed his hand. Jaw tight, he snapped, "What?"

She looked up at him with her painted lips curved in what would have been a pretty smile had it been on any face but the one he was staring at. On Debra it just came off as arrogant. "You could do so much better, you know?"

"Is that so?"

"You're a distinguished author, you're handsome, you're rich. You could have any woman you want," she said as she stepped closer, her outrageously overt cleavage invading his personal space.

"Your point?"

"Why on earth are you wasting your time on Abby Bennett?"

"When I could be with someone like you?" he said, keeping his voice deliberately bland. Unfortunately, the ridiculous woman was completely oblivious, either too stupid or too drunk to recognise the subtle sarcasm.

"My thoughts exactly," she purred as she pressed herself to his side and raked her nails down his bicep. "She's not the only girl in town who's into all that"—her voice dropped to a whisper as she leaned in closer—"kinky stuff."

"I don't know what psychotic little game you and Dick are playing, but I'm not interested."

Debra laughed, her smug smile and smoky breath

causing his features to twist in disgust. "I'm not playing games, Mr Wolfe."

"Neither am I, Ms Melville," Wolf said as he extricated himself from her taloned grasp. He didn't have time for this shit. "I'll tell you why I'm with Abby Bennett. It's because she has more heart, more courage, and more dignity than a pretentious bitch like you could ever hope to emulate, and you're deluding yourself if you think otherwise. And wanting to fuck your cousin isn't kinky. It's creepy. And illegal." Ignoring her outraged gasp, he turned away and stalked to the kitchen.

With his hand poised to push the door open, Wolf stopped for a moment and listened. He couldn't hear much over the sound of the party—apparently ruining a woman's reputation was no reason to let good champagne go to waste —but he could hear Jane's ranting well enough. At least he wasn't the only one who was pissed off.

"Selfish brat!"

"I'm selfish?" she demanded. "You ruined my engagement party!"

"She broke my nose, Jane!"

"Be thankful it was only Abby who punched you," Wolf said as he quietly closed the door behind him.

Dick's eyes widened and the ice pack he'd been holding to his face fell to the floor with a wet *slap*. "You!"

Wolf crossed the room in two steps, latched his hand around the smaller man's throat and squeezed just hard enough to make breathing a chore. "Why couldn't you just leave her alone?" Dick grabbed at Wolf's wrist and tried to pry him loose but to no effect.

Jane moved into his line of vision, her voice quiet. Calm. "Wolf, babe, you have to let him go."

Wolf stared down at his captive and bared his teeth, like an animal hungering for the kill. "Why? He's a parasite."

"True, but he's also my brother." She laid her hand on his arm and looked up at him. "Let him go, Wolf. Please."

Wolf closed his eyes. "She was happy with me," he said quietly, and then he let go.

Dick slumped against the kitchen bench. "I ought to sue you for everything you're worth," he said, sucking air into his lungs with exaggerated gasps.

"Oh my God, really?" Jane said to her brother with a shake of her head. "Do you have no sense of self-preservation at all?"

Wolf's lips twitched as Dick scurried to the other side of the kitchen, and he flashed a brief albeit grateful smile at Jane.

"Where's Abby now?" she said.

Wolf sighed and rubbed at his temples to ease his sudden headache. "She left."

She tossed him her car keys. "So why are you still here?"

Chapter Nineteen

Wolf sat in Jane's old Jeep and stared at the house, his feet as heavy as lead and his heart beating faster than a hummingbird on speed. Why was he so nervous?

Stupid question.

He knew why. He'd fucked up. Big time.

There was nothing he could do now but apologise and pray Abby was in a forgiving mood.

As he opened the front door and walked inside, the chill of the house enveloped him. Abby had doused the fire before they'd left for the party and obviously hadn't relit it on her return. Assuming she was even here.

He hadn't seen her car outside and could see no lights in the house, nor hear any sounds, certainly nothing that would indicate a fully grown, extremely pissed-off woman was anywhere nearby.

The lack of light made for slow progress as he groped along the hallway until he found the light switch, and as the yellowed bulb above his head flickered into wakefulness, his heart sank.

His backpack and all his clothes, his helmet, riding leathers and boots sat in a crumpled pile in the middle of the hallway, silently damning him. "Shit."

He knelt and opened the backpack.

Everything was there, laptop included. Even the little black box with the butterfly vibrator inside. He swore again as something squeezed around his heart. Something painful. He needed to find Abby—*now*—and beg her to forgive him. He allowed himself a small smile.

Beg.

No woman had ever made Wolf beg. For anything. And yet there he was ready to fall to his knees and crawl over broken glass if it meant healing the hurt he'd caused her.

"Abigail?" he called out as he wandered farther into the house. "Abby, come out and talk to me. Please." But no answer came.

Then he saw a glint of light through the window behind his desk. A bright, dancing firelight flickered and flared, and then the clanging sound of metal on metal met his ears. He should have known she'd be out in the forge. It was her safe haven, her refuge.

Wolf took a steadying breath and braced himself for battle. He entered the forge, prepared to do whatever it took to fix his mistake, but when he saw her, when he saw the woman he loved, her face red and blotchy from crying and her dark eyes narrowed in anger, he knew he faced a war.

A war he might not win.

"You're not welcome here," she said quietly, and he saw her grip tighten on the menacing-looking hammer in her hand.

Wolf swallowed hard as his apology dried in his mouth. What was he supposed to say? What was he supposed to do? His brain had gone numb from fear, his body stiff with apprehension. He was floundering, drowning in the depth of emotion he felt for this woman but couldn't put into words.

He'd never stumbled for the right thing to say before, had never not known how to diffuse a tense situation. He felt an urge to laugh at the absurdity of it all, but tamped it down lest his lover felt the urge to throw that hammer at his head.

"Did you hear me?" she said, her chest heaving with every measured breath, her sequins and finery replaced by denim jeans and a faded heavy metal T-shirt. "You're not welcome. Please leave."

"No," Wolf said as he straightened to his full height and lifted his chin. "Not until you hear me out."

"I don't have to listen to anything you have to say, Wolf."

"I could tie you up and make you listen," he countered.

Her eyes narrowed. "Try it. I'll scream my safeword so loud it'll make your eardrums bleed."

And she would too, stubborn nymph. Wolf gritted his teeth and growled, his frustration palpable. "You drive me crazy, do you know that? And can you put the hammer down, please?"

Abby looked positively evil as the corners of her mouth kicked up in a wicked little smile and she made a point of laying the tool aside. Her gaze never left his, and he knew that *she* knew exactly what he'd been thinking. Wolf relaxed a little once she was unarmed, but he was not so stupid as to think he was completely out of danger, especially when she asked him the million-dollar question.

"Why didn't you tell me Richard saw us?"

He'd been asking himself the same thing from the moment that prick had blurted out his insults at the party, and knew his original answer was woefully inadequate. But he offered it nonetheless. "Because I wanted to save you the embarrassment."

Abby laughed, a disbelieving cough of breath. "Embarrassment? Oh, well good job," she said and slowly clapped her hands. "Because not telling me worked out perfectly, didn't it? I'm not a child, Wolf. Yes, I would have been upset, but at least I would have been forewarned and could have taken steps to avoid what happened tonight."

"I'm sorry, okay?" he said, his anger at his own stupidity spilling over. "I'm sorry I forgot to close the bloody curtains. I'm sorry I didn't tell you he saw us making love. And I am sorry that I underestimated exactly how much of a colossal arsehole your ex-husband is. Because obviously I'm the only person who's ever done that!"

She gasped at the sarcastic sting he'd thrown at her, the look on her face a mixture of outrage and hurt, and he instantly regretted his thoughtless words.

"Abby—"

"Get out," she whispered through clenched teeth. When he didn't move, she screamed the words at him instead. "Get out!"

"*Liebchen*—"

"*Don't* call me that. Don't you dare pretend that you care about me."

"Of course I care about you, Abby. I'm in love with you."

She paused and sucked in a gasp of air as if taken aback by his declaration, but then her face twisted like she was in pain. "You don't love me," she snarled. "You can't love someone you don't respect."

"I do respect you."

"Then why didn't you tell me about Richard?"

Wolf groaned and scrubbed a hand down his face. "I was trying to protect you."

Abby folded her arms over her chest. Her eyes narrowed. "And how was exposing me to ridicule supposed to protect me? Please, do enlighten me."

Wolf hung his head as he remembered. "I wanted him to see that he couldn't have you anymore," he said as he leaned his knuckles on the workbench between them and lifted his gaze to hers, fighting to keep his frustration from showing in his voice. "I wanted him to know that he'd never be able to satisfy you, that he'd never be able to give you what you need, and he would never make you happy." He pushed away from the bench and shoved his hands through his hair. "I was going to tell you after the party. I thought if he saw you with your head held high, thinking that you knew about him, that he'd leave you alone, that he would let you go."

"Brilliant plan. Except for a few tiny details." Abby's eyes grew glassy with tears, but she lifted her chin and held his stare. Fierce little nymph. "Richard never cared if I was satisfied, or about what I needed, or if I was happy. So would you like to know what I think? I think you let Richard see me like that not to show him he couldn't have me anymore, but to show him you had all the power, that I was yours now. But what you don't seem to understand, Wolf, what none of you do, is I am not some *thing* to be owned. I am not your plaything. I am not your property. And I am not the prize in some idiotic dick-measuring contest."

"That's not—"

"Shut. Up. I don't want to hear excuses, Wolf. This is all on you. You chose not to tell me about Richard, and as such you chose to set me up to be humiliated in front of half the fucking town, making you no better than him."

"You know that was never my intention."

"And yet that is exactly what happened, because you

didn't respect me enough to tell me the truth. How am I supposed to trust someone... *love* someone... who doesn't respect me?"

Wolf's heart and mind seized upon the one word that mattered most, and he swallowed hard past the lump in his throat.

Love.

He loved this woman and she was hurting. A Dom helps his submissive, that's what he'd told her, and yet there he was arguing with her as if he had every right to do so when he knew full well he did not. How was that helping either of them? Wolf gritted his teeth. He was a Dom, and it was about bloody time he acted like one. His pride was a bitter pill to swallow, but one best choked down before it did any more damage.

She was right.

He was not.

His shoulders slumped as he admitted defeat, and this time his apology—a proper apology—spilled from his mouth with the ease of truth. "*Liebchen*, please... I am sorry I hurt you, that I allowed others to hurt you, that I put my own selfish wants above your needs. You're right. I should have told you about Richard, but what's done is done and I can't take it back no matter how much I want to. All I can do is beg your forgiveness. Please, Abby. Tell me what I can do to make this right."

Abby relaxed her arms and they fell to her sides, and she tilted her head slightly as she considered him. "What are you willing to do to prove yourself to me, to show me you respect me and that I can trust you?"

Wolf breathed a shaky sigh of relief and smiled. "For you, *liebchen*, anything."

She walked around the workbench and slid her hands

over the hard planes of his chest. "Kiss me," she said, her voice wavering slightly. Wolf obliged her and gently brushed his lips over hers. Her mouth was soft, so full and lush and welcoming. He deepened the kiss and she moaned her pleasure, the sound igniting every lustful impulse he owned and coaxing them to action, but as his tongue stroked along the length of hers, she broke the kiss.

"Anything?" she said as she toyed with the collar of his shirt.

Wolf leaned his forehead against hers. "Yes, my love."

"All I want," she said quietly, "is for you to leave. Your book is finished. It's time for you to go. And please," she added as she lifted her tear-glazed eyes to meet his own, "don't make me beg."

Abby slumped down to the cold forge floor and let her tears overwhelm her.

She'd held them in for as long as she could—as she'd watched her lover walk away, as she'd heard the back door slam shut, even as she'd listened to the sound of his motorcycle growing ever more distant in the black of night—but now her tears were a veritable torrent, flooding down her cheeks and splashing onto the sandy floor, creating tiny craters where they fell.

She touched her fingertips to her lips. The ghost of Wolf's kiss still lingered, and she mourned his warmth.

Never again would she feel the heat of his skin pressed against her own. Never again would she scream his name in ecstasy as he held her body hostage to his own personal brand of pleasure, and never again would she trust another man with her heart.

Her stupid, masochistic heart.

Her fingers scrunched against the grainy floor as her anger stole her grief, and she flung fistfuls of sand into the forge, causing the fire to splutter and pop.

She screamed her outrage, a primal cry of loss and anguish before the tears came again, sapping her strength and putting her back on her arse in the corner of the forge.

She had no idea how long she sat there before Paul and Ollie found her, but she guessed it wasn't long. Her face was still wet with tears when they helped her to her feet and half carried her inside the house.

"Do you want a drink?" Ollie said, seating her on the couch. "Water? Coffee? Hard liquor?"

Paul knelt in front of her, tucked her hair behind her ear. "Or a shower, perhaps?"

Abby stared at her brothers without seeing them, then blinked and looked away. But everywhere she looked filled her head with memories of *him*. And every memory punched another hole straight through her heart.

"I'm tired," she said, and it wasn't a lie. "Can I sleep in your bed tonight?"

Ollie sighed loudly and forced a smile. "Sure."

"Aw, just like when you were little," Paul said.

"Don't remind me," Oliver grumbled, and then to her he added, "If you kick me again, so help me God you'll be sleeping on the floor faster than you can say 'Ollie, get your foot outta my back'."

Abby snorted. "I'll bear that in mind."

She tried to stand up, wobbled on her feet. Two pairs of strong, warm hands caught her and helped her stay upright, and she almost burst into tears again because the hands holding her up weren't Wolf's.

Taking a deep breath to steady herself, she rubbed at

her eyes to brush away the fresh tears that were filling her vision. And when she caught her brothers sharing a worried glance, it grated at her nerves that she'd allowed herself to be reduced to this weak and whimpering mess.

I am not weak.

Now all she had to do was prove it.

Chapter Twenty

Abby lay awake, staring at the ceiling as Oliver snored. Sharing a bed with her big brother had always made her feel better as a child, her ever-watchful protector and confidant keeping her safe from harm. But she didn't feel better this time.

She just felt... alone.

Ollie had held her for ages after they'd gone to bed, stroking her hair while she'd cried on his chest, soaking his T-shirt with her tears.

Paul had offered to call their father for her, but what could he do? She wasn't even sure where he was at the moment. He and his current mistress had been travelling north, chasing warmer climes for a few months and hadn't bothered to check in with anyone for weeks, which wasn't unusual.

No, all she needed was a good cry. She was sure of it. In the morning, she would get up and clean the house from top to bottom, removing all evidence that Wolf Adams had ever existed. And then everything would go back to normal.

As her eyes filled with tears again, she realised she had a

better chance of seeing pigs fly than she did of forgetting the man who'd made her feel happier than she'd ever felt in her adult life, then destroyed that happiness when he'd broken her trust.

And her heart.

Her stupid, stupid heart.

She clenched her hands into fists, punched the mattress and flinched when she grazed her knuckles on the cotton sheets. Her hand still hurt from earlier, but the pain was totally worth it. The look on Dick's face as he'd tried to stop the blood from pouring down his chin was an image she'd not readily forget. He'd been furious, but no more so than her. Or Wolf.

As upset as she'd been at the time, she'd not consciously noticed the look of sheer fury on her lover's face as he'd stopped Richard from striking her and slammed him face first into the wall. But she remembered it now.

His hazel eyes had darkened with his anger, his strong mouth nothing more than a thin slash across his face, and his jaw had clenched so tightly it caused the muscles in his cheek to tick.

He'd looked like a man ready to commit murder, and all because of her.

He'd protected her from Richard's wrath. But not from his insults and gossip-mongering. Why hadn't he told her? Why hadn't he trusted her with the truth? Was he just trying to protect her, as he'd said, or did he think her too weak to handle it? The thought grated her already frayed nerves.

I am not weak.

Abby was tired, so very tired, but with a throbbing hand and an overactive consciousness ticking away, sleep still eluded her, causing her to feel restless, so she slid from the bed and returned to the lounge room.

Someone had relit the fire—Paul, probably—but the embers had burned down to little more than ash and produced little warmth, so she stabbed at the fire with the iron poker and fed it bits of kindling, stirring the flames back to some semblance of life.

If only her own life could be rebuilt so easily.

She sat on the couch and stared at the ceiling, her gaze falling upon the chains Wolf had wrapped around the oaken rafters, the chains she'd dangled from on more than one occasion, and usually more pleasantly than not.

Casting her gaze to the floor, she stared at the Persian rug they'd made love on one night when he'd taken her without a single word spoken between them, without any preamble or pretence but simply because he'd wanted her with an all-consuming passion.

The desk by the window, the table in the kitchen, the shower, the bedroom, and even the forge—they all held memories of him. Memories that flooded her brain and heart with every emotion she owned and threatened to crush her under the weight of them all.

She'd never forget the feel of his hands on her skin, the way he made her shiver in anticipation, the way her blood heated with lust. And she would never forget the sound of his voice, so smooth and deep as he whispered his dark commands in her ear, or the rumble of his laughter as he read the morning funnies in the newspaper over breakfast.

How would she ever forget the feel of his lips on her body, of the decadent eroticism that had laid her soul bare before him in a way no one else ever had?

The depth of sensation Wolf's dominance had wrung

from her had made her feel vulnerable and overexposed. But he'd also made her feel wanted and cared for.

And loved.

I'm in love with you.

Had he actually said those words to her? And how was she supposed to believe them? How could she trust him to mean those words when he didn't even trust her enough to tell her about Richard spying on them?

She pushed the heels of her palms against her eyes and groaned as indecision warred with ire and flooded her with grief.

"Still awake?" Paul flopped down on the couch beside her and handed her a beer.

"Couldn't sleep," Abby said as she stared at the shabby brown glass bottle in her hand. "Dad's home brew? You don't think he'll be pissed we got into his booze?"

"Nah. And if he is, I'll just tell him what I always tell him when he grumbles about his beer going missing."

"Oh?"

Paul shrugged. "I'll tell him Ollie did it."

"Dickhead," Ollie said, his sleepy voice coming from the hallway.

"Bastard," Paul shot back.

Oliver grunted. "Takes one to know one," he said as he stomped across the room and swiped Paul's beer from his hand.

Abby took a swig from her own bottle and gulped down the cold amber liquid, then immediately stuck out her tongue like she'd tasted something awful. "I'd forgotten how much I hate this stuff."

"Waste not, want not." Paul held out his hand for the bottle, which Abby gladly relinquished.

Ollie took a seat in the armchair by the fireplace. "Do you feel like talking now?"

"Do I have to?"

"No," Paul said. "But do you want to?"

Did she? "Yes."

"And?"

Staring at her brothers, she tried to focus on the jumble of doubts and insecurities swarming inside her mind, tried to silence the anxiety and muscle past the heartache.

"Why me?" she finally cried out, unable to hold the question in any longer and desperate for an answer. "What is it about me that makes men think they can treat me this way? Is there a giant neon sign over my head that only men can see that says 'doormat'?"

Ollie yawned loudly. "Wolf didn't treat you like a doormat, Abbs."

"No?"

"No."

Abby scowled at him. "If you're just going to take his side, you can bugger off," she said, her head falling back against the couch as she returned to staring at the ceiling... and those chains.

"I'm not taking anyone's side, but you know as well as we do that Wolf never meant to hurt you. He underestimated Richard, and now he's paid the price for that decision."

"He should have told me Richard saw us."

"Yes. He should have," Paul said. "But Wolf is a good person, and like so many other good people, he expects others to behave the way he would. *He* would have kept his mouth shut. Wolf was blindsided by Richard's behaviour just as much as you were."

Abby could hear the logic in her brother's words, but her exhaustion was making her argumentative. "It's not as if we didn't warn him," she grumbled. "I told him, you told him —hell, even Toby told him that Richard is a wanker of epic proportions, and everyone knows Toby doesn't speak unless he has something worth saying."

"Telling someone something and showing someone something are two very different things. Wolf fucked up, Abbs, and he knows it. But any idiot with eyes can see he's in love with you."

Abby flicked her gaze to Paul before quickly looking away again, as if afraid that acknowledging her brother's observations would make them truer. She hadn't finished sulking yet. "He humiliated me in front of half the town."

Ollie sighed, an exaggerated sound. "*Richard* humiliated you in front of half the town."

"The gossips will be having a field day."

Paul laughed. "Like that's anything new."

Abby continued to list her concerns, and her brothers continued effortlessly picking apart every argument she could think of.

But then another thought assailed her. "You think I'm overreacting, don't you?"

Paul finished his beer and set the bottle aside. "Why do you say that?"

"Because men always think women are overreacting, even when we're not."

Ollie snorted. "Did you ever think maybe we're right?"

Abby glared. "Did you ever think maybe you're an idiot?

"Children, please," Paul said, his voice raised, and then he turned in his seat to face her head-on. "Abbs, there're really only three questions you need to ask yourself. First and foremost, do you love him?"

The answer hit her with such astounding force that

even in her argumentative state of mind it wouldn't be denied. "Yes."

"Good. Second question, can you forgive him?"

This question was harder to answer. She'd told Wolf that he couldn't possibly love her because he didn't respect her, and if he didn't respect her, did he really deserve her forgiveness? But by that same argument, if she loved Wolf, which she knew in the depths of her soul she did, then that meant she respected him. And if she respected him, then she must still trust him, too.

She hated to admit it—and she'd never say it out loud—but Oliver was right. Wolf wasn't the one who humiliated her. And he wasn't the one who cheated on her, or tried to hit her, or threatened to cut her nipples off with a pair of scissors. He'd never made her feel anything less than worthy of being loved. He was a decent man, and he expected others to be decent, too.

Could she forgive him for being naïve about Richard, for expecting him to be better than he really was? Hadn't they all committed that particular sin at some point?

She certainly had.

Abby took a deep breath. "Yes."

Paul smiled. "Last question. What are you going to do about it?"

By the time Wolf arrived at his destination, it was late afternoon. He'd ridden almost non-stop since leaving Melville's Cross, stopping only for fuel or when he needed to piss. He was tired, down to his bones tired, but he couldn't go home yet.

He parked his bike in front of a row of old Victorian

terrace houses, removed his helmet and pressed his fist to his mouth as he swallowed down the urge to vomit. He felt miserable, as though his insides had twisted into tightly bound knots. And he had no one to blame but himself.

Wolf had known how fragile Abby's trust in him was, knew what it cost her to give so much of herself, and that she'd given it so freely should have humbled him. But he'd taken that trust for granted, he'd taken her for granted, and he'd hurt her.

The look in Abby's eyes when she'd asked him to leave... his heart had broken at the sight. He'd put that look of torment on her face. He'd left her reeling in anguish, the sadness he'd helped her conquer enveloping her once more.

He'd promised to protect her and he'd failed.

Maybe that was why he felt so angry. He'd failed the woman he loved, and as much as he wanted to lay the blame solely at Richard Melville's feet, he knew he owned a part of it.

A big fucking part.

Abby was right. He should have told her. *Before* the party. He should have trusted her with the information, should have trusted that she wouldn't let Richard intimidate her instead of worrying that she might use it as an excuse to scurry back inside her shell and hide away from the world again.

If she'd known about Dick, she could have used the information to empower herself instead of being blindsided by it. If she'd known what he knew, she could have beaten that arsehole at his own game, won the war before he'd even fired the first salvo.

By not telling her, Wolf had taken those opportunities away from her. By trying to protect her, he had only caused her more grief. Worst of all was that if he was being completely honest with himself, it wasn't even Abby he'd been trying to protect.

It was him.

He'd been so afraid of how she'd react to the knowledge that he'd let Dick see her in a compromising position that he'd kept it to himself, convincing himself it was in her best interest, telling himself he'd tell her about it later, after the bullets had been dodged.

His ego had blinded him to the fact that you can't dodge a bullet you don't know is coming.

Realisation gripped him tight. "I really am no better than him," he said, the words spat from his lips in a harsh whisper.

With this newfound sense of self-loathing, he swung himself off his bike and shoved his keys in his pocket, then walked along the row until he came to the house with a broken wrought-iron gate. The baleful-looking thing lay flat in the tiny front yard, a spotty carpet of grass and weeds growing up around it, poking their bright green blades up through the rusted iron work.

Abby could fix that, he mused, forgetting for just a moment that the woman he loved had kicked him out of her life.

He took a deep breath to settle his nerves, but it didn't help. His thoughts were unsettled, chaotic even, but he'd avoided this for long enough, and this at least was a promise he could keep. It was time to make amends.

He only hoped she didn't slam the door in his face before he could say what he'd come to say.

Even if she did, he wasn't going anywhere. He'd camp out on the porch if he had to, until she relented and let him inside. Because he didn't want to be alone.

Not tonight.

He needed to feel her arms around him. He needed to feel loved, needed the comfort he knew she'd provide.

He lifted the tarnished brass knocker and rapped three times. The sound of footsteps echoed from within, and a moment later the door creaked open, narrowed eyes meeting his downcast gaze.

"Well, well. The prodigal brother returns."

Chapter Twenty-One

"Where will you go if this all goes belly-up?"

"I've booked a hotel room just in case."

"Why not stay with Sally?"

"Wolf is her biggest client. If my plans go south, I don't want her doing something stupid out of a sense of family loyalty. No, it's best to leave her out of this."

Abby replayed the conversation in her head as she walked along the street, her nerves churning in her gut. Twice already she'd stopped, debated turning around and going home. And twice she'd told herself to suck it up and put one foot in front of the other.

Maybe I should have called Sally.

No. As much as she craved some moral support right now, she couldn't involve her niece in this. Abby had made this mess, and she had to clean it up. Like a grown-up, not like the childish moron she'd been in Melville's Cross.

As much as she was loath to admit it, Ollie was right. Again. She had overreacted. Not about Wolf keeping secrets from her and her subsequent humiliation; in that regard her anger was completely justified.

But she shouldn't have kicked him out.

Yes, she'd been hurt, and yes, she'd felt betrayed by the man she'd fallen in love with, but instead of talking to him about it like an adult, she'd reverted to her tried-and-true solution of running away, then spent the rest of the night taking out her frustration and anger on her brothers.

Eventually she'd been forced to own her emotions, admit that yes, actually, she did love him enough to forgive his foolishness, and hope he loved her enough to forgive hers.

Two days had passed since then.

Two days to book a flight and find a hotel near Wolf's house. Two days to decide what to wear, two days to think about what she was going to say to him—she still hadn't figured out that last part.

As luck would have it, she did manage to stumble across his glasses. She'd found them wedged between the couch cushions, although how they managed to end up crammed down there she had no idea. If nothing else, she supposed they'd make a good ice-breaker.

And if worst came to worst, she'd be rid of every last piece of him from her life.

As she turned the corner into the laneway where Wolf lived, she slowed her pace. She saw his terrace house at the end of the row and it was exactly as he'd described—faded dark grey paint, trimmed in white, a dark red door and a polished brass knocker in the shape of a dragon's head. It was very him, a tall, imposing exterior hiding what she suspected was a very warm and comfortable home.

A smile slowly spread across her face as her confidence forced her nerves into submission, and with his glasses gripped firmly in hand, Abby gathered her courage, walked up to his door and knocked. The sound of footsteps coming from within had her biting her lip in anticipation, and she had to stop herself from bouncing on the balls of her feet like an overexcited child.

The soft feminine voice that greeted her, however, was not what she'd expected.

"Hello. Can I help you?"

Abby stared at the woman peeking around the edge of the door, her lovely face staring back at her expectantly.

"Oh, hello. I'm sorry, I think I have the wrong house," she said with a slight frown, very certain she was exactly where she was supposed to be. Who was this woman? And how did she know Wolf? Erring on the side of caution she continued, "I was looking for Adam Wolfe. The author?"

"No, no. This is the place," the woman said, then opened the door wider. "But he's indisposed right now. Perhaps I can help you?"

Abby's gaze swept over the lovely woman standing in the doorway, but as she neared the woman's waistline her blood ran cold, freezing her in place even as her brain screamed at her to run. Hot tears threatened to spill down her cheeks and a lump formed in her throat.

The woman was pregnant. Four or five months, at least.

"Who are you?" she said, her voice quiet, strangled by her welling grief.

"I'm his wife. And you are...?"

Abby sucked in a breath as she tried not to vomit. "No one," she said, her gaze travelling from the woman's swollen belly to the enormous diamond ring on her left hand. She swallowed hard. "I'm no one." And then, as if her whole world wasn't falling apart, she lifted her chin and thrust the embossed leather case at her. "Here. Mr Wolfe left these at the café," she said and nodded in the general direction of a café she'd passed on her way to the house.

"Oh, thank you!" the other woman said, offering Abby a huge smile. "He's been looking everywhere for these. I swear he'd forget his head if it wasn't screwed on."

Abby forced herself to breathe, and then she forced herself to smile. "Yes. It's amazing the things men forget, isn't it?"

"Well, thanks again."

Abby watched the door close and heard the lock click into place, the sound acting as a catalyst, triggering the shock that now worked its way through her body and mind and left her reeling where she stood. She knew she had to leave, knew she couldn't just stand there in the street, staring at his house all day like a fool, but her feet were made of lead.

Tell her.

Tell her.

Tell her.

The thought screamed inside her head, causing her chin to lift and her quivering lips to firm in determination. But then the image of a swollen belly full of innocent life swam into her vision and she knew she couldn't do it.

"No."

If he's done it before, he'll do it again. He'll ruin her life and the life of his child.

Her feet seemed to move on their own, as though she had no control over them, and her hand joined the rebellion, clenching into a fist and slowly rising in preparation to knock on the door.

But that was as far as she got.

Abby stared at her fist, hanging in mid-air, a mere inch from the wood. Silent tears fell. Suddenly that fist was an open hand clutching at her chest, attempting to hold her heart intact, failing miserably as it fell to pieces all over again.

With one last look at the dark red door, and longing for the life that would never be hers, she turned on her heel and walked away, putting much-needed distance between herself and her never-ending nightmare.

Wolf tucked a towel around his hips and slowly walked down the stairs, the smell of coffee and bacon pulling him forwards. His first night back in Sydney, he'd stayed at Kristin's.

They'd talked for hours, caught up on the last few months of comings and goings. Wolf had apologised for being an arsehole and pushing her away after the Beth incident, and Kristin had apologised for not pushing back and giving him the smack up the back of the head he'd so desperately deserved.

The next night she'd stayed at his house, had kept an eye on him as they sat on the couch watching horror movies and eating Tim Tams and Lolly Gobble Bliss Bombs, a habit they'd fallen into as teenagers whenever one of them had had their heart broken.

But Wolf wasn't a teenager anymore, and watching zombies and vampires tear people limb from limb hadn't calmed the aching in his chest the way it used to.

Maybe I've finally matured.

Or maybe his heart really was broken this time.

Beyond repair.

After Kris went to bed, Wolf had wandered around the house, going from room to room in search of... something.

Something that would help fill the hollowness inside him. But he'd found nothing.

He'd tried reading a book, tried writing a book, stood staring into the fridge for so long the little light went out. He'd made himself a sandwich but then lacked the appetite to eat it. He'd hunted for his missing glasses—he was sure he'd seen them in his bag when he'd left The Forge....

And he'd picked up his phone, pulled up Abby's number and let his finger hover over the call button, but lacked the courage to push it.

She'd probably hang up on me anyway.

God, I miss her voice.

He missed her breathy moans as he fucked her from half asleep to wide awake, and he missed the sound of his name on her tongue as she nibbled his earlobe and drove him crazy with wanting. He missed her yelps and cries when he smacked her beautiful arse, missed the jiggle of her ample flesh when he fucked her hard from behind.

He longed to hear her breath catch with lust when he ordered her to go down on him, and craved the sound of her screaming in ecstasy. He missed her smell, the scent of smoke and heat that clung to her after a day in the forge, the rose-scented soap she used to bathe at night.

Mostly he just wanted to be near her again, to listen to her hum as she pottered around the house, watch her pull weeds in her garden. He'd never known such contentment before, to simply sit beside her and talk—or not. Sitting in silence as they read books together, or as he read and she doodled on her sketch pad, was a lesson in serenity, and it was in those moments that Wolf had known true happiness.

He wanted to feel that again, and by the time he reached the kitchen he'd made a decision. "I'm going back to Queensland."

"And a good morning to you too," Kris said as she handed him a cup of coffee. "Do you have time for brunch first?"

"Brunch?"

"It's after ten, brother dear. You've officially missed breakfast."

"I didn't realise it was so late."

"I didn't want to wake you. Not after listening to you haunt the house all night."

Wolf winced. "Sorry. I didn't realise I was keeping you awake."

Kristin shot him a bemused look and ran her hand over her swollen belly. "It's okay. This little bloke gets me up every hour on the hour to pee anyway. Now go, eat, before it gets cold."

Wolf walked through to the dining room and took a seat. Kristin had turned the lights on because even at this time of day, the old house he'd been meaning to renovate for the past decade was still shrouded in darkness. He looked around the room as he ate, at the dark-panelled walls and outdated wallpaper trim the previous owner had obviously thought would brighten the place up.

He shook his head. "Fucking ducks." Then he heaved a sigh and reached for his coffee.

His house had a very different aesthetic to The Forge. Even with its hodgepodge of styles and the endless extensions needed to accommodate the extensive Bennett clan, The Forge lived up to its name. The house was filled with light and warmth, and not a single inch of space was wasted. Wolf had felt more at home in that place in three weeks than he'd felt here in ten years.

The realisation made him sit up straighter, eat a little

faster and grin broadly as a plan of action formed in his head. He had a bag to pack and a flight to book and—

His eyes narrowed, snagged on something curious. "Kris?"

Kristin stuck her head around the corner. "What?"

Wolf held up the embossed leather case he kept his glasses in. The case he'd just now noticed sitting on top of a folded newspaper. "Where did you find them?"

"Actually, they found me." At his raised brow, she continued. "Some woman dropped them off, said you left them on the table at the café up the road."

"What are you talking about? What woman?"

"I don't know. Some random woman. She didn't stick around long enough to introduce herself, and I certainly wasn't going to invite her in. Not after last time."

Wolf's gut clenched around his half-digested breakfast at the memory of the fangirl who'd lied through her teeth to gain entry to a soirée at his house one night, then stole his dirty bed sheets.

Even so, hope bloomed in his chest. "Kris, I haven't been to the café since I got back."

His sister came fully into view in the doorway, her brow scrunched. "Then how did she get your glasses? I don't understand."

"What did she look like, this 'random woman'?" Wolf said as he rose to his feet.

Kristin shrugged. "Tall, I guess."

Wolf straightened to his full height, stared down at her, and demanded an answer. "Don't guess, Kristin. Details. Now."

Kris pursed her lips and tilted her chin up. Her response was sharp. "She was tall, taller than me even. She had dark hair and eyes, a pretty face, and was a little overweight. And don't pull that Dominant shit with me, Wolfram. It's weird."

Wolf's jaw clenched as he tried to ignore his sister's disparaging remarks and headed for the front door. "How long ago?"

"Just before you came downstairs. Why?"

"If she passed the café, then she's probably headed back towards Booth Street. Shit."

"What?"

"I need shoes. Where are my shoes?"

"Shoes? You need pants. Wolf, what is going on?"

Wolf found his joggers sprawled in the corner and frantically tugged them on his feet. "The last time I remember seeing my glasses with absolute certainty was before I left Abby's house. I thought they'd fallen out of my backpack somewhere, but what if they were never in there to begin with?"

"You think she intentionally kept your glasses so she could return them later? That's insane. You don't really think she'd do that, do you?"

"Not intentionally, no, but she was pretty upset when she kicked me out. It would have been easy enough for her to miss something. What I do know," he said, excitement licking along his veins, "is the woman you just described is Abigail. To a tee."

Kristin worried at her lip. "Oh...."

"What?"

"Now, Wolf, this is *not* my fault," Kristin said, straightening her back and anchoring her fists on her narrow hips. "She never said who she was, and let's face it, random women turning up on your doorstep isn't exactly out of the ordinary, "Mr I need to update my security". Besides, you're my big brother and I love you." For all his sister's bravado, she avoided his gaze.

"What did you do?"

She squirmed under his glare. "When she said she was looking for Adam Wolfe, I *might* have assumed she was another one of your fangirls, and I *maybe* told her I was your... um...." She laughed nervously. "Wife?"

As his eyes panned down to Kristin's pregnant belly, the full ramifications of her words became blindingly apparent.

"Fuck."

Shoes laced and tied, and keeping a firm grip on the towel tucked around his waist, Wolf yanked the front door open and ran outside, ignoring his sister's plea to put on some pants, and chased down the woman he prayed wouldn't murder him before he got a chance to explain.

Abby held herself tall as she walked down the blissfully deserted street, determined to walk away with what little dignity she still possessed.

She honestly didn't think she could handle interacting with other people right now. Whether it be as aggressive as a bumped shoulder or as innocuous as a smile in her general direction, her tears burned beneath the surface, just begging for an excuse to fall.

Several times she stopped, needing to suck the air back into her lungs before forcing herself to keep putting one foot in front of the other.

Forcing herself to walk away.

I just need to hold it together until I get back to the hotel.

And that's when she heard her name called out in that all-too-familiar voice. "Abigail!"

She quickened her pace and cursed herself for

wearing a dress. As if she hadn't humiliated herself enough for one day, now she couldn't even walk away from the bastard with any discernible grace because her panties were riding up her backside and her thighs were beginning to chafe.

Fan-fucking-tastic.

The footsteps behind her gathered in pace and volume. "Abigail. Stop." And then a hand was grabbing her shoulder.

"Don't touch me!" she snapped as he whirled her around to face him. She raised her hand to slap him, but it never met its mark. Wolf grabbed her wrist and pulled her into his arms, pinning her back against his strong—*naked*—chest.

"Would you please calm down for a sec and let me explain," he said quietly by her ear.

"Calm down?" she said through clenched teeth. "Calm this!" And she slammed her heel into his toes.

"Fuck! Me!"

Abby moved out of Wolf's reach as he hopped about on one foot, and it was then she noticed the only clothing the man wore was a pair of sneakers and a towel wrapped around his waist. A towel he was desperately clinging to as he hobbled over to the nearest fence and leaned against it. He glared at her as he cradled his foot.

"Ouch."

But Abby felt no sympathy for his pain. Not after what he'd done. "Be thankful that's all you got, you lying, hypocritical scumbag."

"I never lied to you, Abigail," he said as he pushed away from the fence and limped closer.

"A lie of omission is still a lie. And stop calling me Abigail. I hate that name, and I hate you," she said, finally letting loose her tears.

Great sobs heaved from deep inside her, from the place

where all her hurt had piled up and hardened into some great weight, determined to drag her down in despair.

"Why?" she said, tears streaming down her cheeks. "Tell me why. Why do men feel the need to lie and cheat? I trusted you. After everything I've been through, I took a chance and trusted *you*. I told you things I've never told anyone, not my brothers or even my best friend. You could have stopped it, and you know that. You could have done the right thing and ended it, but you didn't. And now *I* have to live with what *you* did," she said and jabbed her finger into his chest.

"Abby, please. Just come back to the house with me."

"And what? Have a cup of tea with your wife? Oh yes, won't that be lovely. How do you do, Mrs Adams? I'm Abby, the stupid whore your husband's been fucking behind your back."

Wolf grabbed her upper arms in his firm grip and stared down at her, his expression frightening. "Stop it, Abigail. You're not my whore. You're the woman I love. And the woman in my house is *not* my wife. But she can explain why she felt the need to lie to you."

Abby shrugged him off and hiccupped as she wiped at her dripping nose. "What are you talking about?"

Wolf rubbed the back of his neck and sighed, and it was then that she noticed the dark circles under his eyes and the scruff lining his jaw. He looked like he hadn't slept in days. He looked exhausted.

"The woman who answered my door was Kristin, my overprotective little sister."

She eyed him warily. "You never told me your sister was pregnant."

"Because I didn't know she was pregnant. She hasn't spoken to me in six months. But I kept my promise, Abby.

As soon as I got back to Sydney, I went to see her, to make peace. That's when I found out about the baby." He tightened the towel around his waist. "Please come back to the house, *liebchen*. I promise you, this is all just one big misunderstanding."

Abby stared at him and frowned while her brain tried to process this new information. The woman in his house was his sister. His sister was pregnant. And his sister had lied to her, but Wolf had not.

Shifting uncomfortably as she muscled past her own insecurities, she recognised the truth in his words. Why else would he be standing in the middle of the street wearing nothing but a towel and a pair of sneakers, trying to convince her to go home with him? If what he was telling her was all a lie, why bother to chase after her at all?

Still, after all the crap she'd been through in the last few days, hell, the last few years, she wanted to be sure.

Needed to be sure.

Remembering what she'd said to him the night she'd kicked him out, she repeated those same words now. "What are you willing to do to prove yourself to me, to show me you respect me." She took a breath. "And that I can trust you?"

Wolf took her hands in his, smiled as he kissed her fingers. "For you, *liebchen*, anything." But then his smile slipped, his grip tightened and his voice dropped to a harsh growl. "Except walk away from you. I'm *never* making that mistake again."

Abby straightened her back and lifted her chin. "Okay then," she said. "Beg me."

Wolf's brow shot up. "Say what now?"

"You heard me, handsome. Beg me," she said. "On your knees."

"On my knees?" he asked, disbelief colouring his voice.

Abby folded her arms over her chest. "On. Your. Knees."

A slow grin spread across Wolf's face and he shook his head, the action unhurried and deliberate. "You're getting spanked for this. You know that, right?"

Abby flicked a non-existent piece of lint off her shoulder and sighed, feigning boredom. Gave her lover a taste of his own medicine. "I can wait *all* day, handsome."

"You stubborn little—" Wolf rolled his shoulders, popped his jaw. His grin dissolved into nothing. "You really do drive me crazy," he said, "but *fuck* I have missed you." And Abby had to hold back her shock when he actually got down on his knees and stared up at her. "I don't beg for anyone, for anything. But I'll beg for you. Only you. Please, *liebchen*, please come back to the house with me. And please forgive my selfishness."

He sighed heavily and ran his hand through his hair, it stuck up in little spikes. "You were right to be angry with me. I should have told you about Richard *before* the party. I should have trusted you with the truth, trusted that you wouldn't use it as an excuse to... push me away. I am sorry I hurt you, Abby. Please come home with me. Please be mine," he said. "You already know I'm yours.

Abby reached out and stroked Wolf's cheek as he'd done to her so many times in the past, but instead of leaning into the warmth of her palm he turned his head and pressed his lips against her flesh. Instant heat flooded her and she felt ready to burst with the riot of emotions coursing through her, most notably lust and longing, but under all of that was the belief that everything would be all right.

They had a future together.

She smiled at her lover. "Okay."

Wolf tilted his head. "Okay?"

She nodded. "Okay."

"Thank you," he whispered, then stood and held out his hand. "Shall we?"

Tentative but determined, Abby slipped her fingers through his. His palm was warm, his grip firm, and as they started back towards his house, she took a breath and let the tension of the past few days ebb away.

Until Wolf reminded her of why she'd come in the first place.

"So, are you going to tell me why you're really here? And don't tell me you came all this way, to a city you detest, just to return my glasses, when we both know it would have been ten times easier to chuck them in the post."

Abby's mouth flapped open and shut but no words came out. And then she saw him raise one dark brow in silent challenge. A challenge she felt obliged to answer. She had come all this way, after all. And she really should do it now before she lost her nerve, before she was introduced to his sister and awkwardness ensued. Her pulse kicked up and she felt a flutter of excitement in her chest.

She took a deep breath. "I came because I needed to tell you... something, and I didn't want to do it over the phone."

Wolf hooked a knuckle under her chin, his intelligent hazel eyes watching for her every reaction. "I'm listening."

"I came because... it turns out being humiliated in front of half the town was more bearable than the thought of never seeing you again, of never telling you...."

"Yes?" he whispered as he cupped her cheeks in his big hands. "Telling me what?"

Abby stared into those warm hazel eyes of his and felt all the tension leave her body. It was now or never, and she was sick of running away, of hiding from the world and never being true to herself. Of living in misery and loneliness through the fear of rejection. Wolf hadn't rejected her. He accepted her, adored her, loved her—and it was beyond time she let him know she felt the same way.

"That I am head over heels in love with you."

Wolf yanked her into his arms and brushed his lips over hers. "Say it again," he said, the desire in his voice as obvious as the erection stabbing into her lower belly.

"I love you."

A firm hand spanked her arse and she melted between her thighs. "Again," he ordered in a rumbling growl.

Abby threw her head back to yell at the sky. "I love you!"

Lips hot and hungry claimed her mouth in an all-consuming kiss, and she returned his hunger in kind. She tightened her arms around his neck and lifted her leg around his hip, knocking the towel free of its moorings. His body shook with silent laughter, but he refused to let her go and retrieve the makeshift garment.

"Reminds me of the day we met," he said with a broad grin. "I'm naked in public and you're wearing that dress." He nodded towards his house. "And while I don't have a creek, I do know where we can find a wall."

She dared to raise a brow at him. "You're not going to punish me again, are you?"

"Now you mention it, I still owe you for that 'dirty old cunt' remark."

Abby spluttered. "But... that was said in the heat of passion."

Another smack landed on her arse, its delicious burn making her moan and shiver with anticipation. "I wonder what else I can make you say in the heat of passion."

Abby slid her hands over his hard chest and leaned up to nibble the strong corded muscle of his neck. "Only one way to find out," she purred.

Wolf scoffed. "One? *Liebchen,* if I haven't thought up at least half a dozen ways by the time we reach our front door, I'm not doing my job properly."

Abby startled at his words. *"Our* front door?"

Wolf smiled and tucked a stray lock of hair behind her ear. "Yes, my love. You didn't really think I'd let you get away from me a third time, did you?"

"Third time lucky, eh?" she said as she snuggled against his naked chest, caring as much about propriety as she ever did. Country road or city street, it made little difference.

Wolf kissed her hair and she heard the smile in his voice. "For you and me both, little nymph. You and me both."

The End

I hope you enjoyed Abby and Wolf in

THIRD TIME LUCKY

Please consider sharing the love by leaving a review for other readers to find. It doesn't need to be very long, and every review is greatly appreciated.

Want something sexy yet sweet?
Check out Jennie Kew's steamy romance series,
The Brisbane Bachelors Series.

Want something short and not-so-sweet?
Check out Jennie Kew's short erotic stories,
The Q Collection.

For more information about
The Bennett's Bastards Series visit
www.jenniekew.com

More from Jennie Kew

The Q Collected

Dirty: 3 Short Contemporary Stories

Grind: 3 Short Paranormal Stories

The Whole Shebang (2021)

Acknowledgements

To my family for all their encouragement, their love and understanding, thank you for being you and for putting up with me being me, especially when deadlines are involved.

A special thank you to my crit partners, my cheer squad, my sisters-in-arms, Bec McMaster and Kylie Griffin. You always challenge me to be a better writer and I really couldn't do this without you. Thank you for keeping me sane...*ish*.

To my editor, Kristin Scearce, who accepts my weird writing style and quirky humour as canon and is still willing to work with me, you rock!

And finally to my readers, thank you for taking this journey with me, and for allowing me to share with you all the people and places who occupy my head and my heart. I hope you enjoy reading about them as much as I enjoy writing about them.

Meet the Author

Jennie has always enjoyed reading but is a relative late-comer to writing. She never had aspirations of becoming a published author until a dance with death made her ask herself what she really wanted out of life, and she's been writing ever since.

When not sitting in front of her computer, Jennie can usually be found reading a book, watching a movie or building stuff out of Lego.

She lives in regional New South Wales, a stone's throw from Australia's capital, Canberra, with her husband, her husband's magnificent beard, a teenage giant and their feline overlords, Max and Tallulah.

www.jenniekew.com

Glossary

As all of my books are set in Australia and use a lot of Australian terms and slang, I've created this guide for my readers to keep you on track when you come across any Aussie-isms in my books.

A bit of all right: If someone is 'a bit of all right' they're considered to be very attractive.

Ambo: Short for ambulance, the term has come to mean anyone associated with any of the public or private ambulance services, their drivers and paramedics.

Arse: Aussie spelling of ass, aka buttocks, bottom, booty and bum.

Arvo and *Sarvo*: Afternoon and 'this afternoon'.

Copper: On occasion, Australians will actually lengthen words or use them in their original format. Cops (i.e. The police) was originally 'copper'.

Fashion Rag/Local Rag: Fashion magazine, any locally produced magazines or newspapers.

Fierie/s: Firefighter/s.

Fuck-knuckle: An idiot.

G'day: Pronounced 'gidday', this official Australian (and Kiwi) greeting is a contraction of the words 'good' and 'day'.

Kiwi: Pronounced 'kee-wee', A person from Middle Earth (New Zealand).

Larrikin: An unruly, boisterous but generally good natured person, usually male.

Mate: Unlike paranormal or sci-fi erotic romances where your 'mate' is the person you're fated to be with for the rest of your life, in Australian culture 'mate' could mean anyone from your best friend to some random bloke you just met.

Pav: Pavlova, a dessert made from baked meringue, topped with cream and fresh fruit, particularly popular around Christmas. We nicked it from the Kiwis.

Phwoar: An estimation of the sound one makes when a bit of all right enters your vicinity. See also, 'panting' and 'drooling'.

RFS: Rural Fire Service.

Sanga: Sandwich.

She'll be right, mate: Usually given as a response when someone is offering aid of some kind, it means 'Everything will be fine but thanks for asking'.

Togs: A swimsuit.

Tradie: Any tradesman.

Uni: Pronounced 'you-nee', University aka College.

Yeah, nah and *Nah, yeah*: Another instance where Australians have made something sound more complicated than it needs to be, is 'Yeah, nah' and 'Nah, yeah'. Whichever word the phrase ends on, is the affirmative answer, therefore 'Yeah, nah' means 'No' and 'Nah, yeah' means 'Yes'.